JUST RIVER

A NOVEL

SARA B. FRASER

Black Rose Writing | Texas

ISBN: 978-1-68433-814-6
PUBLISHED BY BLACK ROSE WRITING
www.blackrosewriting.com

Printed in the United States of America
Suggested Retail Price (SRP) $19.95

Just River is printed in EB Garamond

*As a planet-friendly publisher, Black Rose Writing does its best to eliminate unnecessary waste to reduce paper usage and energy costs, while never compromising the reading experience. As a result, the final word count vs. page count may not meet common expectations.

For Colin

PRAISE FOR *LONG DIVISION*

"I love Fraser's mastery of the complexity of these invented folks ... how she calls for my sympathy for them, and then so quickly undercuts it in order to show me how difficult, how wounded they are -- how fully human."
—**Sue Miller, Author of** *The Good Mother*

"The novel is both quiet, focused on domestic moments and small details, and melodramatic, full of infidelity, bad parenting, and strong emotions. Fraser has an excellent sense of place, and her Cape Cod and North Shore settings are alive with detail. An engaging story with a satisfying resolution. A troubled woman makes peace with her family in this well-written and introspective novel."
—*Kirkus Reviews*

"*Long Division* is a multi-generational tale of dysfunction and hope echoing from grandmother, to mother, to daughter....The storytelling is incredibly human and honest, exploring how a person can be blinded by their own intentions....[it] is a novel whose fluid narration and rich imagery carries a story that is deeply personal to its characters but universal in its themes."
—*Indie Reader (5 stars)*

"*Long Division* deals head-on with issues like abuse, alcoholism, and statutory rape. However, at its very core, this is a book about human understanding. It's a book about recognizing that human beings, even those who are parents, are flawed individuals who don't always make the right choices."
—*Online Book Club*

"An exceptionally well-written novel, giving the reader an insight into the lives of the characters with a style and grace that would be the envy of many writers."
—*Sublime Book Review*

"*Long Division* is narrated in beautifully told interweaving storylines, where the past and present come together in a nuanced, heartfelt drama about everyday people living everyday lives."
—*Authors Reading*

"*Long Division* is a powerful story about three generations of women who share the same bloodline; their inability to deal with their past has inadvertently affected one another."
—*New England Book Critic*

"*Long Division* by Sara B. Fraser was a delightful, character-driven read.... It's a story about family, heartbreak, and finding peace amongst life's broken pieces."
—*J.L. Cole Books*

"I loved this insightful, moving, brilliant novel, reminiscent of Meg Wolitzer's novels."
—Stephen Russell, Wellfleet Marketplace Booksellers

"The three generations of women in this book are connected by shared trauma and also by Fraser's insightful storytelling. The book moves elegantly between narrators and through time, and addresses the far-reaching consequences of alcoholism and childhood abuse with intensity, balanced by a gentle touch for the subtleties of family dynamics."
—Tim Boomer, *New York Times* Modern Love column and podcast contributor

"*Long Division* is as much about the treacherous but essential landscape of love as it is about the narrative webs we often spin to survive and then must find a way to dismantle."
—Tehila Lieberman, winner of the Katherine Anne Porter Prize for short fiction and author of *Venus in the Afternoon*

"*Long Division* is a touching, subtly poignant, and unflinching take on the ties that bind mothers and daughters... and often unmake them."
—Nicole Galland, author of *On the Same Page*

JUST RIVER

How did we get in this state?
We started early. Remember?
Were you holding me up,
Or were you dragging me down?
Were you saving my life,
Or were you helping me drown?
–Alun Smyth, *Staggering*

THE END

The Otis River, upstate, was once a cradle of industry. Its rusty water and yellow-tinted foam lips are partly a legacy of that past, and partly the simple fact of high iron content in the earth. In the small—and getting smaller—city of Wattsville, which straddles both sides of the Otis, all the manufacturing plants were closed by the 1970s, but the redbrick buildings that line the river's banks make visitors—if there ever are any—hearken back to a time when machinery screamed under giant wooden beams, trains pulling into the station were regularly delayed by slow-moving freights, and leaded shop windows rippled the fedoras, furs, and crocodile purses of wealthy shoppers downtown. Now, like every other small city in the area, Wattsville struggles. Wages are stagnant. Industry is gone.

The city is kept on life support by a few small businesses serving an agricultural sprawl, a couple of penitentiaries, and several old-money families that live in the picturesque neighborhood of White Hills. In these families, many fathers spend the workweek in Manhattan, coming home on Fridays in time for cocktails at sunset.

Ethan Thaxter comes from one such family.

Ethan is the owner of a Volkswagen New Beetle that is upside down at the bottom of the Otis. The bright-red paint is in stark contrast to the brown water. Before long, the paint will fade from gumball to cinnamon, and finally be indistinguishable from the rocks around it. Ethan wouldn't have any appreciation for the way nature subdues and incorporates humanity's shiny refuse, but it happens anyway. The car scarcely rocks with the current and a curious fish swims inside, drawn to the graduation tassel attached to the rearview mirror, with its shiny '95 badge.

Several miles north of the VW, where the river widens and flows around the women's prison on Stratton Island, the diary of Ethan's ex-girlfriend, Garnet Harlow, spins in gentle eddies before lodging between two rocks on the eastern shore. The river has claimed Garnet's writings and erased them. Even if someone were to find the diary, the pages would be too warped and stained to be legible.

Within view of the prison, Garnet's mother, Carol, parks near an overpass and wades into the river. Larry Stall, who'd been following her, slows to a crawl. He must be in love, he thinks, giddy with the realization that he might be her savior. He parks at the end of the bridge, scrambles over the guardrail and down to the riverbank to save her.

On the south side of Wattsville, in a place where the river runs narrow and fast, Carol's best friend, Sam Berry, struggles to stay afloat. Blood leaks from a bullet hole in his calf and swirls like beet-colored smoke before fading into the water. He has kicked off his favorite cowboy boots—turquoise with pink stitching—and squirmed out of his angora sweater, which had swollen like a sponge.

There is a wooden dock behind the Sheraton Hotel and Wagonwheel Pub. It is usually empty, except for the occasional fisherman, or sometimes a couple of kids will hang out there getting stoned. Today, a waitress named Simone is gazing at the water, smoking a cigarette, when Tommy Stall stumbles down the ramp. He is weak and nearly knocks her over when they hug. They embrace for a long while before Tommy turns and leaves her there.

Most of the eastern states have been experiencing an early spring heat wave. There have been drought-like conditions, but the weather is beginning to change. A quick storm has shattered the dry calm and left puddles that reflect the sky. There will be more rain: spongy clouds droop with the weight of water and electricity.

THE BEGINNING

The courtroom was fluorescent lit, jaundiced. The whole city felt the same: plywood windows, dog piss in melting snow. The cold carpet, the drab walls, oblong tables strewn with oblong pads of legal paper—everything seemed yellow. Even the judge shone a mustardy hue: it reflected off the face of his gavel and the top of his head—bald but for several strands of hair that he'd combed over from above his right ear.

Carol and Sam feared the worst. From a seat toward the back of the gallery, they watched the judge's expressions: disdainful toward Carol's daughter, Garnet, who was being accused of attempting to harm her boyfriend by attacking him with an armoire. When addressing Ethan, the judge comported himself as though the boy were his own mischievous kid brother or nephew. Garnet's shoulders were uncharacteristically slouched beneath the cotton-candy blouse Carol had brought for her. On the stand, uncomfortable but affably protected by a system of justice that would always have his back, Ethan nodded and pointed at Garnet when his lawyer asked if the person who had fractured his arm and given him a near-fatal concussion was in the room.

"Pissant, sniveling son of a bitch," Carol whispered in Sam's ear. Ethan's limp finger was directed at Garnet, but his eyes gazed into the distance above her head. The judge nodded at the right moments and tsk-tsked when appropriate. Garnet, sneaking a glance at her mother and Sam, made a face indicating her distaste for the judge. Sam picked up a strand of his hair and pulled it across his forehead to mimic the judge's comb-over. Garnet was able to smile.

Ethan explained in a shaky voice that Garnet and he had fought, and when he'd moved close to her, to try and talk to her, to make up with her, she'd pushed the armoire over on top of him.

"He's lying," Garnet said. "Ethan, you know what happened." Ethan shrank into his seat when she said this, and Carol and Sam sat up, hoping he would be a man and admit his role, accept some blame.

The judge said, "The jury should do their best to ignore the defendant's outbursts." He turned to Garnet's lawyer. "Please try to control your client." Garnet's eyes grew wide with confusion, rage, and shame.

"Outburst?" Carol growled. "How was that an outburst?" She turned to Sam and wiped her eyes roughly across his shoulder.

"Careful," Sam whispered, "it's dry-clean only." Carol nudged him with her elbow.

Ethan stuck to his story: that Garnet was unreasonable and "hysterical."

In his final argument, Ethan's lawyer gesticulated, his glimmering cuff links peeking out from under the sleeves of his jacket. "Ms. Harlow is a menace," he was saying, "and she will come after my client again if allowed to roam free."

Carol whispered to Sam, "Roam free? Are we on the frickin' savanna?"

Sam put his arm around Carol's wide shoulders and said, too loudly, "A menace, ha. He's the menace."

The judge thumped his gavel. "If observers in the gallery cannot keep their thoughts to themselves they will be asked to leave."

Seeing that Margaret Thaxter, on the other end of the benches and farther forward, was smirking, Sam caught her eye and stuck his tongue out of his mouth, curling it down his chin like Gene Simmons. Mrs. Thaxter gasped and turned back to the proceedings.

Sam leaned toward Carol. "That woman's gotten so much Botox, her eyebrows have fused to her skull." He recrossed his legs and pulled his shoulders back and away from his ears—thinking for a moment of the latest yoga video he'd taken out of the library and the calming voice of Poppy, that video's instructor. He'd recently discovered yoga and was loving it, though he still wasn't practicing as much as he'd like.

***

At Dunkin' Donuts, after all of the evidence and the testimony had been presented and the wait had begun for the jurors to make their decision, Sam and Carol sat at an orange table eating ham-and-egg croissants.

"We'll see," Carol said between bites, "if money can buy you a judge and a jury too."

"Anyone with half a brain should be able to see that Garnet was defending herself."

Carol shook her head. "They're supposed to disregard any evidence of stuff he did to provoke her."

"They've been told to, but they're only human."

"I hope you're right. I do. But people usually follow the rules. They'll do what the judge wants them to."

"Even if they find her guilty," Sam said, "there might not be jail time."

"It would ruin her life, having that over her head. Never mind if they send her to Stratton Island. Jesus. That would destroy all of us."

"Nothing could destroy her," Sam said with a smile. "You raised her well and she's strong. Really strong. Don't forget that. I never knew anyone so her own person."

"Except you, of course."

"Except me." Sam winked. "Anyway. What a prick."

Carol knew he was talking about the judge. "That's what worries me. If they find her guilty, I bet he gives her the maximum. Prison time." They both winced at the words.

"Imagine calling an armoire a deadly weapon," Sam said. "As if she could bring it with her to rob a bank or something."

"Ridiculous. You gonna eat that?"

Sam shook his head, and Carol picked up the rest of his croissant sandwich.

They were quietly shredding their Styrofoam cups when Sam's cell phone finally rang. He picked it up, squinted at the number, and handed it to Carol.

"Hello? Yup. We're across the street. Okay. Be right there. Well," she said. "I guess it's time."

***

When the judgment was read, the lead juror pronouncing her guilty of first-degree assault, Garnet stood stock-still. When the judge pronounced her sentence right away, as if he didn't even have to consider it—two years in prison—she dropped onto her chair, shaking her head wildly as though trying to dislodge something stuck inside her ear canal. She looked at her mother and Sam with such desperation that Sam's eyes welled up. Carol mouthed the words Don't worry, don't worry. It's going to be okay. Sam rummaged in his purse for tissues.

After the courtroom had emptied, Carol and Sam sat for a long time on a bench in the hall. The marble walls were dulled with age and cigarette smoke, and there were photo portraits of President Clinton and Vice President Gore. "Look at them," Sam said. "They can get away with anything. Do anything they want. All of them . . ."

Carol blew her nose one more time, stuck the tissue into her pocketbook, and stood up. "I guess there's only justice for the people who can pay for it."

She slipped her hand into the crook of Sam's elbow as they made their way down the wide steps to the parking lot.

OTHER SINISTER CREATURES

Sam

Sam plucks a hair from his left eyebrow, moves his face closer to the mirror, sighs, settles glasses onto the bridge of his nose. He looks up into his nostrils, at several magnified hairs, long with scattered droplets of moisture clinging to them like barnacles on seaweed. After two quick, deep breaths he fastens the pincers of an antique pair of tweezers—his grandmother's, rest her soul—onto a wiry hair and pulls.

"Eeeooowww!" he cries, leaning over and clutching the edge of the sink. He shudders as he uses a fingernail to knock the scoundrel free from where it clings to one side of the tweezers. He leans in close again and repeats the procedure several times, then wipes the tears from his eyes and the sweat from his armpits with a piece of toilet paper and sets to work with his makeup bag.

Carol has told him that glittery eye shadow is too young for him, that he should be subtler with his makeup now that he is in his forties. He swipes purple over his brow defiantly, thinking that, at forty-three, Carol sometimes acts as though she were already dead. She had been sliding into a funk even before Garnet's conviction, but since then she's become more and more listless. He doesn't mean to be impatient with her, but she can't seem to pull herself out. It hasn't been much fun being with her lately, he thinks, and then scolds himself. She needs him, but sometimes he wonders if he's enabling her depression by continuing to mask his impatience.

He stands back with his hands on his hips and turns side to side. With his palms covering the crullers that have begun to form just above his hip bones, he looks slim. He is long through the torso, like a pale eel; his belly button is an attractive innie, and his stomach is flat.

He's never grown much hair on his chest and considers himself lucky that he can wax with Sally Hansen strips—a money saver compared with going to a salon.

7

He smiles at himself in the mirror, tipping his chin toward his chest, concealing the walnut-size Adam's apple that is his most egregiously male feature (of those that are visible when he is dressed). If he could alter anything, it would be that: he dreams of having a willowy neck that would swallow sexily, daintily.

In padded bra and lace undies, Sam stands at the door to his closet, throwing item after item onto the floor and the unmade bed behind him, at last settling on a silvery blouse and plaid skirt. His penis hangs from the side of his loose panties, like a secret. He likes the feeling of it there, loose in the warm spring air. Finally, he pulls on his lucky cowboy boots and strides to the full-length mirror in the corner of his bedroom. He squares his shoulders, looks into his kalamata eyes, and recites, "I am worth something. I say yes to life." He grabs his raincoat from where it is draped across the back of the sofa, takes the elevator to the first floor, and waits at the bus stop across the street from the manila brick apartment building where he lives. He checks his watch. If the bus comes on time, he will get to his job interview a good twenty minutes early.

***

Larry Stall, manager of inserting, runs his thumb and forefinger down a pencil, flipping it over and tapping it against the desk as his fingers reach the end. He strokes the sides of his mustache with the eraser, petting them gently like cherished pets. His office is in the corner of the *Chronicle*'s basement. A diploma from Holbrook University hangs on the wall, and on his desk is a framed picture of a little boy in a baseball uniform. Behind Sam, inky machines slam newspaper pages around the cavernous basement.

"You only worked at the Red Rock Grill," Larry says, "for two months. What happened?"

"This is embarrassing, but I got plantar warts. How utterly ridiculous, right?" It was unfortunate. He'd done a good job at the Red Rock. They liked him. But when he got the warts and found it hard to walk, they found someone to replace him. It didn't pay well anyway, and he didn't like working nights—it interfered with karaoke nights at the Wagonwheel Pub. He points at the framed picture on Larry's desk and says, "Cute. Is he yours?"

"He works here," Larry says and points out one of the young guys on the line. Sam can see that the boy has inherited his father's thick orange hair and fair complexion. "He's twenty-one now. It's an old picture." Larry hikes up one

8

haunch and digs a crumpled handkerchief out of his back pocket. After blowing his nose, he puts both elbows on the desk, the handkerchief between his palms. "Here's the thing," he says. "You're not going to work your way up out of inserting. People think this is a foot in the door, but it's not. So, don't get any ideas about working upstairs, journalism, any of that. All you gotta do is be able to lift stuff. You've got strong arms? Can you come in tomorrow?"

"Yes. Thank you. Wonderful." Sam straightens his skirt as he stands and holds his hand toward Larry, who is shuttling papers into a folder and doesn't notice. When Larry looks up, Sam is still there, standing awkwardly, his hand lingering in front of his body as though it doesn't really belong to him.

Larry directs his nose at Sam's boots. "They're a nice color."

Sam tucks his chin and smiles. "Thank you."

***

Carol comes to Sam's apartment for *Law & Order* and *Third Watch*.

"Damn elevator is broken again," she says.

"Good thing it's only two floors."

"Fine, but I gotta get back up there in a couple of hours."

Sam bites his tongue instead of pointing out how much she could use the exercise. She sinks into one end of the sofa and starts pulling chips and popcorn and candy bars out of the paper bag she's brought with her. "So? How'd your interview go?"

"Well it's not exactly the best job ever, but I got it." He tosses a pillow into the corner of the armchair and sits down. "I'll pay you back soon, I promise."

"Don't worry about that," Carol says. "It wasn't much."

"No, but still. It'll be good to have some money coming in."

"You can rack up some more unemployment at least. What did you decide to wear?"

"Gray. Very flattering, if I do say so. Businesslike. Not too flirty. The boss said my boots were nice."

"Sounds like your day was a lot better than mine."

"Oh dear. What happened?"

"Nothing happened, same as always . . ." Potato chips rustle as she unsticks the seam of their foil bag.

"You visit Garnet?"

9

Carol nods. When she doesn't offer more, he says, "We should go out. Dancing or something. Remember we used to go out on Fridays?"

"Yeah," Carol says. "Maybe."

"I know I've said it before, but it's not good for you." Animated, he scoots to the edge of the chair. "You're a young woman still with a lot of life in you. Garnet would want you to have some fun. I know she would. Ask her."

"Sam. You said you wouldn't. No lectures."

"It's just . . ."

"Uh-uh. No lectures."

He slides back and sinks in. Carol crunches on chips.

"Anyway, when do you start?" she says.

"I'm training tomorrow."

"Great."

"It's just inserting," Sam says. "I have to lift bunches of ads into a machine that puts one in each newspaper. I mean, duh."

"It's a job."

"Oh honey, I'm not complaining. You know I'm at the end of my rope, so I'm happy about it, I am." He looks at Carol, who, having moved from salty to sweet, is prying chocolate from the top of a Milky Way with her teeth. "Besides, maybe I'll meet some new people." He grins and nibbles the edge of a potato chip.

Carol considers the Milky Way in her hand—a block of nougat paved with caramel. "It's nearly nine. Change the channel."

"Or maybe I'll get a promotion, who knows? You never know."

Carol's face is shiny, and it reflects the glow of the television.

"If I do a good job, show up . . . it's hard to find reliable people . . . Okay. You're not interested. What is it?"

"Nothing. I don't want you to get your hopes up, is all. A job. A guy. Whatever it is. I hate to see you let down."

"I know it's just a job. I know that." He goes to the kitchen. "Why can't I be positive? You never know, you know." And with a hint of accusation as he reenters the room with two mugs, "We attract what we put out there."

"I guess." She peers into the cup. "Tea, huh?"

"You can have coffee if you insist, but it'll only make your day longer." She raises an eyebrow. "No. No booze," he says. "C'mon, honey, we're doing great!" He puts the mugs on the table and pats her knee.

"Well I sure as hell don't want coffee. I live for going to bed."

10

"It's good tea. It's Darjeeling," Sam says. "Very little caffeine. So. Anything new at work?"

"Same old, same old," Carol says. Sam hasn't been to the community college cafeteria where Carol works in a long time. He used to visit and she would give him free food, but he finds the place depressing, with its high barred windows and dusty posters of food pyramids and babies dressed as vegetables. "There's a new entrée—shepherd's pie."

Sam snickers, his knuckles to his lips. "See? That's exciting. Whoever said things could never change?"

Carol snorts and they quiet down, drawn into the familiar *Law & Order* theme music.

***

Early the next morning, Larry shows Sam around the basement of the *Wattsville Chronicle*: where each inserter is supposed to stand, where to get the bundles of ads, the break room. He shows him his spot on the line.

"You pick them up from the skid, here," he says, hoisting a stack of ads. "Tap them. Make sure they're even, and then slip them in here. Got it?" Sam nods and takes up his position. There are three young guys already at their stations; Sam waves to them.

"This here's Sam," Larry points at him with his thumb. Sam is wearing slacks and a fluffy black sweater. He has on a pink stretchy headband and gray eyeliner that extends the corners of his eyes up into his temples.

"Whatever," one of the boys says. Another coughs loudly into his fist.

"Don't mind them," Larry whispers. "My son. Tommy. He's a good kid. I could do without the others, to tell the truth." Tommy acknowledges Sam with a gesture that is meant to be sarcastic or dismissive, a toss of the head like a horse that doesn't want to be petted, but the way the edge of his mouth pulls up reveals a friendly disposition.

"Okay?" Larry calls.

The boys on the line nod; Sam readies himself. The monstrous conveyor belt shimmies to life, and the inserters begin putting stack after stack of advertisements into the hopper. The newspapers rumble past and the ads get sucked into them.

"Don't forget," Larry calls over the thumping machine, "one weak link breaks the whole chain." Sam has Rite Aid, and he watches the grainy photos of paper towels and laundry detergent and pain relievers get whizzed out and into the newspapers. It's hard work, but the morning passes relatively quickly.

At break time, Larry gives Sam a tour of the editorial offices. "Most of the kids, they don't really care, but I figure, you know, as an older person, you might be interested." He leads Sam up the cement stairway.

"Thanks so much," Sam says. "You know, as a child, I idolized Lois Lane."

Larry clears his throat. "Well, it's nothing that glamorous."

As they pass through, Larry says hello to some of the people. They are writers, editors, marketers, salespeople. He whispers their job titles reverentially. It is a noisy beehive, with people talking on phones and typing in cubicles that stretch across a wide room. "I used to work up here before I went down to inserting," Larry says. "As an intern. I was an intern." He holds the door for Sam, and it clangs behind them as they start down the cement stairs.

"You've been here a long time," Sam says. "I mean, not that long, of course, because you're hardly old . . ."

Larry laughs and runs a hand over his hair. "Don't worry about it. They didn't have a job for me when I finished my internship, so then I was a DJ. I used to be a DJ. For a long time. Then I came back here."

"That's exciting. Where were you a DJ?"

"KLMN."

"I listen to them! 'The top six at six for your afternoon commute!' I must have heard you."

"It was a long time ago, and I had the two-to-six a.m. slot, on weekdays."

"Did you use your own name? Or something else?"

"Just Larry." He pushes open a heavy metal door that brings them outside. "A lot of people never heard me. Anyway. We've still got about ten minutes before we start her up again, so go on and have a rest. There's vending machines inside the door."

The *Chronicle* is housed in a sand-colored brick building surrounded by parking lots. The inserters, in good weather, take breaks in the north lot, which is bordered by plots of faded pink mulch.

Sam gets a bag of pretzels and a soda from the machine and sits on the edge of the curb with his legs stretched in front of him. Two of the young guys are smoking on a bench. They wear oversize jeans, hoodies, and have lasso-length wallet chains. What lousy fashion sense, Sam would like to be able to say to someone. He smiles at Larry, who is sitting at a picnic table eating a sandwich.

Larry smiles back, seems a little flustered, and looks down at a newspaper spread on the table, wipes mayonnaise from the corner of his mouth with a napkin. Sam shakes the hair away from the back of his neck and approaches the young guys.

"Hey, do you have an extra cigarette?"

They look at each other and raise their eyebrows.

"You speaka da English?" Sam says. "Ciga-rette? Smokey smokey?"

One of the boys stands up, pats his pockets, but doesn't take anything out of them. Though he is a full head shorter than Sam, and thinner, he looks ferocious and wiry, full of jagged angles and steely bones. "Looks like I'm all out."

"Oooooh," Sam waggles his fingers at the two of them. "You boys are too cool for school, aren't you?" With intuition honed over the years, Sam is pretty sure they're not dangerous.. They'll leave him alone, but he'll never win them over. He retreats to where he'd been sitting. He's been trying not to smoke anyway. Larry is studying his newspaper.

Soon Tommy comes out of the building and nods at the guys, then sits at the table with his father. Father and son both seem tinged with discomfort: Tommy's hands shake with what Sam recognizes as hangover jitters and Larry fidgets as though the inside of his clothing were lined with straw.

Sam thinks about his own father and tries to conjure a happy memory of him, but can't. His father died young. Sam's mother later joked that if he'd lived, he'd probably have killed them both, especially when Sam started insisting on dressing up as Cinderella and his mother would brush and braid his hair for him, the two of them snuggled up on the couch watching *Ozzie and Harriet*.

His mother had wanted a daughter and, from as far back as Sam can remember, he'd been happy to oblige. His grandmother and his mother were both inspirations to him. They had exceptional senses of style—his mother slightly more androgynous, like Georgia O'Keeffe, and his grandmother with a lipstick collection that would fill the double bandoliers of Frito Bandito. He loved them for their acceptance, not just of him, but of everybody. His mother tolerated his father's temper and insults while he was alive and then accepted his death with the same humor. Everyone was okay in her book—and she loved Sam unconditionally. His grandmother died while he was still quite young, but he remembers her as being the same. He credits his mental well-being to both women's love and support.

Watching Tommy and Larry in their awkward father-son dance is entertaining to Sam, and a welcome distraction from the antagonistic smoke blowers, carbon copies of all the small-minded people who have looked at him with blind hatred. There have been more times than he can count when he'd nearly decided to give up, dress like a man, bury himself in a normal existence. He glances at the young smokers and feels proud that he never did give in, despite the danger he's managed to skirt, for the most part.

He knows that by being himself, he's much braver than those boys. Too bad they don't know it and maybe never will.

Between the two smoking boys and the father and son, Sam feels a little lonely, and he wonders, for the millionth time, whether he should have tried to adopt or otherwise become a parent. But the world is a dangerous place, and he's glad he doesn't have to try and protect anyone. His thoughts turn to Garnet. He misses her. He feels vaguely guilty that he hasn't been to visit, but he hates going into that place. In his regular circles—his neighborhood, downtown, even at this new job—he feels comfortable. People may not be his friend, but he's part of the fabric of Wattsville and they know who he is. Out at Stratton Island, well, he's out of his element. Carol visits her daughter all the time anyway, so he figures he's not really needed.

***

On his way home, Sam cuts through the woods along a path that used to be a road, before they'd built Route 22 to replace it. It is overgrown but there are remnants of human activity—a fossilized car frame, fragments of old stone walls, a rusted-out storage container, and farther along, where Route 22 swings close to the Otis River, the old mill. Sam notices the ferns that are beginning to unravel on the forest floor. "Fiddleheads," he says out loud, and remembers the only time he'd tried eating the springtime delicacy. He'd thought they'd tasted like chalk and had the consistency of tangled thread, but he'd been at a fancy restaurant in Montreal with his ex, Davide, and had been too timid to admit his distaste for them.

The old mill is like a movie set—a little spooky, intricate in its disintegration. Some corporation recently bought the building and is going to renovate it. They've already laid a pitch-black parking lot with bright white lines.

He's always loved the old building and had fantasized having the money to take it over himself. If he owned it, he'd make it into something that celebrated its heritage, its connection to Wattsville's past, something tasteful and culturally inclusive. An arts center, a bed and breakfast, or a chic café. Or why not all of those things at once? The corporation that bought it will probably fill it with something boring and profitable: offices and a D'Angelo's.

There is a truck parked on the new blacktop, and Sam can hear the voices of men inside the building. They are far away but he can tell they aren't speaking English. His curiosity pushes him toward the building and as the voices of the workmen become somewhat clearer, a more distinct noise comes hurtling over a nearby hill: two ATVs ridden by young guys in sunglasses with close-cropped hair; they remind Sam of his unfriendly coworkers. They veer in his direction. He stands his ground as they approach and then, at the last minute, jumps into the trees at the side of the path. They pass so close he can feel the warm wind of their exhaust. He isn't sure if they are his coworkers or not but their aggressive presence gives him a surreal feeling—as though other sinister creatures will be popping out of the forest and chasing him down.

He picks his way through the trees toward the river, hoping to hide in case the ATVs return from the other direction. He steps over low-growing bushes and between wiry limbs that brush at his hair and his sweater. He holds his hands in front of his face, fending his eyes from the branches. At the river's edge, a plastic tampon applicator stuck between two rocks is the color of the underside of a person's eyelid. He moves away from it and crouches until he is sure the boys on ATVs are far away. He can hear the river lapping at the rocks, the distant hum of cars on Route 22, and the faint, foreign voices of the workmen renovating the mill.

CRUSHING

Carol

At midday, Carol sits on her stool in the cafeteria of Wattsville Community College, ringing in students' lunches with fed-up fingertips. The high windows look out at ground level, and feet and bicycle wheels shuffle and slide by—their colors dulled by a patina of grime. Carol shifts on her stool and looks down her nose at a sandwich.

"Tuna melt?"

A girl with braces nods and works some dollar bills out of a Mickey Mouse change purse.

"Three-fifty."

Across from her, stationed between the hot premade food and the wide, flat grill, stained brown from years of burned fat, Ron is sliding a grilled cheese onto a plate.

"Look at that beautiful day, Miss Carol," he calls, motioning toward the windows. A student slides a tray toward Carol and waits, timid but superior, hands resting lightly on a plastic box of salad.

"Why the hell are you so happy, Ron?" She hopes he knows she's teasing him.

He sucks air through his imperfect teeth. "Why not? It's a beautiful day."

Carol jams in the price of the salad, doles out change. The student takes the coins and hustles to the condiment table. "It's beautiful outside, Ron. It sure as hell isn't beautiful in here." Ron laughs: hearty, clear, openmouthed.

As the students in line at the grill wait for their orders, they seem happier, friendlier than when they pay Carol at the cash register. The lighting is brighter over there, but Carol knows that isn't why. She knows, too, that it's not just that they spend more time with Ron, watching him as he cooks their orders. Ron has a way with them, and she doesn't. She tries to be at peace with it, but because she's worked at the college for so much longer than he has, it stings.

A couple of students laugh at something he says. A girl slides her hand into the back pocket of the boy standing next to her as she waits for Ron to push french fries across the counter. As the girl and her boyfriend move their trays toward Carol, she tries to exude something like the kind of frivolity she imagines will make them like her too. She puts on a smile as she reads the green numbers from the screen at the top of the register. It feels odd, smiling at them, like something might escape her mouth if she doesn't keep her teeth clenched. But they don't even look at her. The boy pays for his meal, waves to some friends, and meanders toward a table while the girl counts change in her palm, distracted by the whereabouts of her boyfriend.

After the lunch rush has died down, Ron comes up behind Carol as she is shuffling ketchup packets into a cardboard box. He sits on a stainless-steel table and swings his legs back and forth like a child in a grown-up's chair. His eyes push into smile crescents, his arms folded across his chest. She knows that he works another job in the afternoons when he's done with this one, and that he is also taking advantage of the free class per semester he can take as an employee. On top of that, he sends a portion of his pay home to family members in Colombia—a mother and a sister, maybe others.

"What?" she asks.

"Carol, my friend. I hope it's okay. I want to say . . . You don't take well care of yourself." Carol grips the edge of the condiment counter.

"You want to say I'm fat?"

"No, no. Not that, you look good," he says. "You just not taking well care of yourself."

She sighs. "I know, Ron. I know. And . . . I appreciate your concern."

"Sorry," he says. "Hey, we friends, right? I know you been sad since this with your daughter, but you are a beautiful woman. You shouldn't, how you say, allow yourself go."

"Let myself go," she corrects him, thinking, *beautiful woman?*

They are silent for a long moment. Finally, she says, "Thank you. Really. It helps." She is still holding ketchup packets. "We've been working here how long, Ron?"

"I am here almost a year."

"Yeah, and I've been here since I was born."

He looks at her quizzically, then smiles when he understands her sarcasm.

"Thing is, it's a shithole," she goes on, tucking the slippery little packets into their box.

"A what?"

"Shithole." She closes the box of ketchups. "The best part of my job is teaching you new vocabulary."

"Shithole. Ha ha. That's a good one." He slides off the table.

"Useful in this world."

"Yes, Miss Carol. It is a shithole."

Ron finishes cleaning the kitchen while Carol straightens the cutlery.

"I go to my other job," he says after he's finished. "See you tomorrow, Miss Carol."

"Bye, Ron. See you tomorrow. Hey, *hasta mañana*, right?"

He flings a denim jacket over one shoulder. On his way past a group of students, he taps his fingertips on the middle of their table. The kids react with friendly commotion and one lifts his hand for a high five, which Ron executes with precision.

Carol waits for the last couple of students to approach the register. There isn't much left for them to choose from now that the grill is closed, just a few Colombo yogurts and waxy red delicious apples. After she pulls the grate down in front of the grill and refrigerators, she counts out her drawer and locks it away. She grabs a plastic-wrapped peanut butter cookie from a three-story pastry shelf and pushes it into the pocket of her button-down smock. On her way past the tables, she slows down, looks at the students from half-lidded eyes to see if any might give her a high five, or even look her way, but none of them does.

***

Route 76 between Wattsville and Stratton Island Women's Correctional Facility is a scar through the woods. The trees are budding under a scalding blue sky. Carol's hands grip the steering wheel, and her eyes are fixed on the road. She's used to the drive and expects the numbness that normally settles on her, but today is different. It hits her all at once, and it's weird: like she isn't sure if the feeling has come from inside her, or if it was sprayed over her by some mischievous god. It's been so long, she has trouble recognizing it. A crush. She has a crush.

She tries to think back to any other crushes she's had in her life, but her mind won't land on anything other than her eighth-grade social studies teacher, Mr.

Muldoon. Mr. Muldoon was in his fifties but was kinder than anyone she knew. The evening after her junior high graduation she cried, clutching the handkerchief he'd given her one day during recess when she'd fallen and skinned her knee. He'd told her she could keep it and she had: a cheap bandanna, probably infused with his mucous and sweat. She never washed it and had tucked it between her pillow and pillowcase. She is a tiny bit surprised at herself as she remembers this detail. How had it gotten lost? At the time, it was her most prized possession, though she wouldn't have ever shared that with a soul.

Did she have a crush on her ex-husband, Beaver, before they'd gotten together? She can't remember but wonders now how she'd gone from idolizing a social studies teacher with thinning hair and kind eyes to getting pregnant by and marrying Beaver, about whom she can't think of a single positive thing to say.

She hates this drive, but today, with Ron on her mind, things are feeling a bit easier. Their conversation replays in her head and his interest in her feels like a tenuous lifeline that might pull her back from the despondency she's inhabited ever since Garnet's incarceration. She watches herself with interest to see how she will deal with this development. She hadn't even recognized it until today. This thing, the crush, has been there for longer, but only now does she recognize it as such and wonders if he feels it too. She's so out of practice it's hard to say. She should tell someone, but she already knows how each of the people closest to her would react: Sam would push her to do something she's not ready to do, and Garnet would encourage her to buy some new clothes and doll herself up. She'd even tell her to get her nails done.

Carol knows that to speak of her crush will cheapen it, so she decides to keep it to herself. She's good at that.

The parking lot is a giant shortbread cookie that crumbles under the Buick's tires. She always parks in the same spot—halfway down the row, next to the building. The car stays in the shade if she's visiting in the afternoon, and there are no potholes here, so no puddles form when it rains. There is no sign of rain anyway—and hasn't been in weeks. Forecasters are worried because it's early in the season for drought, but she likes it to be dry. Rain depresses her and makes her hair frizz.

Carol waits, chewing a piece of gum, while the guard goes through her pocketbook. He's new. Usually they ruffle through quickly and send her on, but this guard is examining every tiny scrap. And because Carol doesn't like to litter, her pocketbook often stands in as a trash can. The guard pulls out a key chain that Sam gave her—a bear that poops a rubber bubble when you squeeze its belly.

"I love these," he chortles, pressing it so the balloon inflates out of the bear's ass. "My cousin has one." He drops it and continues his exploration, pulling up anything that weighs more than a piece of paper: half a pack of Mentos, loose rectangles of shellacked Trident, the cardboard backing of a used-up checkbook. He takes her nail clippers and puts them into a plastic bag, pries open the corner of the Tupperware container of Rice Krispies treats, sticks his nose in, and hums approvingly. Carol knows that it's against official rules to bring in food because once a guard took away the cookies she'd brought, but other than that one time, they always let it go.

"You want one?" Carol says.

"I got allergies." He refastens the top of the plastic box. "Thanks though."

Garnet is already waiting. Carol hasn't allowed herself to cry since the day of the trial, but every single time she enters this room and sees her daughter at the table in her orange prisoners' uniform, she feels a lump rise in her throat and stinging behind her eyes. She approaches quickly. Inmates and visitors are allowed one three-second hug at the beginning and end of each visit, and Carol has to focus hard on something else to make it bearable to so quickly let go of her daughter. Today she squeezes Garnet's shoulders with her eyes focused on the vending machine and tries to count how many different snacks are displayed behind the spiral guardrails.

"Christ almighty," she says. "There's a new guard. Went through every little thing in my pocketbook." She scrapes back her chair and tosses the Tupperware onto the table. "I made you Rice Krispies treats."

Garnet's laugh is a low bubble. "You probably haven't even cleaned that thing out since 1980." She stretches her hands along the sides of the plastic box. "Thanks. I love these."

She takes out a buttery square and pushes the rest of them toward her mother, who takes one too, saying, "Easy to make, but they're tasty. No denying it." They chew and crunch, focusing on the flavor and texture of the bars. "So, you okay?" Carol says finally. "Everything okay?"

"Sure."

"Good. That's good. No news is good news, right?"

"No news is good news," Garnet agrees.

"You get outside yet?" Carol asks. "It's nice. The spring's here, finally. It's getting hot."

"Nope. Not yet."

"Got something to look forward to then, huh?"

"Yeah. Best part of the day, when it's nice out."

Carol wipes her fingertips down her thighs. "You'll be getting out soon." Garnet nods. "Bastard is doing fine now anyway," Carol goes on. "Hundred percent recovered."

"We don't need to get into that whole thing." Garnet sighs.

"Asshole should've been the one in here, not you."

Garnet presses her lips together.

"I mean, how they figured, how his fancy lawyers figured a way to make that stuff . . . not . . . relevant?" Carol's voice is rising in frustration. "I mean, it was . . . God, it makes me so . . ." She hums, like she's trying to keep the noise inside her body but it escapes anyway, through her nose.

It's a conversation they have often, even though Carol knows that Garnet is sick of hearing it. Carol understands her daughter wants to move on, put it behind her, but she can't help bringing it up. It feels like a balm because it puts her and her daughter squarely on the same team. But today Garnet's not taking the bait.

"Mom. We've been through this. Again and again."

"It still makes me mad."

"Ethan isn't so bad, you know. He put in a good word for me, to the parole board. Through his lawyers." Garnet sits on her hands, her shoulders curled over.

Carol has to catch her breath. "He. What?"

"Put in a good word."

"And . . . you know this . . . how?"

Garnet chooses that moment to have a coughing fit. Carol waits for her to finish and then repeats the question: "How do you know he did this?"

Garnet points at her throat. "I got a tickle. I hate that. All right, he wrote me a letter." She puts her fist to her mouth and coughs one last time.

"Are you out of your mind? Garnet. Did you forget what he did to you? And then he let you get punished for defending yourself?" Carol is on the verge of standing, ranting, pacing, but she stays put.

"But if he's gonna help me get parole . . ."

"If it means you're going to get back together when you get out," Carol interrupts, "then I'll have them keep you in here."

"Don't be stupid," Garnet says.

"I'm not being stupid."

"He's doing well, you know, at Holbrook. Getting good grades. Anyway, he's just helping me out."

Carol leans back and laughs bitterly. "Oh yeah. He wants to help you out! Help you out. That's like . . . that's like . . . it's like the murderer doing a good deed by . . . paying for his victim's funeral. Or something." Carol breathes heavily. "You'd be at Holbrook if we could afford it. And you'd be doing well too. Better than him."

"I did nearly kill him, Mom. Don't forget that."

"Self-defense."

"Still. The trauma to his head."

"Like the Thaxters don't have enough money to cover hospital costs." Abruptly, Carol cocks her head and squints at her daughter's black curls. "Your hair looks fancy."

"What are you talking about?"

"Just, it looks like you got your hands on some product. I hope he's not bringing you stuff."

"One of the girls gave it to me," Garnet says meekly.

"You've always been a terrible liar."

"It's only a little mousse. Nothing to get worked up about."

"No, it's not only a little mousse. I don't know why you can't see that. It's not so simple. Honey. It's not so simple. It's. God. It's. How can you be so"— and her voice rallies to a hoarse shrillness— "stupid!"

"God Mom, relax. It's a little canister of foam. You never thought of bringing me any."

"I'll bring you some stupid product, Garnet. I didn't know you wanted to do yourself up in here. I don't know why you'd want to do that. I'll bring you whatever you want." She shakes her head, frowning.

Garnet runs a palm along her fluffy hair. "He's being nice. Why shouldn't I let him be nice? If it's gonna help me? He's trying to help."

Carol's hands are stretched on the tabletop, her knuckles white with anger.

"The better I do with the parole board, the more likely I'll get out."

Carol leans forward like a sumo wrestler, her expression threatening.

"Fuck you, Mom." Garnet rocks back and forth in her seat, angry but cowed. "I know what I'm doing."

"It's wrong. You're wrong."

"I'm gonna get back," Garnet says, pushing herself up. "I love you." She pistons over to the exit, but remembers the Rice Krispies treats and turns around. She takes them quickly from the table and kisses her mother's immobile cheek.

Carol watches her daughter recede through the wire-inlayed glass. "God dammit," she says, too forcefully, and the couple at the table closest to her, a gigantic Mr. T and a petite white woman with straw hair gathered into a plastic clip, turn to stare at her.

BREAKING UP IS HARD TO DO

Garnet's Diary

Dear Diary,

I'm in love. I have that song, "Breaking Up Is Hard to Do," rolling through me like it's melted butter and it's greasing up the gears inside my brain. "You know that breaking up is hard to do. Now I know, I know that it's true, cuz breaking up is hard to dooooooo!"

So much joy in that song. Sometimes I think that getting back together after splitting up is even more romantic than when you first meet someone, first fall in love. Because you have to be more real. You can't pretend, and you know each other's dark sides. I know Ethan's dark side, and I think I can love him anyway.
☺

I feel so alive with it.

Shanise is sleeping. She looks pretty, like a baby. Her lips are loose and full like raw calamari. There is a wisp of saliva starting to dampen the My Little Pony quilt she keeps on her bed. She looks so peaceful.

It's nice sometimes when one of us is awake while the other is asleep. It's the only private time we get. Well, she doesn't like it the way I do. She usually coughs or drops something on the floor when I'm dozing because she doesn't like to be alone. Luckily, she needs more sleep than me. If she's awake when I'm writing, she keeps asking what I'm writing about. "What're you scribbling at, Gar?"

"Just keeping track of stuff." I guess that's what I'm doing: keeping track.

Two girls sharing a room with the toilet right in here, with no toilet seat cover. The smells are pretty gross, being so close to someone's well-you-know. I won't burden you with a description of that. Not even you, and you're only a book half-full of empty pages.

Ethan sent me hair mousse and chocolates. Two fantastic smells. Mousse reminds me of Saturday nights. Chocolate is love.

Right now, it's warm out, so the window is open. Not that we can see much. Last time I tried to see anything outside, besides the rectangle of sky I can see from my bed, Shanise's back had a spasm from me standing on top of her. But it was cool. Before I got down, I could see woods and mountains as if someone had tossed them across the horizon like a comforter. I can smell the Otis. I'm not an outdoorsy person, but it's hard to beat the smell of springtime near woods and river.

I'm smooshing a waxy wrapper from the chocolates up against my nose and inhaling. No more chocolates left, but still a lot of good smells today. Days are good when you can smell good things. On the outside, I never would've imagined that. Smells making or breaking a day. And what else? Ethan coming Saturday. Ethan coming Saturday. Ethan coming Saturday!

So okay,

Ethan loves me. It's like this. I'm better than he is and he knows it. That's the way it should be, right? He says he doesn't know who he is without me. What is love? Making each other better people, right? Okay, so I make Ethan better. Does he make me better? He's got money. Maybe that can be his contribution. Seriously. It sounds bitchy and shallow, but maybe it's a fair trade-off. I make him a better person and he can support me. Maybe he'll pay for my school now that I won't be eligible for loans. Which is his fault, so it's fair. That's balance. Balance is life.

It was weird, after not seeing each other for so long. We kissed. We only had the couple of seconds before the guard told us to let go of each other. Ethan's lips were hungry but mine were shy. He tasted weird. I love him. I get butterflies when I see him. He's handsome. He takes care of me. I guess he makes me a better person too, because he loves me so desperately. Yes, so desperately he did some bad stuff. But he promised never again. He's promised before, but I'm leaning in the direction of believing him, this time for real. This time for real.

I think a lot about his mom. I wonder if she's been trying to win a battle for his soul. Against me. She's a bitch. I had her for Home Ec (which boys don't even have to take—so dumb). That was before I knew who Ethan was. Mrs. Thaxter. If there was an award for most-hated teacher, I would put my money on her.

She used to go on about how us girls were going to need to be able to do things like cook and sew because our lot in life wouldn't allow us to do much more. Those of us lucky enough, she said (pretty enough, is what she meant), would get to be wives. The rest would be cleaners or cooks or nannies or, if we were gifted, secretaries. She was a mean bitch and you could tell she only liked a couple of the prettiest girls. Now that I know her better, I think they reminded her of herself: beautiful and not much else. She would let those girls do whatever they wanted. They could listen to their Walkmans or go off to the bathroom for nearly the whole class, while, if the rest of us acted like that, we'd get detention. I guess she knew they didn't need skills, because they had looks.

You know, Diary, I think she didn't want them to have skills or brains or anything else because that would've meant that it was possible to have it all, and since Mrs. Thaxter didn't have it all, then nobody else should either. If they'd been smart, it would mean they were better than her, and she wouldn't have been able to stand that. I never thought about it at the time, but it's possible that some of them were very smart. So smart they knew to pretend they weren't in order to stay on Mrs. Thaxter's good side. Maybe they didn't even know that's what they were doing. Boy, people sure can be complicated—and clever, without even knowing it.

I remember the first day I met Ethan. I was leaving school, late because I'd had detention that day (ha! For skipping Home Ec!) and I was digging through my book bag for a lighter or matches. I used to smoke, but I quit. That's a good thing that Ethan did for me: he got me to quit smoking. I guess in that way he makes me a better person! He hates cigarettes—they make him wheeze and his eyes water. The first time I met him though, there I was, with a ciggy hanging off my lip and looking for a light. He was sitting on the wooden rail that goes along the driveway leading up to the school. I asked him for matches and he said he didn't have any.

When I got to the counter of the Sunshine Mart, next to the school, he came in after me. "Are you following me?" I said and he looked so shy. When he blushes it's like two pink creatures are snuggling underneath the skin in front of his ears.

"I'm getting a Pepsi. You want one?"

"You buying?" I said, and he said sure so I let him get me a Mountain Dew. We stood in the parking lot, drinking. I asked what grade he was in. I'd never seen him.

"I'm up at B-squared," he said and I looked confused so he explained. "You know Buckingham Browne? Two Bs?" Everyone knows what Buckingham Browne is, but I'd never heard it referred to as B-squared, and it made me laugh. I guess I used to feel sorry for myself that I couldn't afford to go somewhere like B-squared, but Ethan says it's full of drug-ridden fucked-up kids who are all near

geniuses and totally misunderstood by their families. He meant it in a bad way, but to me that sounds fun and I still kinda wished I went there!

"What are you doing hanging around here then?"

He explained that his mother taught Home Ec at my school and I said, "Holy shit. You're Mrs. Thaxter's son?" and he nodded. "But Mrs. Thaxter is . . ."

I trailed off and he said, "a bitch," and I laughed so hard and decided right then that I wanted to date the guy. You know, it's weird, but sometimes he wants to be his own person, screw what his mom thinks, right? And then other times, he seems disgusted by me just like she does. And he'll treat me like he deserves a hell of a lot better. In those times, I hate him, I really do. I write about those times so I won't forget, but I write down the good times too.

I can't imagine having a mom like his. My mom is so nice and I love her so much. But Ethan never got that. That's why I wouldn't trade places with him in a million years—no matter how much money and cars and fancy schools and clothes and whatever. That woman robbed him of something by being such a selfish and material bitch. She robbed him and I'm trying to fix it.

Take for example when Ethan and I had just started dating. I don't know if it was the very first time he brought me home but it was early on. Sunshine, his dog, was nicer to me than anyone else in the house—meaning his mom. His dad wasn't there. I only ever met that guy once or twice. He brings home the paycheck, but he's never home. We walked into the kitchen and Mrs. Thaxter was chopping something on a cutting board. Probably babies' feet or frogs' intestines.

"Hey, Mrs. Thaxter," I said.

Ethan was trying to be cool and make her seem cool and he goes, "You're not in school, Gar, so you can call her Margaret." He picked up an orange from the perfect, shiny fruit bowl and tossed it into the air.

You know, like anyone would do in their own home and she goes, cold as ice, "No, that wouldn't be appropriate," and then her voice goes up high and squeaky: "Do not toss fruit. It bruises." So he starts to peel it and she says, "Do that over the sink."

Their kitchen is like something out of Better Homes and Gardens. She's a Home Ec teacher so it stands to reason that she does a fair amount of cooking, and she does, but she has people who come in and clean up after her. Then there are people who take care of the yard, and do all the laundry, and everything else. I wonder what she does with her time because she doesn't have to do any of the stuff that most people spend all their time doing. I said it to Ethan once and he told me she was always going to the hairdressers and the nail salon and stuff.

Ethan went over to the sink to finish peeling the orange. Then he ate the thing, without offering me any.

When that woman speaks or breathes, a layer of ice covers everything touched by the air that comes out of her. I pulled my coat tighter around me. No one had offered to take it from me so I was still wearing it. I got bold for a second and picked up another orange. The witch watched me take it and said nothing; her face was a plastic mask. I started to peel it, and I was looking out the window at their amazing yard that stretched down the hill, dotted with perfect trees.

"Garnet," Ethan reminded me. "Peel it over here, okay?"

Now, I could be wrong, but the look of satisfaction on her face, like she'd won something, was creepy and horrible, and I just wanted to get the hell out of there.

On a normal day, Ethan would say bad stuff about her behind her back, but when she was there it was like that: a silent battle that she always won.

Ethan is sorry for what he did. Prosecuting me. But now here he is again, and he admits it all. He defends his mom though, sometimes. He says she pushed him to press charges because she had been so petrified when he was concussed. He was unconscious for more than an hour and it was really touch and go. She thought he'd die and even if she's a bitch, she still loves him.

I'm confused. Maybe it's just being here, after seeing him in the visiting room, with the guards and the other people talking to their loved ones in hushed tones— some of them in love, some of them pissed off as hell, but all of them missing each other. Other girls have talked about the way, when you're in the visiting room, it's like your former life comes to meet your current life and it can be wiggy.

He gave me some money, so I can buy some stuff from the store. I'm going to get myself a bottle of perfume. And Kit Kats for me and Shanise.

God.

I've been here five months. A lifetime. I never wrote about my first days. It seems like such a long time ago.

When I arrived, the jumpsuit they gave me felt scratchy and stiff. I'm used to it now, and I've nearly forgotten what it was like to wear clothes that were washed with regular detergent—not the metallic-smelling chemical stuff they use that leaves the fabric feeling like sandpaper. Anyway, the guard that led me to my cell was nice. He chatted to me the whole walk, and I know he was trying to calm me down. It was like he understood what it feels like on the first day—he didn't ask about my home life or my family or anything, just talked about the weather, and, of course, Monica Lewinsky, everybody's favorite conversation topic. Listening to him kept that big empty fear factory inside my head from dragging me into total darkness.

"If the president was French," he said, "he'd get a medal."

"Yeah, it's scummy," I might have said. "Who knows what any of them are up to."

I was answering distractedly; my memories of that day are all echoey like this building. I remember numbness and fear and disbelief. I remember that I nearly smiled when the guard said, "I liked her dress though. Nice color." So funny, all the hype about that dress! Anyway, he kept talking calmly until sliding open the door and putting me in here with Shanise.

Shanise wasn't very nice when we first met, though I can't blame her. I guess she was worried that I'd be a crybaby or crazy or something. After a while, when we finally started becoming friends, she told me about her last cellmate. The lady had some mental health issues and Shanise woke up to find her doing all kinds of weird things. Like the time she was playing with Shanise's toes. That's how she woke up: the chick was pulling at her feet. She was having some kind of flashback of a dead little sister or whatever, and she was playing this-little-piggy-went-to-market, this-little-piggy-stayed-home.

Shanise said she never wanted to look into the eyes of somebody so gone like that again.

When I think of gone, I think of Shanise's second cousin, Eloise, and her friend Molasses. Oh and Margaret Thaxter, of course! By the way, you might think it's a coincidence that Shanise has a second cousin in here. Small world, right? Well, Black girls are much more likely to end up here than White ones—through no fault of their own. I mean, they make up, what, 20 percent of Wattsville's population but 60 percent of the inmates? Yes sir, there's something seriously wrong with that. When I feel sorry for myself for whatever injustice I've had, I just think, well, it would've been a hundred times worse if I'd been Black. Everything's been easier for me, because I'm White—not that things have been that easy! Ha! But at least I can travel outside the city and walk around without people assuming I'm a criminal. Shanise and I talk about that stuff a lot. She's actually the best friend I've ever had and we can talk about absolutely anything.

Anyway, Eloise and Molasses are gone. In the head. It's drug-fueled goneness, though, which, even though I know addiction is an illness, still makes me have much less sympathy for them than I might have for someone like Shanise's old cellmate. Their eyes are only able to see opportunity for getting high. It must be exhausting. Shanise says Eloise wasn't always like that. Who would be? Kids aren't born addicts. Duh. They used to play together and go to each other's school dances and such, and then Eloise started in on the drugs and she got lost. And now, in here, where the drugs are a little harder to get, she's gotten meaner. A lot of women are gone on drugs or just gone on bad luck or craziness or whatever. Thank God I got put in here with Shanise. Shanise is a special person. She'd tell me to shut up if I said that out loud. But she really is.

At first, she didn't want to open up to me. Not until she knew how things were going to be between us. I understand that. I could've been like any of them.

I remember she just sat there reading magazines and I would ask questions and she'd give me one-word answers and nothing more. Like, here's a typical exchange from those early days:

"So," I'd say, "how long you gonna be here for?"

"Seven to ten."

"You grow up around Wattsville?"

"Yes."

"What are you reading?"

"Magazine."

"Okay. Okay. You don't want to talk."

"No."

So that was in the beginning, but then, after some time, she started to defrost. "Well we might both die of boredom," she said one day, turning onto her side and looking at me. Finally. I think that was the first time she ever looked at me. It was like I'd started to wonder if I really existed and then she looked at me and I knew I did. "You got a boyfriend?" she asked, and that was it. I started in on the story of Ethan and we've been friends ever since, sharing stories about boys and family and everything else. And I appreciate her advice, that I should forget about him. But, for better or worse, I do love him.

I wonder if me and Ethan will have kids. I'd like to one day. I wonder what kind of a father he'd be. And what kind of a mother I'll be.

I hardly ever think about my own father. I barely know who he is, and I don't think it matters because I have Mom. But I guess no one is complete without thinking about their two halves. And nature versus nurture. Mom was my nurture 100 percent but my dad is 50 percent of my nature; that's just the way it is. He left when I was a baby, and he was a substance abuser too. I didn't figure it out until I was a teenager. I don't know what I thought when I was younger. He'd show up once every six months or so and I'd just look at him—pudgy cheeks, red face, really red nose, and a mustache that drooped down at the sides toward his chin. He smiled and tried to get me to sit on his lap but I clung to Mom's leg and she didn't make me go near him. He'd get mad and leave, but Mom always made sure to tell me he was mad about something else, and that it wasn't my fault. I honestly don't remember having any emotions at all except that I was happy after he left because Mom would cut up apples and sprinkle them with cinnamon sugar and she'd let me eat them in front of the TV.

The first time I started thinking about him was when I was in eighth grade. I went through a phase when I'd threaten to go find him. I guess I was just trying to get my way with Mom, but she was cool and said, "Sure. Go find him," which wasn't the answer I was looking for. In my immature head, she was supposed to say, "Oh no honey, don't go! Stay here with me and you can hang out as late as you want with your friends."

And then there were the times I'd ask questions about him. I guess I was starting to think that I must be broken because I didn't have a father, so I'd ask. She'd say things like, "He loves you, of course, you're his daughter, but he doesn't know how to act." Or, "He's good, deep down, but he has some problems." Ha. That's sort of like what I say about Ethan. Life's funny, isn't it? It's hard to know what's right.

Mom used to drink too much, but my father did drugs. Mom wasn't going to tell me that but I asked outright and she said yes, he was an addict and probably wasn't going to live too long, which is why she thought it was better that he wasn't around. But she was in denial that she had a drinking problem. She was controlled about it, but she'd drink nearly every day. She'd never pass out or anything, and she was always able to take care of me, but she rarely went to bed at night without a few drinks in her. Most people probably wouldn't even call it a problem, but I challenged her to stop and so she did. She says she's still not drinking, and I hope that's true, but part of me thinks, what the hell? She's got no kid at home anymore, so why not have a few?

She doesn't look so good lately. She's gotten pretty heavy. I mean, we're big-boned women both of us, but I can see she's having trouble walking and she wheezes when she walks too far. I wish she'd find a boyfriend. I never thought about it when I was growing up. She was always there for me. Made dinner every single night. Now that I'm grown, it would be great to see her with somebody. Somebody nice, and good. Somebody who treats her right.

Truth is, when I think of me and Ethan and a family, I can't picture it. I guess it's because, in my experience, it's just a mother and a kid. No father. At least I have that in common with most of the women in here, Shanise included. Makes you think, huh? I just hope, if me and Ethan work things out, we'll be different than most of the marriages I know. I guess the odds aren't in our favor. Stay tuned!

BIG FISH, SMALL POND

Sam

Sam walks toward the old mill, shaken by his run-in with the ATV-riding hoodlums and thankful to have avoided any altercation. The voices of the workmen become clearer and he can make out a man giving orders to several workers: "We'll start in the back," he is saying, and one of the workers translates into Spanish for the other two. The boss has an Irish accent, unkempt strawberry-blond hair, and a lumpy potbelly like two buttocks resting in the hammock of his T-shirt. The one who'd been translating for the others—early-forties and attractive—is still tying his work boots. The other two wait for him: A slightly bulkier man with a dollop of gray at each temple and a pockmarked face, and a younger guy, with thick, waxy hair and earnest eyes. The three of them grab shovels; they start filling industrial trash bags with splinters of wood, nails, metal, and chunks of crumbled cement.

"Hello," Sam says. The boss jumps a little and Sam apologizes. "There were some scary people on the path. Riding those four-wheeled motorcycle thingies. They're gone now." The man shakes his head and turns away. "It's not the first time I've been harassed anyway, I can tell you that." Sam fans his face with an open palm, then motions to the gutted mill. "It looks good." He is sweating, so his eye shadow is dulling and starting to droop. "Um, the mill. You're renovating?"

"Yup. We're renovating," the man says.

"Can I . . . look around a little? It's just that . . . I always loved this place. I like to imagine it, you know, when it was a mill and with people working in it . . . So, what are they going to make, condos or something?"

The mill has brick walls that are a couple of feet thick, and the beams in the roof and the second floor are sturdy and rustic. Since the crew has started renovating, it looks less dilapidated—the sagging wooden floors, the splintered window frames and broken glass, all the parts that had given it the quality of something in decay, are being stripped, leaving the skeleton. The Spanish-speaking workers are carrying refuse to a dumpster and they stop to watch Sam and the Irish boss.

"Yep, condos upstairs, some shops and all on the first floor."

"You're Irish," Sam says, a little flirtatiously.

"You can't be looking around here, miss . . ." his tongue skids at the *s* sound, unsure where to go with it. Mister or Missus. "It's a hard-hat area."

Sam looks at the man's bare head and squints. "Right. Well. You've got a lot to do. I shouldn't bother you."

"You're brave to do it."

"Brave? Why?"

"Well, like, you know," he laughs. "Look at the state of you. What are you? Girl or what?"

"I enjoy being a girl." Sam aims a finger at the man's belly bulging over his belt. "When are you due?"

Two of the workers are carrying a heavy old beam. The handsome one translates for them, and he has to cover his mouth to keep from laughing out loud. The boss moves toward Sam, his hands forming fists.

"Come on now," Sam says, backing away. "You wouldn't hit a lady."

"I think you should get off of this property." He stops about three feet from Sam. Sam moves back. He steps forward again and Sam steps away, but his heel catches a rock and he falls, in slow motion at first while his other foot tries to get into place to catch his balance, but suddenly time speeds up and he lands with a thud on his side. The man laughs. "And you're not even wearing heels."

Sam is clutching his ankle and whimpering.

"Alright, alright, don't go getting your knickers in a twist, like. I didn't mean for you to fall down."

"I think it's sprained." Sam purses his lips. He slides off his sneaker and sock.

"Oh for feck's sake. Ron!" The Irish man calls. Sam touches his ankle gingerly. "Ron's good with this stuff. Jesus but you're a girl's blouse." He turns and walks toward his truck.

The worker named Ron crouches and takes Sam's ankle in his hands, runs his thumb over the outside of it.

"It hurts here?" he asks. Sam wipes a finger along the lower rim of his eyes. "Or more here?"

Sam yelps. "I don't have any health insurance . . . and I can't afford to miss work. I hope it's going to be okay."

Ron turns the foot in small circles, his thumb resting on the joint.

"Do you know about these things? Are you a doctor or something?"

"No. I'm not a doctor." Ron's eyes meet Sam's for an instant, and he turns away quickly.

The boss comes back with a cigarette dangling from the corner of his mouth. "That'll do, don't need a doctor."

"Oh, go get stuffed." Sam waves his hand as though he could shoo him away. The boss mutters and lights his cigarette. Sam turns his attention back to the man cradling his foot. "Well, if you're not a doctor, what did you do . . . wherever you're from?"

Ron pushes his thumb into Sam's outer ankle.

"Oh!"

"I worked."

"Mmm. Mysterious."

He lowers Sam's foot to the ground and hands him his sneaker. "It will be okay. Just try to rest."

"Thank you." Sam leans in the direction of the sock that lays crumpled on the leaves. "Could you just—?" Ron takes the sock between his thumb and forefinger and drops it onto Sam's lap.

***

Later, Sam is in front of the TV, a bag of frozen peas on his foot, when Carol knocks at the door.

"Christ, what happened to you? You're not going to eat those things, are you?"

"They were old anyway." Sam kneads the softening peas. "I think I bought them during the Carter administration."

"What happened?"

"Just twisted. Not sprained. So said . . . a very handsome Latino."

"Who?"

"Oh Carol, you should have seen it." He tells her the story. Carol chews her nails and listens, looking periodically at the television screen. "He was so . . . chivalrous."

"I'm glad you had a good time twisting your ankle. You need anything?"

"No honey, no thanks."

"There's a South American guy works with me in the college," she says.

"Ooh, Carol he was so sexy. Is yours sexy?"

"He's not bad. Yes. He's handsome."

"I think we had a connection."

"You'd think you had a connection with the pope."

"I probably would."

Carol laughs through her teeth, making a hissing sound.

"You just never know who you're going to meet. Oh Carol, life can be so full of wonderful things."

"I guess."

"Listen. I'm not lecturing, but I'm singing on Friday. Why not come? You could use a night out."

"I dunno. It's all gay guys when you do your karaoke thing."

"Well, you think about it."

"Yeah, maybe. I know you'll want to go back and see that guy but I don't think you should be walking in the woods."

"I'll be careful, I promise."

"You sure you don't want anything? To eat?"

"I guess I am a little hungry."

"I've got lasagna upstairs. You want me to bring some down?"

"No, that's okay . . . except . . . I guess, if you don't mind. Would you?"

"I'll be back in a minute."

"You're a doll, Carol. You know I love you."

When she leaves, Sam flips through stations, stopping when he comes to a telenovela. A woman in a stunning cobalt dress and heavy makeup is going from angry to irate at a black-haired man in a white suit. Finally, mid-rant, the man pulls the woman into his arms and kisses her passionately. Sam sighs and changes the channel.

"I have to upgrade," he declares as Carol returns with a plate of lasagna.

"No shit. I don't know how you live without any of the good channels."

"It's expensive."

"You make it work. Cook more," she says.

Sam nods and looks guiltily toward the kitchen, where his routine consists of pouring the contents of takeout containers onto plates or microwaving frozen meals. He blows on a forkful of lasagna to cool it. "Oh honey, how could I start trying to cook? You have me spoiled." He chews and makes an appreciative humming sound.

"Maybe I'll bring some to Garnet. She loves my lasagna."

Sam nods. Carol's eyes are trained on the plate of lasagna. "She's been in touch with Ethan. By the way."

"What?" Sam shrieks. "Why didn't you tell me?" The plate nearly slides from his lap.

Carol shrugs.

"But why?"

Carol shakes her head.

"Carol!"

"I know. I know. She said he apologized. I didn't even want to tell you." Carol recounts her visit to Stratton Island: Garnet's hair product, her defense of Ethan. "God dammit, Sam. Is she gonna get back together with him? Honest to God, I don't know what she's thinking. I just don't know what do with her."

"Can . . . Ethan . . ." Sam has as much trouble spitting out his name as Carol does. ". . . really help?"

"Maybe. I don't know. I'd prefer her to stay in that place than to get out and get back together with him." Carol puffs up like a scared cat.

"I'll go with you this weekend. Maybe I can talk to her," Sam says.

Carol brightens a little. "I'll make cookies."

"You should have had a great big family on a farm somewhere, honey."

"Yeah, coulda shoulda woulda." Carol stands up. "I'm gonna go back up and watch HBO. You wanna come? The elevator's fixed."

"Thanks honey. I better rest my ankle. I have to work in the morning. We'll go this weekend, to see Garnet. Maybe together we can, I don't know, do something."

"She loves you," Carol says. "Maybe she'll listen."

***

The next day, the warm weather continues and his ankle feels better so, after work, Sam decides to walk home. Near the old mill he stops and listens. The Irish boss's truck isn't there, but Sam can hear voices, so he approaches. The three workmen are shoveling debris. Sam has several copies of the *Chronicle* under his arm.

"Hellooo," he sings out. "I was passing by and I wanted to say thanks." He extends folded newspapers toward the men.

The handsome one takes the papers and hands them out to the other two men, introducing them as Jorge, the older of the two, and Jaime, Jorge's nephew. "And my name is Ronaldo," he says.

"Hola! Hi!" Sam smiles and waves.

Jorge shrugs. "No speak English," he says.

"Oh yeah, oh gosh," Sam says. "I know poco Spanish. Hola. *Me llamo* Sam."

"You are a funny man," Ronaldo says.

"I know," Sam laughs. He is wearing a pair of khaki culottes and a fern-green sweater that crosses between stuffed breasts. "That's just me." He looks over his shoulder as if to see if he's been followed. "The woods can be a dangerous place, but I feel so much safer knowing you're all here, you know? When I'm walking home?"

Jaime mutters something in Spanish, drops his copy of the *Chronicle* into a trash bag, and plucks a broom off the wall.

"No problem," Jorge says. "No problem. Is okay." He scolds his nephew in Spanish, but Jaime shrugs him off and starts pushing the broom.

"Oh, I'm not offended," Sam says quickly. "I talk fast and he doesn't understand."

Ronaldo translates and Jorge nods.

"Your ankle?" Ron asks.

Sam puts his weight on one foot and then the other. "Much better, a little weak, but fine. Thank you. Oh, this place. Such a marvelous structure. So. What are you going to do after it's cleaned out?"

"We just demo. Subcontracting. After finish, another construction company will come."

"Oh that's too bad. Demolition doesn't seem as much fun . . . or maybe it is fun. God knows I'd like to demolish something sometimes!"

"We better get back to work."

"*Sí!*" Sam says. "Don't let me bother you." He wanders through the mill, stepping lightly around the men as they sweep and shovel and haul.

"As someone who probably would've been hanged or shot if I'd lived then," he says to the ceiling, "I do love to think about a simpler time." The men keep working, unsure whether they are expected to be listening. "Maybe I'd have been masculine in a simpler time. I would've had to work all day long—in the fields or something—and I wouldn't have had time to think about my identity." He turns suddenly. "Would that have been a good thing or a bad thing?"

Ronaldo looks at him quizzically. Sam explains, "Would it have been better to live back then, in the past, when things were simpler? Or is it better to live now? *Mejor*, right? Better?"

"Yes, yes. *Mejor*." Ronaldo has a thoughtful look on his face. "In the past. Yes. *Cierto*. I think."

Jorge and Jaime glance up, trying to make sense of the words.

"I don't know," Sam says. "I think that too, a lot of the time. But I'd have been killed! Not that I haven't been almost killed now! And also, back then, everyone had to work all the time, just to survive."

"No, no. People did good work. Work for themselves."

"Well, not here. Not in this factory. They were all working for the man, you know what I mean?"

Ronaldo nods. "I guess I mean more long ago. Not so long in my country."

"Where are you from?"

"Colombia."

Sam shudders. "Oh, that's a dangerous place. From what you hear."

Ronaldo motions toward the other two. "They are from Honduras. Thank you for ask. Most people don't. They think we all Mexican. And the *jefe*. Boss," he looks toward the road. "McMaster. He from Ireland. I return to work."

"Oh, yes, gosh. I'm sorry. I didn't mean to keep you." Sam wanders on through the mill. The workers' shovels and voices become fainter as he walks.

He stretches his arms out like a child pretending to be an airplane. The structure makes a ninety-degree turn toward the river and Sam can hear the rush of water. He leans out a hole in the wall where a window once was and watches the water charge by, all mossy gray and cappuccino foam. The river is narrow here, so it is faster and more intense.

He turns and goes back toward the men but stops short when he sees they are huddled around their boss, McMaster the Irishman, whose truck Sam hadn't heard over the sound of the river. Jorge sees him but looks away quickly, and Sam makes a dash for a tower of concrete bags against the wall. He can hear the four men moving closer. McMaster is giving directions and inspecting their work. Sam sits on his haunches, knees up, culottes sagging down to his hips, and hugs himself as he used to do as a child when his father would come home in a rage—shrinking himself into a corner to escape the sound of things breaking and his mother crying.

McMaster's boot stomps in front of him.

"Holy fecking Christ!"

"Oh, my heavens. You scared me." Sam stands, brushing the dust from his behind. "I was just. I was looking . . . for . . . well, I just left something, before."

"I don't know what you're after, but you're not gonna find it here."

"Don't get all upset, okay? It's not a big deal. I came to say thank you to your kind worker who examined my ankle when I was in distress."

"I've got enough troubles," McMaster says. "And you're trespassing."

"I'm just walking home."

"If I were you, I'd get home as fast as your fecking girl legs will carry you."

"All right, mister. Listen. I'm going, but there's no need to be rude."

"No need to be rude," McMaster mimics. "You know what? You need to learn a lesson. Today I'm in a mood to teach it to you." His arm hinges out to the side, his fist floating menacingly. He steps forward and Sam steps back, palms out.

"Take your feckin hands down. Ye cunt. Ye fecking freak."

"That is not a word we use in this country." Sam straightens. "I don't want you to talk to me that way. You know that? I really don't." He pushes the hair from the sides of his face. "You . . . fatso."

Jorge and Jaime giggle a bit. They understand the gist. McMaster becomes even more enraged. He grabs the sleeve of Sam's shirt until the neckline pulls down over his shoulder, revealing a black bra strap. Sam swings around after his sleeve. Ronaldo puts his hand on McMaster's arm. McMaster turns and elbows Ronaldo across the jaw. Jorge catches Ronaldo as he stumbles backward and Jaime, not amused anymore, takes three steps toward McMaster, cocks his arm, and knocks him out with one blow, leaving him unconscious on the floor while the three workers and Sam hover in stunned silence.

***

Sam gets to work early the next morning, before any of the other inserters. The sun has begun to bleed inky blue light into the darkness but hasn't yet cracked open the horizon. Larry is at his desk with his hands wrapped around a mug of coffee.

"Good morning!" Sam yodels as he plucks his time card from the holder on the wall.

"You're early today."

Sam scratches his fingers around the bottom of his nylon fanny pack until he's collected two quarters, slides them into the coffee machine, and waits for the Styrofoam cup to fill.

"You look good," Sam says. "Have you been dieting?"

"I've been trying not to eat desserts. If that counts as dieting."

"Oh are you kidding?" Sam says. "Everything counts! Especially if it's working!"

"Well thanks," Larry says, returning to the papers in front of him.

Sam looks right and left as though making sure he won't be hit by traffic, then scurries to Larry's desk and sits down. "I have a sort of favor to ask. Well, I mean, it might be a favor for me and it might be a favor for you." Sam tells him about the incident at the mill, how he'd gotten into an altercation with McMaster, how the South Americans had helped him, how strong and capable they are. How, after they saved him, Sam had been struck with the idea of getting the men jobs, better jobs. And how they were hard workers, and good people. He leaves out how hard it had been to get them to understand him. The one who speaks good English didn't want to leave his job, and, while Sam had instructed the other two, through slow, loud English and lots of hand gestures, when to meet him at the *Chronicle*, the other man had attended to McMaster and told them all to run when McMaster started to regain consciousness.

Sam motions toward where the nasty young guys usually stand on the line. "Those . . . hooligans . . . are unreliable," he says. "I mean, they don't even show up half the time. Not Tommy, of course. But those others." He looks to Larry for some encouragement. Larry shrugs to indicate that Sam is right.

"I mean, I'm not going to tell you to fire them, Larry. But we both know that they don't deserve those jobs. They're terrible workers."

Their conversation is cut short by the squeak of the door opening. Tommy comes in and drapes his hoodie on a hook. Sam stands, brushes the wrinkles from his capris, and moves toward his station. "Give them a chance," he stage-whispers. "I give you my word you won't regret it."

The other boys don't show up for work—again—and Larry has to fill in on the line.

When the work is done, Sam and Larry are sitting on boxes of the next day's circulars. Sam likes to be around the hulking inserting machine after it has gone to sleep. He likes the dusty, oily smell and the peacefulness that comes when the loud monster is at rest.

Larry concedes that he hasn't been having much luck with hiring. "When the Anamax plant shut down," he says, "things went downhill around here. You know that. You remember."

"I understand how hard it must be. The guys who had union jobs, they don't want to be here."

"And young people are entitled and lazy. I hate to say it, but it's true."

"That's why I think you'll be glad," Sam assures him.

"It's a risk," Larry admits. "I don't like to make it a habit. But, if they're hardworking, like you say, and we make deadline without having to kill ourselves, like we did today, it will be . . ."

"Worth it," they say in unison, then laugh, a little awkwardly.

"Great minds think alike," Sam says.

***

With Sam's help, Jorge and Jaime fill out applications.

"*Muy bien,*" Sam says with an accent that gives *muy* two syllables. "Moo-ee bien. You'll like it here." He looks at Larry and winks.

Jaime asks his uncle what to write, pointing at the part of the application that asks for previous experience. Jorge tells him something.

"What what what?" Sam says. "What is it? Do you have a question?"

"A-okay," Jorge says.

"I feel like we're in this together, you know what I mean? Like it's a karmic connection."

"I sorry," Jorge says. "No understand."

"That's okay," Larry laughs, "he doesn't make sense to a lot of people."

Jorge points to where it asks for Jaime's social security number and says something. Jaime nods and writes numbers in the squares.

Sam smiles at Larry. "I think they're happy," he says. "I think they're saying they're happy."

***

Curiosity about Ronaldo, who had declined to come for a job interview, makes Sam sneak close to the mill again on his way home. He smiles to himself as he thinks about Jorge and Jaime but, at the same time, cautions himself against feeling too much pride over having helped them out. After all, it's his fault they got in trouble in the first place. Still, he can't help but feel a little heroic.

McMaster's truck isn't there, so he figures it's safe to have a closer look. He can see Ronaldo moving around inside the building; dust rises up around him like clouds in a Hollywood heaven and the way his jeans hang reminds Sam of April in the Firefighters of New York calendar that is propped on the windowsill in his apartment. Ronaldo leans over to pick something up and Sam can make out the contour of his bicep; it moves against his arm like something that has a life of its own. Sam acts like a statue, partially hidden by a tree, and watches, half-hoping that Ronaldo will look up and see him and half wanting the perfection of the moment to never end.

He is about to make his presence known when a car pulls off of Route 22 and eases into a spot. Sam crouches by the base of the tree. Behind the tinted window there is the quick pulse of a cigarette being lit and the window lowers for an arm to throw a match onto the pavement. The car is shiny and black, but Sam doesn't know what make it is. He's never cared much for cars; he doesn't own one and isn't interested in fancy ones. This car, however, is obviously expensive. The grate on the front is like a silver doorway, the right size for a hobbit, and the headlights are two white streaks that resemble war paint on the car's face. Ronaldo gets in on the passenger's side. The car continues to idle, cigarette smoke wafting from the sunroof. Then Ronaldo gets out and the car backs up and pulls away.

Ronaldo walks unsteadily to the doorway of the mill, out of sight of the retreating black car, puts his fist against the wall and leans his forehead onto it. His whole body—that beautiful calendar-worthy physique—clenches and doubles over and shakes and Sam can see that he is crying. A twig breaks under Sam's foot as he shifts position, and Ronaldo swings around. Sam approaches, trying to be as nonchalant as possible.

"Why are you here?" Ronaldo demands, his voice nasal from crying.

"What, me? What do you mean? I'm just walking home."

"Please go away."

Sam takes a step closer. "Are you okay?"

"You already cause enough trouble. You should go home."

Sam stands still, unsure whether Ronaldo is actually angry, or whether he should read his anger as a call for help. "Maybe I can help you, the way you helped me?"

"Go away now. Please." Ronaldo picks up a shovel and holds it in striking position.

"I was just trying to help."

Ronaldo makes a move toward Sam with the shovel and Sam, though certain that he wouldn't actually hurt him, turns and jogs back toward the path.

***

Karaoke night. Sam is drinking club soda with cranberry and lime and listening to his friends, Francine and Chloe, complain about what a provincial and small-minded city Wattsville is. It's hard to disagree, but he feels defensive. He wishes he could explain to them about the people he knows, humble and complicated in their own ways, and how fulfilling it is to be him: he is sure that his mere presence improves Wattsville. He brings diversity and encourages tolerance, though his acceptance has been hard-won.

He and Francine and Chloe have shared their coming out stories—all three are from small towns, but Sam is the only one who elected to stay where he grew up. Dressing as a woman in public was a slow evolution, beginning with letting his hair grow long, then putting on some eyeliner, his fashion slowly becoming more feminine, until, under the noses of everyone in Wattsville, he'd become who he is. And he usually feels safe—despite the antagonism of some people, like the young guys at the *Chronicle* or that Irish contractor. In general, Wattsville has become used to him and he's comfortable here.

Chloe and Francine live in the city, capital C, and their sarcasm toward the locals is hard to stomach. They usually spend the weekend in nearby Patten-on-Otis, relaxing at their favorite bed and breakfast during the day and coming to Wattsville to shop and go out at night. Sam has known them for almost ten years—since the Sheraton first listed karaoke night in *After Dark* magazine. And he's grateful. Attendance by people like them has made this twice-a-month, gay-friendly sanctuary possible in the midst of this blue-collar, politically red, socially conservative area.

"It's a culinary wasteland," Chloe is saying to Francine. "If I lived here, god forbid, I don't know what I'd do without authentic sushi."

"Yes, that's true, but it's so relaxing. You don't have to eat, it's only a weekend! So many trees in one place—it's good for the soul. One couldn't be an artist without being able to recharge the batteries. Breathe good air. And the Otis is ... so quaint, compared to the Hudson. It is worth the drive."

Chloe has a Vera Wang purse and her shoes are Jimmy Choo, but Sam knows, despite her glamorous trappings, that she lives in a tiny studio apartment and sometimes has trouble making rent. Francine, however, who recently had gender-affirming surgery, is an acclaimed abstract artist, and a millionaire.

"It's fine for a weekend, but I don't know how anyone would choose to live here. Aside from the complete lack of culture, the economy's the pits and it's impossible to even make a living. No. The city is the only real place to be."

"Wattsville is a city too," Sam says, and they snort at him.

"You can't call this a city with a straight face."

"Well, it has a city hall. And that's what it is. It's a small city, that's true. But a city nonetheless. It's not so bad when you get used to it."

"Well," says Chloe. "I'd rather stick pins under my fingernails. I suppose one could get used to that too."

"Tracheal shave," Francine says to Sam, who has been admiring her neck. "It really does make a difference, doesn't it?" She looks frankly at Sam's Adam's apple.

"And your breasts are fantastic," Sam says.

She grins widely. "Sam, it's so completely worth it. I'm finally the me I've always dreamt. You know what I mean?"

Sam doesn't. He loves being a gay man who feels like a woman and dresses like a woman, but he doesn't mind treading water between the two sexes. It's hard to understand why anyone would need to tie herself so irrevocably to one shore. Especially when it means having a surgeon cut you up. He loves the body he was born with, respects it (Adam's apple notwithstanding). But he nods. He knows some people are simply born into the wrong body, and that the biological parts identifying them as one sex or another are completely alien and distressing to their owners. "I'm happy for you. And I'm glad it wasn't too traumatic. You know, the medical intervention."

"Intervention my ass, Sam. Medical savior of my very soul."

Chloe puts her hand on Francine's shoulder. "It's incredible and wonderful that you can do it."

"Well, I have the means," Francine says. "I am captain of my own ship." The waitress, a girl barely into her twenties, picks up the empty glasses from their table and balances them on a tray. "Another round, dear," Francine says. "My oh my."

She is looking at a table full of young guys across the room. "You have some admirers."

"I don't know," the waitress says quickly. "I don't know them." She fumbles and nearly tips the tray onto the floor. "I'll get your drinks."

"Youth truly is wasted on the young," Chloe opines.

Sam rests his elbow on the table and fiddles with his straw. He turns to look at the boys who had been admiring the cute waitress and recognizes one of them as Tommy. He pulls his purse onto his forearm, says, "I'll be right back, ladies," and makes his way over. There are four of them, and they're drinking bottles of Genesee.

"Well, well, well. Hello, Tommy!" Two of the boys snigger. Tommy says hello and the fourth boy turns away. "Are you going to introduce me to your friends?"

"Wow, Tom, you're making some interesting acquaintances since you got back," one boy says. He has a cowlick that makes the hair at his forehead grow backwards so he looks a little like the Fonz.

"Thank you," Sam says. "Actually, we work together. Who are you?"

"I'm his roommate." The boy squeezes Tommy's shoulder as if to say thanks for bringing the entertainment. "Hanky." He sticks his hand out and Sam shakes it.

Sam looks at each boy, taking his time. He's enjoying watching the other two squirm, their inability to decide whether to be friendly or not. One of them has acne scars and a crew cut. He smokes aggressively. The other wears an expensive-looking leather jacket; his face is turned away. Sam waits for them to say hello. Finally, the boy in the expensive jacket stands up, facing Sam. His eyes are stony.

"Anyone wants a ride, let's go."

"Ethan?"

"You know each other too?" Hanky laughs. "Small town, huh?"

"No. We don't know each other," Ethan says. "Let's go."

"Oh you do know me." Sam's surprise makes him unable to decide on anything else to say.

"Whatever," the boy says, and walks briskly toward the door. The other three follow, muttering about Ethan being the one with a car.

"See you tomorrow," Tommy says.

"Actually I have the day off," Sam says faintly, watching them leave. "Well, what do you know about that." He feels like his insides have been stirred up, and it takes some time to regain his equilibrium.

Francine and Chloe are chuckling when he returns. "My goodness, but you scared them away!"

"One of them works with me. Another was Ethan."

"The Ethan!" They gasp, having heard of Garnet's troubles.

"The one and only."

"Darling, if he were still here, I'd claw that boy's eyes out for you," Chloe says, looking at her manicure.

"I don't know what I could've done, but I feel like I should have done something."

"Nonsense," says Francine. "If you'd done anything, you'd only have ended up getting yourself into trouble."

"Francine's right," Chloe says. "What on earth could you have done? There were four of them!"

Sam slides a cigarette from Chloe's pack and lights it. "I'd love a drink."

Chloe lights his cigarette. "I'm not going to tell you anything, Sam. It's your life."

Sam unzips his purse and takes out the piece of paper that reminds him why he quit drinking. He reads it to Chloe.

"Dear self. Remember this: I quit drinking because I woke up in an apartment that I didn't recognize, next to a man I didn't recognize. I don't know what I did, but I feel like a huge pile of shit. Period. Don't do it."

"Everybody makes mistakes, but all right." Chloe takes a long sip of her vodka tonic and then a caressing drag from her cigarette, and it all seems to visibly unwind her. "Oh look, they're setting up shop." Sam turns to see the karaoke machine blinking to life. "That will make you feel better."

It's true. Sam loves the feeling of the mic in his hands and the dim suggestion of people looking up at him from beyond the spotlight's glare. He loves the way his voice gathers itself from the bottom of his lungs and pulses up and out of his throat in euphoric waves, his wide mouth shaping the wrenching lyrics. The applause, the feathers of hair tickling his shoulders as he bows and stands up again. And the way he feels afterward, as though he'd been scrubbed clean, energized.

He doesn't even need to sign up—Barry, the karaoke master, summons him before anyone else. He sings Tina Turner's "Better Be Good to Me," and the crowd loves it. Once, a woman told him that he was as close to the real Tina Turner as a white man could get. Levitating on applause, he floats back to where Francine and Chloe are ordering another round.

"I know I've said it before," Chloe says, "but you could make good money with that voice in the city. I could help you."

"Oh, thanks, honey. But gosh, I don't know. I'm getting old for picking up and moving. I don't know anyone there, only the two of you." He gulps his club soda, forgetting to cover his Adam's apple.

"Honey, you're good," Francine says. "Why not make use of it? Listen, the unemployment rate up here is double what it is in the city and the wages are half. What did you say you were doing? Working in a basement somewhere, on an assembly line?"

Sam looks at their drinks with envy and sucks his straw. How could he explain what keeps him in Wattsville? It seems obvious that he has very little in common with the people around him. In Wattsville he is one of a kind, whereas he would find many like-minded people in the city. But he's afraid. Its size scares him, and furthermore he wouldn't be particularly special. Here, he explains, he's a unicorn, a big fish in a small pond.

"Puddle," says Chloe. "It's not a pond, it's a puddle, my dear. You want to swim or lie there getting splashed? Heavens, the place is bound to evaporate in warm weather."

"Well, it's not that bad," Sam laughs. "I'll think about it though. It's flattering you think I could do it. Thank you."

"Well you could, my dear," Francine says. "But I've gotta tell you there's a whole new generation out there, coming right up behind us. If you want to grab it, then you should act fast."

That's what scares him. If you don't try, you don't have to fail, he almost says, and then realizes with shame that it sounds like something Carol would say. He would tell anyone to take a chance, to grab life by the horns and forget about the risk, but for himself, he has become frightened. "I'm not as daring as I used to be," he admits.

"You're braver than you think," Chloe says. "I mean you live here. I wouldn't have the balls to live here. So to speak."

"Anyway," Francine chimes in, "you can't be brave until you give yourself a chance to be."

Sam is overwhelmed by appreciation for his friends, and ashamed that he'd been annoyed by them earlier. He is warm inside, as though he's been drinking.

"You know," he says, "maybe you're right. Maybe there is a bigger world out there and I could be part of it." The Wagonwheel, with its stained carpeting and unfashionable people scuffling across the dance floor, tonight seems altogether at Sam's feet. He wonders if he'd ever feel that way in a bigger venue.

At closing time, he follows Chloe and Francine to Francine's car. It is white but Sam notices the grate has the same hobbit door as the black car he'd seen pull into the lot next to the old mill—the car that Ronaldo got into and then out of.

"What kind of car is this, Francine?"

Francine giggles and Chloe laughs loudly.

"It's a Bugatti, my dear."

"A Bugatti? Never heard of one. It looks nice." Sam slides onto the back seat and pulls the door closed.

"It's a wonderful way to ride," Chloe says.

Sam can see Francine's proud smile as she puts the car into reverse and pulls onto the main road.

"Bugatti," Sam says, yawning and leaning into the headrest. "Funny the way you never see something and then you see it twice in the same day. Expensive?"

"May be one of the most expensive, isn't that right, Francine?" Chloe is rummaging in her purse for a cigarette.

"Yes," Francine agrees. "There aren't many of them." To Chloe she says, "You're not thinking of smoking?"

"Of course not," Chloe says, clutching the pack and a lighter. "I'm just getting it ready."

***

Stretching his arms between the sheets, Sam glows. He has the day off, and he had another alcohol-free night. Standing in front of the mirror, he puts hands on bent knees and pulls his shoulders back and forth to loosen his spine, just as Poppy has instructed in the yoga video that sits on top of the television.

Later, he takes the stairs up to Carol's apartment. She has a cold. "Damn community college students," she says, standing at the door in a bathrobe like an upended pup tent, a tissue bunched up against her face, "coughing on the money they hand me and wiping boogers under the tables."

Sam takes the cookies she's packed and her car keys and heads to Stratton Island to visit Garnet on his own. Not owning a car, he enjoys the rare opportunity to drive. The freedom with comfort of being able to go anywhere, stop anywhere, eat takeout burgers, and drink coffee from a Styrofoam cup while hurtling down the highway. Lost in thought, he steers with one hand and fingers Carol's rubber bear key chain with the other. He squeezes it to make a poop balloon come out of its butt and remembers the weekend he'd bought it for her.

He'd been visiting his ex, Davide, and Davide's new partner Lucas. Lucas had custody of his five-year-old son, and the three of them were a family, with their intimacies and their routines, and Sam had felt like an outsider.

His and Davide's had been a rocky long-distance romance—full of passion on those once-a-month weekends when they'd meet in an anonymous border town and not emerge from their motel room except to bring in supplies: food, wine, cigarettes, lubricant. When Davide had casually mentioned that he wouldn't be meeting Sam for weekend trysts anymore because he'd decided to settle down, Sam had broken apart, having thought that they were settled, albeit living in separate cities, separate countries. The discussions they'd had about the possibility of Sam moving to Canada had apparently been folly for Davide—who'd callously asserted that there hadn't been anything between them but a little fun. Davide said he never imagined that Sam hadn't also been seeing other people the whole time. "I mean, four weeks between vee see each uzzah," Davide had explained in his French-Canadian accent, "surely you deedn't expect that I could go so long wizout . . . eh . . . sex?"

Lucas's son had ended up being the only bright spot in an otherwise desolate weekend. The little boy, whose mother had recently moved to South Korea after having fallen for her tae kwon do teacher, took to Sam right away—brushing his hair, holding his hand—so much so that Davide might have ignored Sam even more because he was jealous of the boy's attention to him. Davide and Lucas went on with their sickening lovey-dovey behavior, and Sam did his best to withstand his near-crippling heartbreak. The little boy helped, but Sam still cried the whole bus ride home.

When he'd gotten back to Wattsville, he'd gone straight to Carol's apartment, without stopping in his own.

"Hello sweetheart," Carol had greeted him. "Guess what I made for you," and she'd gone to the cabinet and pulled out a plate of brownies. "Homemade."

"Mom!" Garnet had protested, "I can't believe you've been hiding those!"

"They're for Sam. He needs chocolate, because I bet his weekend didn't go as well as he wanted it to. Am I right?" Sam had given Carol the key chain souvenir and they'd laughed—Garnet, sixteen at the time, joining them as a young woman, not a child anymore. "Love's shit," she'd parroted them, taking her turn squeezing the bear's belly and giggling at the rubber bubble ballooning out of its ass.

***

After going through Sam's purse, the guard shakes the Tupperware up and down and peers inside. "Oops. All broken. Anyway, you can't bring in food." Sam gasps but keeps his mouth shut and clenches his jaw to keep his face impassive. He is helpless as the guard throws the whole box of cookies into the garbage. He knows he has to take whatever the guard dishes out; if he doesn't take it quietly, they might deny him entry—the guards don't seem to have to obey any rules or laws and can send visitors home on a whim. Thankfully, without any more trouble, he is allowed in.

Garnet is sitting at a table in her orange jumpsuit, and Sam is shocked to see her looking so drawn and tired. He hurries over and grabs her hands across the table. She looks much older than her years and she's lost some weight, which is probably a good thing, but, together with her makeup-free face, gives her a dull and deflated appearance.

He feels guilty for having been happy, angry at himself for having been able to go on with his own life, oblivious to Garnet's suffering. "It's so unfair," he breathes, his shock and indignation fresh and exposed.

"Long time," she says.

"I'm sure your mom told you I got a job and have to work most Saturdays."

"It's okay. This is not a nice place to come. Even for a visit."

The complicatedness of their relationship comes flooding back to him, pushing out the hazy glow of an idealized quasi-fatherhood. He isn't her father, so why does he feel guilty? He's known her since she was a child, and they've been a part of each other's lives, but he's never been sure about the level of responsibility he should feel for her, and sometimes, even though it has nothing to do with her— she doesn't demand or even expect anything in particular, apart from friendship— he still resents the murkiness of that gray area and the muted guilt it leaves behind.

"I should have come more often. It's just those guards . . . they're horrible and it takes all the restraint I can muster to keep my mouth shut."

"It's okay. Mom comes a lot. I won't be in here forever anyway."

"Your mom says it's only a couple weeks until you find out about parole."

"That's right."

"Garnet, you're not going to get back together—"

She waves, batting away the idea. "Whatever Mom told you. I'm not going to—" She hesitates, tears welling up.

"Gar, don't let him back in," Sam says. Garnet's body, usually voluptuous and solid, wilts even more.

"What if I love him?" She is so earnest that he can't be harsh with her.

"I understand," he says, thinking suddenly of everything he'd put up with from Davide. He'd still be in love with the man if Davide hadn't broken it off. He'd have put up with all of it—the iciness, the infidelity, the emotional withdrawal. "Sometimes we don't do what's good for us."

"I guess. I don't want to give up hope that people can change though."

"Unfortunately, they usually don't. They usually get worse, if anything." He considers telling her how rude Ethan was when he saw him the night before at the Sheraton but thinks better of it, because it might just ignite her interest in him. "I don't want to think that, Sam. Not when it feels like fate. Like something that's not in my control. I feel like, how can I fight this? And I can't fight it. And maybe I don't want to."

"Gar, make a list. Do it soon, of everything bad he's done to you. Then keep reading it. You have to remind yourself." He shows her the note he keeps in his purse to remind himself not to drink. (He wishes he'd made one with all the bad things Davide had done to him, but he doesn't have to keep himself away from Davide—Davide cut him off, after that uncomfortable, failed weekend, and there was no invitation back.) Garnet's eyes glance over the list and she nods, but it doesn't seem to make an impression.

"He's good deep down. It's like he's wounded and—this sounds weird—but I feel like without me he might die."

"Garnet, my dear. I know you're smarter than that. He hit you on more than one occasion. Once is more than enough. He's downright mean, too."

"You're right. I know you're right. But I feel like that's just on the outside. Love is powerful, Sam. Maybe I'll never feel this way again. About anybody."

"Honey, you will," he says, without much enthusiasm. He's told himself the same thing, but hasn't met anyone since Davide and has started to despair of ever meeting anyone. Ronaldo flashes in his mind's eye for a moment like someone has flicked heavy curtains away from a sunny window. It is enough to leave Sam feeling a residue of buoyancy. "You're young," he adds. "There will be others for you. It is hard though, I know. Sometimes love just won't let us go."

When he leaves, he hugs her and strokes her hair. Comforting her feels good, but he is vaguely guilty again about having taken the path of least resistance: he didn't convince her to stay away from Ethan. Instead, he took the opportunity to be the healer, the comfort-giver, the sympathetic ear. He hopes that she makes the right decision and vows to make more of an effort to come visit her.

In the parking lot, Sam upends his purse. No keys. He curses, picks up his wallet, makeup, house keys, Tic Tacs, leaves the crumpled receipts and gum wrappers on the ground, and retraces his steps back to the visitors' entrance, scanning the ground.

At the front desk, the guard, with hairs sprouting from the top of his nose, dangles them. "Yup, they're right here. Someone found 'em and turned 'em in." Sam grabs them with gratitude and moves aside. He is zipping his purse when he hears the person behind him say Garnet's name. He turns to see a sleek leather jacket and adolescent-ruddy cheeks.

"Ethan!" He pokes the younger man's shoulder.

Ethan turns to the guard, "Can I go in?"

"You're on the list," the guard says amicably.

"You're on the list?" Sam cries. "You put her in here. She let you on the list already?" He turns to the guard. "He shouldn't be on the list. This is Garnet's ex."

The guard interrupts. "He's on the list. It ain't got nothing to do with me."

Ethan turns and walks through the heavy doors, past another guard, who pats him on the back like he's an old friend. "I don't know who that old homo is," Ethan says loudly.

"Old? Excuse me? Don't know who I am? I practically raised that girl, for you to abuse her," Sam yells, pointing his finger like a guest on the Jerry Springer Show.

"All right. Calm down, lady."

"He abused her," Sam says as the door to the visiting room closes behind Ethan. The guard pulls bulletproof glass across the counter.

A MOTHER'S PRIDE

Carol

"What the? My cold. Thought you didn't want to catch it." Carol follows Sam as he pushes past her to the kitchen; he leans against the counter, propping himself up as though he were a gymnast about to do a bar exercise.

"He was there, Carol. I met him."

"What? Met who? What's the matter?"

"Ethan."

Carol groans and slumps onto a chair. "Oh Christ. I knew it. I knew it. What're we gonna do? They're back together! When I was in there, she had a head full of product . . . that he'd bought for her. She's gonna be back living with that little bastard soon as she gets out." She blows her nose loudly and stuffs the tissue into her bathrobe pocket.

Sam taps his fingertips on the table. Carol feels responsible. Maybe she should have gone with him despite her cold. Maybe if she'd seen Ethan she could've killed him, and then she could be in prison too, with her daughter.

"We have to stop it," Sam says.

They steep. "I've got it," Sam says, slapping the table. "Tommy."

"Tommy?"

"Tommy from the paper. He knows Ethan." Carol waits for recognition or further explanation. Sam goes on: "At the *Chronicle*, the boss's son, this kid Tommy, who works there. I saw him at the Sheraton with Ethan last night. At first I didn't recognize Ethan. Out of context, I guess. Anyway. They know each other."

"They know each other," Carol repeats.

"Yeah. They know each other. Tommy and Ethan."

"Hmm. Wait. You saw him last night and today? What the hell is that all about?"

"I know. Crazy, right? You know, I hadn't thought about it but it seems like some kind of a sign."

"I'd normally say that's all bullshit," Carol says, "but maybe. Maybe. Okay. If there's a sign and we're supposed to know what it is. Let's see. Ethan and this kid Tommy."

Sam says, "I've got it! I'm gay!"

"No. Shit. Sherlock." Carol's chuckle sounds rusty.

"Well, there must be some way we can make Ethan, I don't know . . . Maybe I should seduce him. He sure comes off as homophobic, probably queer deep down."

"Holy shit. I thought I'd heard it all. You're gonna seduce my daughter's boyfriend to break them up."

"Listen, I'm just throwing ideas out there."

She shakes her head. "Maybe there's some way we can get him arrested."

"You couldn't get him arrested for beating Garnet, what else could you get him arrested for?"

"Yeah. Dumb idea."

"No idea is dumb, Carol. We've gotta figure something out."

They fall silent again. After a while Carol gets up and pours two glasses of orange juice.

"You know. Off topic, but I'm thinking of moving to the city," Sam says, and puts the glass to his lips. He doesn't sip, but waits for Carol's reaction.

"Don't distract me. I've got it."

"What?"

"You're not going anywhere, by the way."

"What's your idea?"

"First tell me you're not moving to the city."

"I might."

She shrugs. "You're going to get that money of his. That faucet of money . . . we're gonna shut it off." Her dry cough has turned productive. It sounds like heavy rain on a plastic sheet.

Sam leans away from the table and pulls the shoulder of his top up to shield his nose from Carol's infection. "No offense, dear, but let's hatch this plan over the phone. It's a germ incubator in here. You know the way I am."

"If you want a germ incubator, move to the city," she calls after him as the door closes.

***

A few days later, Carol is at the register and Ron is behind the glass case that houses stainless-steel trays of macaroni and chicken thighs, drab green beans bathed in melted margarine, and a concrete slab of mashed potato product.

"Three thirty-five," Carol says and the girl pays.

Ron slides a spatula underneath an omelet and flips it over. A hamburger patty hisses and he drops a basket of frozen fries into the fryolator. Carol wipes a cloth over a soda ring left by a sloppy student.

"Tuna?" she says. A professor. Many of the professors dress more poorly than the students. This one is wearing a blazer, and she can see as he thumbs through the bills in his wallet that the ends of the sleeves are worn thin.

"Aren't you Ms. Harlow?" he says as he hands her a ten-dollar bill.

This startles her. "Do we know each other?" She slides the money into the cash drawer.

"I'm sorry. Didn't mean to be rude." He emits a short laugh. "Your daughter, Garnet. She was a student of mine." Carol stares at him. "She was in my English class. Mike Bruss." She wipes her palm down her smock, and they shake hands. "She was one of my best students," he says. "I just thought you'd want to know that."

"Thank you," she whispers. "Oh, your change!" She hands him some coins and a couple of bills.

"You must hear it a lot," he says.

"No, no." She gets her voice back and says, "No. I don't think I've ever heard it before."

"I haven't seen her in a while. How she doing?" he asks, and Carol goes back to looking stunned.

"Oh. Is everything all right? I'm sorry . . . I . . ."

"You don't know?" she says and now it is Mike Bruss's turn to be speechless. "She's okay," Carol says quickly. "She's . . . I guess it wasn't such big news really, it wasn't murder or anything, but, well, she's in . . . Stratton Island . . . she's incarcerated."

Professor Bruss stuffs his change and his wallet into the pocket of his blazer. "I'm . . . I guess *surprised* is the word. And sorry. I'm sorry."

"It's not her fault," Carol says quickly. Professor Bruss seems to want to hear more, but there is a line forming behind him. He moves to a far corner of the cafeteria and sits by himself. Carol rings in orders distractedly. As she works, she is aware of his presence and steals glances. He eats his sandwich thoughtfully; he stares straight ahead as he chews and takes sips of his coffee. Finally, when there is a lull and a work-study student has arrived to man the other register, Carol gets the nerve to approach him. He looks unsurprised as she sits on the edge of a chair.

"She was in an abusive relationship," she says.

"I'm sorry to hear that. I really am."

"They were fighting. She pushed an armoire over and her . . . boyfriend . . . got stuck underneath it. He got a concussion. Thank God he didn't die." She is silent for a moment. "I guess."

He surprises her by laughing and, at first, she isn't sure why, but then she sees the humor in what she said and laughs as well.

"Guess you're not fond of him," Professor Bruss says.

"You could say that."

"Please give her my best," he says.

"I will. Thank you again. It means a lot."

"She has a bright future. Don't think otherwise."

As she stands, her smile is both grateful and doubtful.

With Professor Bruss finishing his coffee on one side and Ron's friendly countenance flipping burgers on the other, Carol feels something like a supportive community around her, and the dark fog she's been living in feels a little bit brighter. The early spring heat helps. Dusty yellow sunlight shines through the windows and crows are yelling outside in the sky.

***

Toward the end of her shift, Carol's cash register reverie is broken when her attention is drawn to three men who have just walked into the cafeteria. They wear chunky gold rings and sunglasses on their heads and two have blue-green tattoos creeping up their necks and down their arms. They are definitely not students. At first she doesn't think much about them. Sometimes delivery or maintenance workers come in and order lunch. But these guys seem to take up more space than their actual bodies require. Ron knows them. He doesn't say hello but makes a movement with his head toward the kitchen, and they follow him back there.

Carol busies herself by straightening boxes of condiment pouches. Soon, the three men leave and Ron starts cleaning the grill. Carol watches him scrape dried cheese and grease and wonders about the strange men.

She's not sure if she knows Ron well enough to ask him about them. Sometimes she thinks that she and Ron are friends; but she's never spent any time with him outside of work, and she actually knows very little about him. She's told him a little bit about her life, but he doesn't ever reveal much about his. He seems agitated now. He finishes wiping down the grill and lifts the square metal containers out of the hot water bath that keeps them warm. She approaches as he is dragging sheets of plastic wrap from a box.

"Hey, Ron."

He smiles thinly.

"You okay?"

He nods and hoists a container of meatloaf slices from the counter, heading to the walk-in. Her instinct is to leave him alone, but she fights it, thinking that, if she wants to know him better, she'll have to push herself to be more outgoing than she's used to being.

Plus, she's getting a vague idea about those men and how they might be able to help her with Garnet's situation.

Ron comes out of the walk-in and pushes the heavy metal door closed behind him. She's looking at him, suddenly aware that she's not sure what she wants to say. Her vague idea had been that he might be able to get one of his scary-looking friends to threaten Ethan—or something. Suddenly, with the opportunity in front of her—Ron blinks at her, looking more impatient than anything—she's not sure exactly how to frame her thoughts. In fact, she's not sure her idea even makes any sense. She stutters: "I . . . ah . . . well . . . so . . ."

She must seem pathetic. He takes both of her hands in his and leads her to the corner of the kitchen, where there are upside down milk crates. They sit.

"What is it?" he asks and his kindness makes her wilt with relief. But she's still not sure what she wants to ask him.

"Who were those men?" she says finally.

He stretches his shoulders back. "Nobody. Just some associates. From my country. You okay?"

"Yes, I'm fine. Are you okay?"

"Of course," he says. "You're a nice lady. I'm sorry your family is having some hard times."

"Did you see the professor that was here before?"

Ron shakes his head.

"He said Garnet has a bright future. Those were his exact words."

"That's good. She does, of course. You're a good mother."

"But, what about you?"

He smiles and stands up, pulls the snaps open on his cook's shirt and throws it into the laundry sack. "Not sure what you mean?"

"Ron, I'm being very forward here. Do you want to come over for dinner sometime? I'm a good cook." She feels currents of electricity from her toes to her scalp, but she holds herself steady and tries for impassive.

He pulls a T-shirt over his undershirt but not before she gets a glimpse of a tattoo on his chest. The combination of his kindness and these hints of a past that she can tell has been full of danger lends her a feeling of importance, of being in contact with a kind of mysterious actuality. Life. She's close to it. It makes her feel courageous.

"Maybe. I'm sure you are."

"You probably get sick of cooking," she says.

"This isn't real cooking."

"Well, let me know. About dinner."

"Okay, Carol," he says and then he is gone, the swinging door to the kitchen huffing back and forth behind him.

***

After being led to the waiting area, Carol stands mute, staring, for a few seconds or an hour—she's not sure which. Garnet's eye is ringed by a purple bruise; a blood vessel has burst and flooded the white of her eye with red. Her arm is in a sling. Without saying a word, Carol puts gentle arms around her daughter. "Three seconds are up!" a guard says and they both scrape their chairs back and sit down.

"It's nothing," Garnet says. "It's not as bad as it looks."

"Sam didn't tell me," Carol whispers.

"It hadn't happened yet. It was right after he came. It's really not a big deal."

Carol leans her head into her hands and closes her eyes. She looks up slowly. "What happened?"

"Mom, really. It's no big deal." Garnet's smile looks forced and she turns away.

Carol squints, thinking, and then says, "Let Ethan help you, Gar. Let him help get you out of here. Get him and his lawyers to . . ." She breaks off, overwhelmed. Garnet is gazing at her incredulously.

"You mean it? Mom? You think I should let him protect me?"

"I can't protect you." She stifles a sob.

"Maybe I don't need protecting. Maybe I can protect myself. Maybe there was a little trouble with some of the women in here. But I can't use a guy just because I need protecting. And anyway, it wouldn't have happened in the first place if he wasn't rich."

"But he has lawyers. His family has connections."

"That's the problem." Garnet sounds suddenly doubtful, and her voice is squeaky the way it used to be when she was a child and was upset about something.

"This was his fault?"

"Of course not. Just someone found out he's rich. I guess they don't like that here."

"Garnet, I feel so helpless. With you in here. This . . ." Carol feels the hot sting of tears as they burst from her eyes and slide down her cheeks. She wants to punch the snack machine, get a big shard of glass, and go in there and kill whoever did this to her baby. She rustles through her pocketbook until Garnet stands up and grabs a box of Kleenex from another table. Carol whiffs several from the box and hides her face behind them. Garnet pushes her hand across, past the halfway mark, and Carol grabs and clings to it. Carol notices how much Garnet's hand resembles her own: ruddy, with deep crevices around the knuckles; for a surreal moment, it feels as though she is holding the hand of her own younger self. If she closes her eyes, she can imagine that they are sitting at the kitchen table. Finally, Carol puts a Tupperware box in between them.

"Tollhouse."

"Thanks." Garnet blows her nose.

"Is it broken?"

Garnet shakes her head. "No, I can use my arm." She lifts her elbow to prove it. "It's just a cracked rib. No big deal. It'll heal fast, they said. In fact, it's feeling better already."

"They got doctors in here?"

"Of course they do."

"What happened?"

"Mom," Garnet whispers, "I don't want to talk about it. I shouldn't. And I don't want to. Not yet. Can we talk about something else?"

Carol leans back and shakes the neck of her T-shirt. "Sure is hot outside."

"Yeah."

She makes a heroic effort to put away her anxiety. "Oh hey. One of your teachers introduced himself to me a couple of days ago."

"Oh yeah, which one?"

"Bruss."

Garnet smiles. "That was a great class." Her voice trails off as the memory clashes with her current predicament.

"He said to say hi. He said you were a really good student."

"He did? Oh, well. I guess not so good, or I wouldn't be here."

"Don't say that," Carol says. "This is not your fault."

Garnet is quiet. Both women spend some time looking around the room. Carol finally breaks the silence. "Sam went out the other night. You know, the Sheraton karaoke. With his friends from the city."

"Oh yeah?"

Carol is silent. She is hatching a plan. She's not going to encourage Garnet to ask Ethan for help. Getting Ethan away from her daughter will also make her safer inside this hellhole. It's beginning to feel like the final, crowning achievement of her motherhood. A plan. She will free her daughter from Ethan. Garnet needs her strength.

"Mom?"

"Sam says he's thinking of moving to the city," Carol says finally.

"Really? He didn't tell me that."

"Yup. I guess he thinks he can sing, in clubs or whatever. His friends told him he should."

"He is a good singer. But he won't. Of course he won't," Garnet says.

"Maybe he won't. You never know though. Sometimes I think he loves Wattsville, and other times, I think he hates it. He got that new job. You know the way he is. Every day is an adventure."

"He told me about the job," Garnet says, "but not much else."

Carol hoists her body up and scoots her chair closer to the table. "Soon enough you'll be out of here. This . . . fight . . . won't affect your parole?"

"No, no. I don't think so." They sit in silence. Then Garnet says, "If Sam goes to the city, we can visit. Visit him there."

"I guess. It's not the same though." Carol doesn't believe Sam will go. Sometimes she doubts herself, however, and can't stand the thought of life without him two floors down. "A friend who's around all the time, it's . . ."

"Like a husband. Duh."

"Yeah, but without the work."

"And without the sex."

"Oh. I don't miss it," Carol declares, and then leans her head on her hand. "Well. Sometimes. I guess."

Garnet laughs. "Damn right you miss it! Don't lie, Mom."

Carol waves her hands in front of her face, an embarrassed grin on her lips. "Anyway, I'll miss Sam if he does go," she says. "That's for sure. Especially with you here."

"It's not the first time he's talked about moving to the city. I mean, the longer he doesn't do it, the less likely it is he'll go."

An inmate and a middle-aged man are sitting at a table close by, and Garnet and Carol fall silent as they eavesdrop on the couple's conversation. The man has a loud voice and doesn't seem to care who can hear him, while the woman whispers most of her responses, so that it sounds like a one-sided conversation. "Yeah, Tony says he's gonna let me in on a deal. A trip thing." The woman says something. "Vacations," the man responds. "I'll be getting a place." The woman asks a question and the man goes on, "You behave yourself honey, I'll have room for you there. Don't worry. I'll get you a nice little French maid number, stick you in front of the sink. You'll like that." Garnet and Carol catch each other's eye and stifle a giggle.

When it is time for her to leave, Carol hugs her daughter gingerly. "Garnet, this won't happen to you again. You'll be safe." It isn't a question and it's not a directive. It's more of a prayer.

STUFFING-STEALING MONSTERS

Garnet's Diary

I haven't written in a couple of days. Because I've been in the infirmary. I'm healing now.

E. and M. beat me up. Cracked a rib. Black eye. Slight concussion. Not terrible, but it's the first time anything like this has happened to me, and it feels weird. Like I'm not sure who I am anymore. I wonder if I'll go back to being myself anytime soon, or ever. Fear has become a part of my muscle fibers. It's all I can feel. Besides that, is just numbness.

Eloise and Molasses. I'm going to write their names out, who cares who finds this. Let them beat me up again.

Eloise, Shanise's second cousin. It all started a couple of weeks ago. We were hanging out on the bleachers at the edge of the dust bowl. I think the dust bowl used to be a field, but nothing grows there. It's dust when it's dry and mud when it rains. Shanise and Eloise were talking about how much they missed getting high. I don't know why Shanise was talking like that. Shanise isn't a user. I mean, sure, she and I both have wished for a little pot or even just a beer. But her cousin is an addict.

I should be mad at Shanise for telling Eloise about Ethan. But I guess she didn't know what she was opening me up to.

"Garnet, can't you get that lover boy of yours to get us a little package of reefer?" She said that in front of Eloise.

"No, of course not," I said.

Eloise got curious and she goes, "Who's lover boy?" and Shanise told her and she said, "White Hills, yeah?" and her eyes went flat like a shark's. Then she must have told Molasses—who is hard as asphalt and everybody's petrified of her—and the two of them started putting the pressure on.

I didn't think anything would actually happen because Eloise is related to Shanise. I thought that would protect me. I refused over and over to get them anything. I mean, I know they get drugs from somewhere, so I figured they'd forget about me.

But then, the other day, when I was by myself because Shanise wasn't feeling well, they cornered me.

And you know what, Diary? The guards let it happen. I think they want to see us beat each other up because they have such a low opinion of us—we're like animals to them, or maybe worse—and they want that opinion confirmed. So there I was, lying under the bleachers and finally Officer Reavy pulls me up and she goes, "I guess you're not going to tell me who did it to you, so let's just get you over to the infirmary."

Nobody even asked who did it! They assumed I wouldn't tell, and I guess I won't because I'd only get into more trouble if I told. But now, I have to ask Ethan to do this thing and I'm worried for him. He's not going to like it. Anyway. I'm feeling a bit better now and he's coming today so I'll ask him. I'll write more later, after he comes. Mom visited, by the way. It was terrible for her to see me this way. I'll describe the whole thing another time. I can't do it now. I have to look away from it, even as it calls me back. Like when you have a sunburn and you can't stop peeling the sheets of skin off yourself. You can't let it be. I'm going to force myself to let this be. Because it hurts to look at it—not like a sunburn. Peeling a sunburn gives you satisfaction, but this—it just hurts.

Hey there,

Ethan and I had a beautiful visit and I'm feeling empty now that he's gone. ☹ It's almost physical, the hole I'm left with. Like all the pink organs inside me have been drained of blood and now are paper thin and see-through. He said he'd do it. What if he gets caught? His whole future could be ruined. And his future has a lot more to lose than most people's, including mine.

He doesn't mind. He's generous. I love that about him. He really would do anything for me, when push comes to shove.

I wish he got along with Mom and Sam and we could all be more like a family. If he would just give them a chance, he'd find them so much nicer than his own family.

He doesn't mind Mom, but he says mean things about Sam. He's going to have to stop that. I only put up with it because I know he does it out of ignorance.

God, I just read that last sentence and it sure sounds bad. Let me explain better. He's mean sometimes because he's been hurt. And because he was raised in a mean atmosphere. Once he feels more secure (with the help of the love of a good woman—me!) he'll be more confident and he won't have to be mean. I really believe that. Shanise says I'm naive, but I do believe in the goodness of people. Even Eloise and Molasses. Well, actually, I'm going to make an exception for them. If you do drugs you lose the opportunity to be saved by love. They're so lost they'll never make it back.

I'm feeling so much stronger after meeting with Ethan.

I can write now about what happened. Before. When they beat me up. Shanise wasn't feeling good and decided to stay inside, so I was by myself. I walked a few circles. There's not much else to do. Some women play hacky sack and others sit in groups on the ground or on the bleachers. There's a basketball hoop and there's always women over there playing. I don't play well enough to join them, so I just walk around, trying to breathe some fresh air, get my muscles moving. I know exercise is good for me, even though I'm not especially fond of it.

Eloise caught up with me. She carries this cloud of tension around with her that you can feel. So, she's walking with me, our arms scissoring like we're soldiers. "Snow White," she said. I used to kind of like that nickname. Now I wish to never hear it again. "My other source is tied up, so you're gonna be a friend and ask your prince to bring in something for me, right?" I sighed in a way that meant we'd been through this before and she'd been told my answer. "Snow White, if you're not going to be a friend and do it because we're friends, then I'll have to try and make you see my point of view in a more forceful way." She said something like that. I slowed down and she slowed down. I sped up and she sped up. The guards were picking their noses, as usual. I had nobody to turn to and then there's Molasses on the other side of me. I can't remember exactly what she said. Something about me having power and her not letting me be the one with power and something else about doing for others, which I may have laughed at because, what had they done for me? Anyway, she did not like me laughing at her one bit.

So I remember this: they each took an arm and we were behind the bleachers and the ladies who were sitting there, they got up and left. Molasses must have given them a look. One of them caught my eye as she walked away. I don't know her name. She's one of the crazies, talks to people who aren't there and picks at the freckles on her arm so she has bloody little spots all over her. She looked at me with what you could call sympathy—I think. Maybe there was nothing in her eyes but my predicament made me want to think that somebody was feeling sympathy for me.

Next thing I know, I'm on the ground. Their feet are coming at me like I'm in some kind of a fleshy-boney machine. Both of them in sneakers, but their feet were hard like they were in Timberlands. My head scraping the dirty ground; hugging myself; crying. God the pain was terrible, both being hit and in the moments between—the anticipation of the next blow, and the pain of the previous one settling deeper into my body—all the way to the marrow of my bones. Then, all of a sudden, it didn't hurt anymore and I went to sleep in the midst of it. It must be the body's way of protecting you when you have no hope of changing things— of surviving. I must have passed out and the next thing they were gone— everybody was gone. I was drawing pictures in the dirt with my finger, humming, not any song in particular, just making human sounds that let me know I was alive. Next thing Officer Reavey was helping me up and bringing me to the infirmary. So that's it. Now I'm someone who's been in prison and who's been beaten up and who is going to have drugs smuggled in. That's who I am. Six months ago I was a college student. Will I ever be that person again?

Well.

He brought it. But he wasn't happy about it. Last time he was here, he was gentle and sweet and said he'd do anything in the world for me, but today he seemed mad that I was making him do something so dangerous. "I'm risking my whole future," he said. I asked him about that other thing he said he'd do: talk to his lawyer, try and put in a good word. He said he was still working on it. Seemed to think that what he's doing now—getting drugs for E. and M. so they don't kill me—was enough. I asked, couldn't he tell the lawyer about the trouble I'm having in here? And he said, "Oh sure, and then tell him about the fact that I just walked in here with drugs tucked into my socks. I don't think I should make any waves."

I don't think Eloise's source has really dried up, because all Ethan could score was pot, and that seemed to be enough; she's been leaving me alone.

Shanise and I took a little and smoked it out the window of our cell with a bong made out of a Coke can, and it was the best day I've had in a long time. We laughed and laughed until our bellies hurt and Eloise heard about our stoned giggling from Nancy, in the next cell, and lucky for me I had most of it to hand over to her or she would've been seriously pissed. Her and Molasses. Shit.

I had a dream this morning. I was a bird. I love dream flying, but this time was weird, because I could fly, but not that well. I was covered with yellow feathers like Big Bird and I sort of fly-climbed up to the tower at the corner of the dust bowl. Fly-climb? What's that, you want to know? I'll tell you what it is. It's like your body is light enough that, like a helium balloon three days after a birthday party, you can kind of hover, not going up, but not going down either. So I made it to the top and I could see Wattsville in the distance and it was all neon colors and there were fireworks exploding and they were reflected off the Otis and I thought, it must be the Fourth of July and I wanted to fly over and find Mom, because we always barbecue in the park on the Fourth, but I couldn't get the courage to jump and fly because, as I said, I was a helium balloon in its death throes and I kept thinking, if only I had the courage. Jump, I told myself over and over. Jump. Just jump. You can do it. The wind will blow you if you can't fly very well. And I was about to do it. I swear I was about to do it, but Shanise, in a typical Shanise move, dropped her magazine onto the floor right near my head so I woke up. I told her about the dream and she laughed and said I was high. ☺

Speaking of Shanise, she seems a little off lately. When I ask what's wrong, she says Officer Frank and her are having some issues. Issues. Whatever that means. What issues can a couple have time for when they only get to see each other for ten or twenty minutes in a supply closet? Seems like they shouldn't have time for disagreements. But she won't tell me more. "Oh nothing, just some stuff we were talking about." She's not shy about physical stuff. She'll tell me anything, but when it comes to feelings, she doesn't say much. I think it must be the way we were brought up. Or just different personalities. I wouldn't describe sex, but I'd talk about my feelings all day long.

I found a picture of Big Bird in a TV Digest that reminded me of my dream and I cut it out and put it in the urinal. Did I mention that Stratton Island used to be a men's prison and so we have a decorative urinal in our cell? We call it the Fountain of Funk because sometimes smells waft up out of it from the depths of the prison's plumbing system. As if our toilet wasn't bad enough. Anyway. I made a base of hair mousse and stuck the picture into it. It's inspiring, spiritual, decorative, and it also covers the drain in the bottom of the Fountain of Funk, keeping out smells. You'd be amazed at the many uses one can find for hair mousse.

It's been a great week, with E. and M. all chilled out and leaving me alone. I was thinking today, during rec, about the way one person can put a hex on a whole community. Granted a prison community isn't exactly a band of angels, but most of the girls aren't so bad. Eloise, on the other hand, and even more so Molasses, make the whole atmosphere kind of poisonous. I don't think I noticed it so much before, but everybody's really tense. Let me tell you, every woman in this place is suffering big time.

Some of us help each other and make things better and some of us make things worse for everybody. It's incredible and maybe because I'm stoned again from the bit we had left over, it seems so deep, but I can see clearly that even though we're all human, some of us have enough inside—like stuffing in furniture—that we can absorb all the shit that's happening to us, and even offer comfort to others, and then there are girls who just don't have enough stuffing—either to comfort others or even for themselves—so that their skeletons transform into these hideous stuffing-stealing monsters. (As if you could take stuffing from another person and put it in yourself.)

Stuffing transfer doesn't work that way. I would gladly give Eloise and Molasses some of my stuffing, if it would comfort whatever bad shit has made them into such bitches, but I can't. I just have to try to protect myself so that they don't whittle me down to a skeleton. Because what they don't know / don't care about is that being mean isn't going to make anything better for them in the end. We all just end up more miserable. Me and them. They can take my stuffing, but it's only going to evaporate into nothingness. A cloud of stuffing that floats in the sky toward the mountains and then rains itself out and disappears. They should ask for comfort, not demand drugs. Idiots.

Ha. I just read over what I wrote and I'm laughing because I sure am stoned. Shanise wants nothing to do with my stoned philosophizing. She just giggles and giggles. Like totally fifth-grade stuff—fart noises crack her up. Who am I kidding? They crack me up too.

She still won't tell me what's going on with her and OF. I'm sad about that and I worry for her, because if she can't tell me, then chances are she's not telling anybody, and keeping whatever it is inside has to be terrible.

Officer Frank. He has grandparents from all over the place. I think from Japan, Puerto Rico, and Turkey. He's a funky dude for a prison guard. He thinks he's deep and super smart, but from what I can tell, he's kind of thick and dull. He has this stringy goatee and his eyes look Japanese but he has kinky black hair, and he's balding on top. Shanise says she's with him for his "sex." That's the way she says it, that his "sex" is "big and handsome." She's funny the way she talks. I can understand though. Sex feels like love—especially if you're deprived of it the way we are.

Speaking of sex. Some of the women fall for each other—even though they weren't lesbians to start with. I can understand that, too. You start to feel so weak and you need something or someone to rely on, to trust. And you just ache for someone to touch you, too. Especially when you don't have many visitors. Shanise brushes my hair sometimes. It's the most wonderful thing and when she's doing it I don't mind the smells or the sounds or anything and I can forget that I'm in here.

Another thing I love is when Mom comes and we shoot the shit for an hour, about whatever. That's the best. And Sam too. He can gab forever and he's so entertaining. He doesn't come much, though.

Sam. About Mom's age. Mom's forty-three. I think Sam is a year younger. He looks kind of like Susan Sarandon. He says he doesn't mind if you call him He or She but one thing he's certain about, and that's that he likes to be with men. And he can sing like Tina Turner.

Mom and Sam both drilled into me from as far back as I can remember that I need to go to college so I don't end up like them, working shitty jobs and never getting ahead. I miss college, especially English class. Mr. Bruss would get us thinking about the coolest stuff, and when I'd say something, he'd really listen, and then he'd rephrase my idea in a way that was much better than what I'd said originally. I'd love to be smart like him one day. He told Mom that I was smart and a good student. One person who believes in you is the difference between life and death.

Signing off, Diary. Shanise is awake again and she's starting to annoy me with "What are you writing about?"

Bad news.

Shanise is pregnant. Well, now I know. She wasn't going to tell me, but I found out. What a day. I'll start from the beginning. Ethan came with shipment number two to keep E. and M. off my back. He had a bad attitude about it. He says I shouldn't ask him. I'm pretty much all healed up so I guess if he can't see a black eye he doesn't believe that the situation is as serious as I say it is. Anyway, he brought it and then he got all horny, made me put my foot on his thing under the table. *Normally that wouldn't do much for me, but, well, I guess it's been a long time. So then he goes to the guard, someone I don't know. New guy maybe, and he gives him money and tells me to go into the bathroom. The door doesn't lock and it's covered in graffiti. "Fuck the Guards." "I love pussy."*

I went in and then he comes and tells me to pull my pants down and we did it on the edge of the sink. And then, after we finished, he was kind of mean. "You shouldn't make me do that," he says, "I could get into trouble." I started laughing, looking around that shithole of a bathroom and I couldn't even express what was so funny, what I was so mad about. Here I am in fucking prison and he's the one worried about getting into trouble! When he left today, he went up to his mansion in White Hills and I came back to this goddamned fucking cell. I didn't make him do anything! It was his idea!

Okay, so the next part of this fan-fucking-tastic day is that I had the package stuffed into my sock and it was Officer Blanchard in the search room. The Butcher, we call her, because when she searches you it's like she's handling dead meat. She pulls your butt cheeks apart and has a good long look in there. Rubs your boobs. So I walk into the search room and there she is. My heart climbed up into my mouth and I swear I was about to puke it out onto the floor. But just as she was getting ready to do her thing, OF comes in and tells the Butcher it's time for her break. He's always been nice to me because of Shanise. I should be thanking my fucking stars that Blanchard didn't search me. I'd definitely lose parole then. Or who knows what.

"Give this to your roommate," OF says, and shoves this little folded-up piece of paper with a pill inside into my hand. "Tell her she takes it or her life will be much more unpleasant than it already is. I won't be able to help her."

So I stuck it in my bra and he sent me on my way to the next guard who brought me back to our cell. I did some Hail Marys to Big Bird before I did anything else. After I could breathe normally again, I gave the pill to Shanise. And then we opened up Ethan's package and got stoned. We both needed it. And she talked. Finally. She didn't shut up for a couple of hours and now she's asleep and I'm watching her and imagining the little person she has in her belly. I wonder if it has fingers and toes yet. If it does, they're the size of sesame seeds. Or smaller. Wow. I can trip out imagining the baby with Officer Frank's stringy little goatee.

I don't know why I didn't guess.

When you spend so much time together, you start having your periods at the same time, but Shanise hasn't had hers for a while. She said that that's the way she is normally, that she'd never been so regular as when she started sharing a cell with me. But when they stopped coming she didn't think too much of it.

She apologized again for that time she told Eloise who Ethan was. She was so freaked out and scared and that's why she wasn't thinking about the trouble it would cause.

And we talked about her family. She has a couple of little brothers and a little sister and she says it's the worst part about being here—that she can't be around to help with them. They all looked up to her and now here she is. Anyway, while we were talking, she was holding onto that pill and staring at it in her palm as if she were waiting for it to wake up and cry.

"I can't," she kept saying, and then, "But I have to." And then she ripped a page from a magazine and made it into an accordion pinched in the middle and started saying, "You must take the pill," "I can't take the pill," "You must take the pill," "I can't take the pill," and then with the glossy paper as a bow tie: "I'll take the pill." "My hero."

We laughed till we were jelly. You know the way tragic and scary things can be funny, like you laugh so hard because on the other side of the laughter are sobs of misery. And fury. The suppressed sobs added fuel and we laughed so hard until when we stopped, we had no idea what to say and the two of us just stared at the walls.

But. I wonder who that hero could be. Who could take the pill for her? Nobody. Just her. She didn't take it yet and there it is, lying next to the pillow. She put it in one of the brown paper wrappers from the chocolates Ethan sent me and it looks like it's in a little cradle.

She used to always say that OF was just a toy. Just physical release, nothing more, but tonight, after we'd laughed our heads off and our high had mellowed out, she started to talk about their relationship in a way she'd never done before. She actually loves him, she says. Honestly, I wonder if she loves him for the sake of the life he made inside her. I wonder if it's really him she loves or if it's just the idea of somehow making things right with a new baby.

"He says these amazing things to me," she told me. But she can't remember exactly what they are, just that when he talks to her it "opens up her world and her heart."

"How much time do you get together?" I asked her. I didn't mean to question it, but seriously couldn't see how it was possible for them to even have conversations when their whole relationship consists of sneaking into an empty closet or cell or office and getting down. Plus the fact that she always referred to him as a sex toy, nothing more. He writes letters to her. She let me read a couple of them before and we would laugh together. Let's see if I can remember anything from any of those letters. Oh yeah. We laughed our heads off over this: "Shanise my love with your eyes of brown sugar. Your sweetness is tantalizing." I think that was it. Man, we laughed over the brown-sugar-eyes line. Shanise'd ask me for a Kit Kat and I'd go, "What do you need those for? You're so sweet, your eyes are made of brown sugar!" She would always laugh but now she's not laughing.

People will do that. They'll make fun of their family member or their boy- or girlfriend, but when you join in, they could turn on you because they might have changed their mind. And then they'll drop you because you remind them of their own hypocrisy. People don't like to be reminded of their own bad decisions.

But you can't question people's loves anyway. Look at me and Ethan. I'm going to have to figure that shit out on my own.

This one time, a long time ago now, right when Ethan and I had started to send each other letters and I'd told Shanise all about him, she said to me: "You know what you gotta do to figure out if he's good for you? You gotta ask yourself, Does my mama like him? If not, then you gotta do some serious soul searching. Your mama always has your best interest at heart."

I asked her about that today. What would her mother think? Shanise waves her hand in front of her face like I have bad breath and goes, "She wouldn't approve of anyone at this point in my life."

"Well she's right about that." I leaned back and stuck my nose into another one of those waxy paper chocolate holders. They're losing their smell. In fact, I don't even know if there is any smell left in them or if it's just phantom chocolate in my head. I wasn't going to argue with her. With her having these big problems, it makes my problems feel smaller, and if I'm going to be truthful, I'm enjoying the fact that she's making mistakes too—so she can't point out the mistakes I'm making. If our lives were a film then the focus would be taken off me and put on her. And I don't have to look in that mirror. You know the one? Your best friend can sometimes put it in front of you. The mirror you really and truly don't want to look into.

So here we are. On the downhill slide from being stoned. Baby in the belly on the bed across from me. Sesame seed fingers and toes. Half Shanise and half Officer Frank. What's she going to do? Boy, I'm tired. I don't think I can write any more today. The pill sleeps and we sleep and we will see what tomorrow brings.

BRITNEY SPEARS AT THE WAGONWHEEL

Sam

During break on Sunday morning, Sam sets his and Carol's plan in motion. He sits next to Tommy at the picnic table.

Tommy pushes an invisible button with his nose. "'Sup?"

"Oh, nothing much," Sam says. "You know, nothing much." Tommy's head is loose on his neck. He fishes a pack of cigarettes from the cavernous front pocket of his oversize jeans and lights one. "D'you mind? Have an extra?" says Sam, who ostensibly gave them up more than five years ago but who has lately come to the conclusion that living without either cigarettes or alcohol is a tad extreme. Tommy puts the pack on the table in front of him, and Sam pulls one out.

"So, Tommy, I'm not supposed to say anything, but you know, where I saw you, you know, at the bar? The Sheraton?" Tommy waits. "I have some information, I have some connections there, and, you know Britney Spears? Well, apparently she's going to play a surprise performance on Friday night." Sam tries to exude a restrained, secretive enthusiasm. Tommy takes a long drag.

"No shit."

"Do you like her?"

"Not really. She's hot, though."

"Well, it's sure to be a good night. A lot of fun. I'm not supposed to say anything." Sam winks against the plume of smoke that roils toward his face.

Jorge and Jaime are sitting on the curb eating doughnuts.

"You hear that?" Tommy calls to them. "Britney Spears? You know Britney Spears?"

"Sshhh," Sam shushes Tommy. "I'm not supposed to be telling people."

"Well you told me. Hey, boys, Friday night, at the Sheraton. Britney Spears." They smile timidly. It's unclear if they understand. "Friday night," Tommy says again.

"So, your friends," Sam says. "You've known them for long?"

"Friends?"

"The guys you were with the other night. When I saw you. At the Sheraton. Karaoke night. I take it you're not a regular. But. Will you . . . bring them?" Sam looks hopeful, his eyebrows arching up into his forehead.

"Bring them where?"

"You know," he whispers, "to see Britney Spears. Friday."

"I dunno. Maybe. You got a thing for one of them? I can tell you right now they're not interested."

Across the landscape of faded mulch and cigarette butts, Larry is ambling over. Sam suddenly feels awkward about the cigarette between his fingers, like a recent grown-up in front of his father. He is surprised that Tommy doesn't seem to feel the same.

"How are you both? Everything okay?" They nod. "Good, that's good." He smooths the ends of his mustache and looks at the sky. "Nice day," he says finally.

Sam answers: "Yes. It's such a relief, isn't it? The springtime?"

"Just that it gets hot so fast," Larry says.

"Hey Dad, Britney Spears is gonna be at the Sheraton on Friday," Tommy says. "Friday, right?"

"Wow, really?" Larry's tone is like that of a kid who's just been told he's being taken for ice cream.

"I'm surprised you're a fan," Sam says. "I told Tommy, because, well, she's more his generation than ours, isn't she?"

"I'm a big fan, in fact." Larry, forgetting himself, does a tiny hip swivel and sings a snippet of "Baby One More Time." "Um. Isn't it, though, I mean I've heard . . . ? Don't they have . . . karaoke . . . on Fridays?"

"Every first and third," Sam says with a smile. "I'm sort of a fixture over there. Sometimes they have it more often. They squeeze them in on the second Friday sometimes, sometimes the fourth. It'll be listed in the . . . oh gosh, you know the *Chronicle*, right?" He laughs a little hysterically and Larry laughs, either with relief or just to be friendly, while Tommy taps his cigarette pack on the table before sliding it into his pocket.

"Well, thanks for the tip," Larry says. "I used to be privy to, you know, surprise concerts, when I was at KLMN, but now I guess I'm out of the loop."

On their way back into the building, Sam whispers to Tommy, "I hope you're going to come still, even though, you know, your dad might be there too. I hope that's not too uncool."

"Nah. My dad's all right."

"Don't forget to bring your friends."

"Yeah?" Tommy readies a bundle of ads.

"But don't tell them I told you! I'll get into trouble, and they won't tell me these secrets any—" Sam's voice is cut off by the machinery as it wakes up, grumpy and boisterous.

The rest of that week, Sam drops casual reminders. "I don't think I can go, but Tommy, if you make it, take a little video, will you? With your phone?"

In the evenings, he and Carol discuss possible ways of framing Ethan and methods of delivering the information to his parents, who will surely put restrictions on his trust fund when they discover he's been cavorting with homosexuals.

In the back of Sam's mind, he is also thinking about his career, and moving to the city, though he doesn't mention it again to Carol. He hopes that Chloe and Francine will shower him with praise again. If Carol hears them tell Sam how talented he is, she might actually encourage him to go for it, to follow his dream to the city. He feels like he might really do it, with a bit of a push.

***

Finally, Friday comes. Sam is wearing a squid-like opalescent dress with synthetic tentacles of blue, green, and pink that breeze around his legs. He has blown dry his hair so it falls gently about his face in downy wisps, and on top of his head, as an accessory, is a pair of white-plastic-rimmed sunglasses with rhinestones in the corners. He takes the elevator to Carol's place, because his shoes are already beginning to give him a blister. He slips a finger behind the glittering heel strap. "Shit," he mutters, missing his Nikes and wishing he didn't.

"You have Band-Aids?" he says as Carol opens the door. She is wearing an elastic-waisted pair of black polyester trousers grabbed off a sidewalk sale in front of the Dress Barn and a black sweatshirt turned inside out so the logo for Titleist golf balls is just a smear of stitching. Tucked among the debris in her pocketbook is a small disposable camera. Sam follows her to the bathroom.

"How's the cold? You better? You ready?"

Carol opens the mirrored cabinet, shakes a flimsy Band-Aid box.

"Wasn't I born ready? Much better."

He sits on the toilet, rips open the paper wrapping, and crunches it and the nonstick bits into Carol's outstretched palm while aiming the absorbent padding toward the pink blister on his heel. He sits up, sighing, hands on hips. "I don't dress up enough. I'm in those sneakers all day, every day. Ugh. Next thing you know, I'll be getting . . . athletic . . . or something."

"God forbid. Not that," Carol drones, stepping on a plastic lever at the base of the trash can and dropping in the Band-Aid wrapper.

Sam tips the sunglasses from the top of his head onto his nose. "Undercover Agent Sam, ready for assignment Fuck Ethan Thaxter. Oooh, we're like Charlie's Angels. Oh honey, I hosey Farrah Fawcett. You can be that tall, serious bitch."

"Don't twist your ankle wearing those things."

"Don't be grumpy. You can be Jaclyn Smith if you want!"

"Christ. I don't care which Angel I am. I just hope it works."

Sam puts his hand on her shoulder. "It was your idea! And you're brilliant. Of course, it'll work!"

"I guess I just don't particularly want to end up on Stratton Island with Garnet."

"No," Sam says. "No, I wouldn't either." He shakes away the thought. "But we won't. We're not doing anything that bad! Ethan would never have the balls to press charges against us."

***

"Mind if I smoke?" Sam cracks the window and pulls a pack of Marlboro Lights from his purse. Carol flips down the ashtray. The sky is a deep, glowing indigo; the moon is a quarter full and the fecund smell of spring wafts in. "This is my favorite time of year." He leans his head back and takes in the rooflines passing blackly against the sky, stretches his arm over his head and inhales his cigarette. "It's like you get a second chance, over and over. You survived the winter and you're new again! I love it!"

"Be too hot to breathe before you know it," Carol says. Sam looks at Carol's hands, pudgy and joylessly hugging the steering wheel.

"Be here now," he says, sweeping his hand across the expanse of windshield and what lies beyond it: a McDonald's on the right, its arches lit from underneath, and on the left a strip mall with a Pizza Hut, a Dunkin' Donuts, a Laundromat. Carol grunts.

"Carol, you've gotta remember how to live in the moment. Life can be beautiful. Look at that sky. Breathe! It's mating season!"

"Mating season, huh? I don't know about you, but I think I'm past that." They leave behind strip-mall territory and enter downtown—buildings that have seen better days; closed-down shops that used to sell everything from hats and dresses to eggs and milk; some funky artists' cooperatives and fair-trade coffee shops that have taken advantage of the cheap rents that Wattsville's poor economic situation affords; and a few scattered restaurants, mostly chains like the Burrito Factory, but some new places as well, none of which Sam or Carol has yet tried. "I'm a downer," she concedes. "Sorry."

"Don't be sorry; I just don't like to see you unhappy."

"I can't help it, Sam. My daughter's in prison. And she's getting back together with the person who put her there. Not to mention that that relationship is getting her . . . oh those women who did that. I'd kill them with my bare hands . . ."

"I know, I know," Sam says, trying for sympathetic but coming off as annoyed.

"Okay." She taps her fingers against the wheel and leans back, pinning her shoulders against the seat. "Tell you what. We keep Ethan away from Garnet, I'll be happy. I promise."

***

The bar is dimly lit by candle-shaped light bulbs screwed into wagon-wheel fixtures. They scope out the floor plan: Carol will stand near the bathrooms and when Ethan arrives, Sam will confront him, and when Carol has moved in close enough, Sam will grab him and hold him in a smooch long enough for her to get a picture. Then they'll use the picture as blackmail, threatening to send it to his parents if he ever goes near Garnet again.

"Lovely to see you," a raspy voice approaches them. It's Francine, and behind her is Chloe. Sam air-kisses them both. They stand awkwardly for a moment and then Sam explains the plan. Carol nods along with Sam's words, as though to music, and has a smile on her face that is stretched tight with anxiety.

Sam has witnessed Carol's awkwardness in social situations before and recalls what usually happens: first he will be embarrassed by her and anxious to make her look good. Chloe and Francine already think he has a screw loose because he lives in Wattsville; witnessing his decidedly un-glamorous best friend at her most socially anxious will make him look even worse. Embarrassment will then turn to anger at them for their judgment (even if he is only imagining it), and he will feel defensive of Carol.

Like a college student who leaves home for the first time, he'll long to return to the ease of being with her, lounging, watching television, eating her cooking. But then, he'll resent her and hold her responsible for his own lack of movement and success. And of course, after he's been through this roller coaster of allegiances, defensiveness, and rancor, he'll realize that the whole darned thing had been in his head and that everybody was just being herself—except him.

Tonight, however, he largely avoids feeling stuck between his two sets of friends, because it is time for Carol to take her place in the dark corner to wait. He establishes himself at the bar with Francine and Chloe, and they become animated with talk of various possibilities: what kind of a kiss he should lay on Ethan, whether or not he should use tongue, whether he should try to bite him and draw blood. Chloe, who's confessed a fascination with vampirism, says, "Is he good looking? Maybe I should be the one to kiss him!"

"It's a risk." Francine's voice is long and deep like a yawn. "Nobody wants to get hurt by this boy. I think we already know he's violent? Too bad that gawky waitress isn't here. They all seemed smitten with her."

"Here they come," Sam interrupts her, waving to Larry, Tommy, and one of Tommy's friends. "He brought a friend," Sam says. "It's not Ethan."

Larry approaches first and nods to Chloe and Francine when Sam introduces them. Tommy rubs his elbows, folding himself in close, and his friend Hanky tucks his hands into his armpits. Their awkwardness amuses Sam and makes him feel confident.

Chloe moves in on the boys and suggests they all get a shot of something. Sam recognizes in Larry's reaction a fellow non-drinker and sidles up to him. "How about I buy you a soda?"

"No, no. I'll buy you one. What are you having?"

"Ginger ale with cranberry. Please and thank you."

Larry slips a bill from a tarnished silver clip and waves to the bartender.

"What time is she going to make an appearance?"

"Britney? Oh, a little later."

Francine leans in. "What are we drinking?"

"One more slippery nipple," Chloe calls to the bartender. "Sorry, dear. I would have gotten you one but I thought you weren't taking alcohol."

"Oh they tell me not to, but, really, what could it do? I mean it's only hormones. Presumably we all have them."

The bartender drizzles grenadine into another shot glass and slides it in front of Francine. She takes the glass and rejoins Larry and Sam, who are discussing work.

"I don't know why it's so hard to find people," Larry is saying. "I guess when the economy's good, it makes everybody think they can be Warren Buffett without ever having to do any work."

"It's so true," Sam says. "It's good for a body to work, isn't it? I mean, what else are we going to do with ourselves? You can't watch cable all day long, you'd be bored. Plus," he adds with a wink, "when you have a job, you meet new people and make friends."

"So," Francine says to Larry, "is your son going to bring any more of his friends?"

Larry looks confused. "I don't know."

"I mean, did he tell anyone about the concert?"

"No, no, he knew not to." Larry looks at Sam. "I mean, he told Jorge and Jaime. I don't know if they understood him, or if they'd even be interested. You hear that Spanish music they play."

Sam scans the room, and then gives a yelp.

"What is it?" Francine says, following his gaze. "Oh good lord."

Sam jogs and Francine strides to where Carol is curled up on the floor next to her chair.

"Carol, what are you doing down there?" Sam says, relieved that she is conscious. "What happened? Are you okay?" He crouches in front of her.

She lifts her head a little and says, "Hey, you don't wax up there, huh?"

Sam slaps his knees together. "What happened?"

"Threw my back out. I was getting ready; I had my camera. I dropped it and when I went to pick it up, well. I couldn't sit up again. So here I am."

"Can I do something to help?" Larry is standing behind Sam.

"This is my friend," Sam says. "Carol, my boss, Larry." They wave at each other.

"We should get her off the floor," Larry says.

"I'll see if I can get some help. Do you think we need an ambulance?" Francine sounds more bored than worried.

Larry crouches and helps Carol into a sitting position.

"I'm fine, I'm fine," Carol says, grimacing.

"You're not fine," Sam says. "Let's get you to the car and I'll bring you home."

"But the plan," Carol protests.

"What plan is that?" Larry says.

"Oh," Sam fumbles. "We were . . . going to . . . see Britney Spears. Of course. That was the plan."

"Yeah. I love her," Carol says. She is leaning back on her hands with knees bent and is breathing little puffs of air through tight lips.

"I'll get my son to help," Larry says. Francine follows him back to the bar.

"Larry seems nice," Carol says to Sam when they are left alone.

"He is nice," he agrees. "He's straight, I'm quite sure. And no wedding ring; I assume he's divorced."

"Remember when people used to stay married?"

"So, what really happened?"

"Who knows . . ."

"I mean, just now."

"I fell off the chair."

"How can you fall off a chair?"

"I told you. I dropped my camera and then when I went to reach it, I couldn't stand up."

"They say most back pain is psychological."

"Sure doesn't feel psychological."

"It never does. But listen. You had a cold, now you've thrown your back out. Think maybe your body is telling you something?"

"No, I don't." Carol coughs and winces.

"I'm just saying . . ."

She is squinting toward the bar. "Hey. Shut up. Is that Ethan?"

"Oh shit."

"I can't get up." Carol is like an insect stuck on its back. Sam tries to help her, but his heel gets snagged in the carpeting and he stumbles. On his knees, he rummages through her purse, looking for the camera. Meanwhile, Tommy and Hanky, over by the bar, are pointing Sam and Carol out to Ethan, who turns and high-tails it out of there.

"Shit. He's gone," Carol says. "He's gone."

"Let's help get these ladies to their feet." Chloe has appeared and offers her hand to Sam; he grabs it, and she helps him up. Larry and Tommy manage to help Carol get back onto her chair.

"We missed him," Sam whispers to Chloe.

"Oh shit. Was he that boy who was with your friends?"

Sam nods.

"Oh sugar. I'm sorry. I wasn't sure . . ."

They stand in an awkward circle for a long moment until Larry says, to nobody in particular, "Well, when do you think she's going to show up?" They all look at him with blank expressions. "Britney," he says. "Britney Spears?"

***

At work the next day, Larry tells Sam what a great time he had with Tommy and Hanky, and with Francine and Chloe. They'd stayed until closing time, singing karaoke songs.

"Well, I'm glad they showed you a good time," Sam says. "And sorry again about being misinformed about Britney Spears."

"You know, that would've been great, but Chloe and Francine, they were so nice. At least they can sing. Not me." He laughs. "I feel like we're friends now, you know?" Larry and Sam are at the picnic table. Tommy, Jorge, and Jaime are on the curb, flipping through old magazines and eating lunch. "You don't meet people like them every day."

"Well . . ." Sam says. "I mean, you do know me."

"No, but they're so . . . I don't know. They're so incredibly . . . cosmopolitan. Yet easygoing."

"They're fine," Sam says. "They're nice enough."

"I guess I don't get out much."

"I'm sorry. I guess I was disappointed to have to leave early, that's all. I really am glad you had a good time. Did Tommy enjoy himself?"

They look over to where Tommy is showing Jaime something in a magazine and cracking up. Jaime high-fives Tommy. They can't speak each other's language, but they are roughly the same age, and they manage to communicate through pointing and gesturing and laughing a lot. Larry shakes his head and looks a little despondent. "I think so," he says. "I'm never really sure what's going on with him."

"What do you mean? You two seem to get along great."

"No," Larry speaks in a low voice. "I feel like I don't even know him. He's been gone nearly his whole life and now I don't even know who he is. I can see some of my features. My mouth. He's a lot like I was at that age." Larry grabs a handful of his own abdomen. "Skinny. Not like I am now. Believe it or not."

"Oh, you're still fit," Sam lies.

"His mother, my ex-wife. She took him to Colorado. She met someone. A Christian. Convinced her I was depraved."

"You?" Sam's eyebrows fly up his forehead in surprise and anticipation. "Why would she say that?"

"I shouldn't be telling you this. Nobody knows."

And you're going to tell me? Sam thinks, flattered. He stays quiet, waiting.

Larry says, "Oh, it's just . . . Well, it's personal. I'm sorry I started talking. My big mouth." He looks thoughtful. "Ha, my big mouth. I hardly talk to anyone, except when I'm at work. Funny I'd have a big mouth."

"Listen," Sam says. "I'll tell you something I haven't told anyone. It's something I've been thinking a lot about."

Larry's grin under his mustache is grateful and frank. "What is it?"

"Well. I'm thinking about moving to the city."

"That's it?"

"That's big," Sam defends himself. "I've never really considered it before. You know, really, like it might happen. But don't worry," he says quickly. "I would give you a lot of notice! And make sure you had someone to replace me."

"Oh, don't worry about that. There's no one lives up here that doesn't half-wish they lived down there, and nobody who hasn't thought about making the move."

Sam deflates. "Well, what's your secret?"

Larry rolls up the sleeves of his shirt. "It's more ... personal than yours. Okay. Well, the reason my wife, his mother, why she left. I used to really like, uh, sex," he whispers.

"Well, there's nothing wrong with that! Unless you were unfaithful?"

Larry chuckles. "No, but I like to do things."

"Things?"

"Dress up, and stuff."

"Costumes?"

"I guess you could say that."

"Trans kind of fun? Dresses?"

Larry's face registers shock, but the shock is replaced quickly by recognition—that here, finally, is someone he can be truthful with and not be judged. "Just for fun. She was into it too—for a while."

"Well, you're human, and humans are sexual. And Larry, you have my word, that no matter what you say, I cannot be shocked."

He shakes his head, wondrous. "She came home early from work one day. I wasn't expecting her. There I was, going through our closet in a skirt, looking for a blouse to match. I'd put on one of her necklaces. Anyway, she actually liked it for a while. She dressed like a boy."

"That sounds like fun," Sam says. "God. Why would anyone think there was something wrong?"

"Well, then she met *him*. Quinn, his name is. In town for a convention. He's a businessman, she told me, a *moral* businessman. The way she said it was like only businessmen are moral and the rest of us aren't.

"He was in town to meet a bunch of other people and talk about disinfectants. That's what his company makes. Industrial disinfectants. We used to have their soap in the bathroom, but I stopped ordering it. That's why I bring in bottles of hand soap. I couldn't bear to look at it. Ah. It's over now anyway. Water under the bridge. But he's back, finally." Larry looks over at Tommy. "And I don't know what to do with him."

"Does he know anything about why she took him away? Did she tell him anything?"

"No. I don't think so. I'm afraid to ask what she might've told him. She's born again now, same's her husband." He gazes into the distance. "'We're not going to consummate our love until we're married in God's eyes.' That's what she said, not long after she'd left. As though it was going to be a comfort to me? Or was it a dig? At me for my sinning ways? I still don't know why she would tell me things about their relationship. Maybe I'm just a pushover. She still calls and tells me things like we're friends. And I take it, I listen, because, you know the truth of it? I don't really have any friends. She was my best friend."

"That's why your partner should never be your best friend," Sam says. "That's why Carol is my best friend. She's reliable. She's not going to leave me."

"Nice lady. Well, we better get back," Larry says suddenly, standing and looking at his watch.

"I've enjoyed talking to you, Larry."

Larry pulls his pants up, running his thumbs around the inside of his waistband. "Yeah. Me too. Um, you won't . . . ?"

"Never!" Sam says. "You can trust me."

***

Sam slips his yoga video into the player and sits down on his mat. He imagines Poppy's life, apart from what he sees of her on the TV screen. He wishes he could meet her, to thank her for her soothing voice. He sits tall, as she instructs, leans from side to side, pulling the flesh out from underneath his sit bones. He wonders momentarily what exactly sit bones are—are they attached to the tops of his legs or the bottom of his bum?—and then focuses on his breath. In, out. In, out. His thoughts drift to Larry's new friendship with Chloe and Francine, and he feels a little jealous but also satisfied that Chloe and Francine had liked Larry, too. That they had found something to like about Wattsville. Maybe now they'd stop poking fun all the time.

That is, if they really did like Larry. Maybe they were laughing? Maybe they found him kind but pathetic, and maybe Sam was wrong to become friends with him. He wonders whether Larry had shared his secret with them. He resolves to ask them about it, but then, is it supposed to be a secret from them, too? Would they think Larry's secret was silly?

Maybe Chloe and Francine are right: maybe all the cool people are in the city . . . He opens his eyes to find that Poppy is already doing cat-cow. He sighs and pushes himself onto hands and knees. He stretches into cat and sags into cow. Up, down. Up, down.

Later, he is watching *Friends* when the phone rings.

"Hey can you go?" He can tell from the tightness in Carol's voice that her back still hurts. "I can't see trying to drive, and I can't afford to miss work Monday, so I gotta rest my back."

"Again?" He had told her last night that he'd go visit Garnet if she needed him to, but he'd forgotten about it. He had envisioned an afternoon on the sofa.

"If you can't, it's okay. I'll get myself there. It hurts, but I'm not crippled."

"No, no. Of course I'll go. After everything you've done for me."

"Sam. Make sure you don't tell her about what we tried to do."

"No, of course I wouldn't. God."

"And find out. What's going on, with him. If they're in contact."

"Carol. I'll do what I can. Okay? Don't worry. Everything's going to be fine."

Sam knows that friendship requires sacrifice, compromise, and being there for someone when you're needed. It's true he's asked for help from Carol many times, and she's always given it willingly—cooking for him, lending him money, taking care of him when he's sick. But this morning, after his yoga and meditation, he is interested in thinking about himself, and his dreams, and his life's journey. He's beginning to feel resentful that he has to think about other people's problems. He has his own life to live. He has a star to follow. Why is it his job to keep Garnet away from Ethan? He may be signing on to a mission that even Carol shouldn't really be on. Garnet is a grown woman, and a grown woman needs to make her own mistakes. You can't control her. Carol is proud of having singlehandedly raised Garnet; but now that her job is done, she doesn't seem able to get on with her own life, preferring instead to keep acting as though Garnet were still a little girl who needed protection. It's not healthy. She needs to live her life and let Garnet live hers. And Sam needs to live his.

"You're sure you don't mind?" Carol asks again. "Someone needs to go. After . . . the last time. Oh Sam, sometimes I'm sick with worry."

"I know you are. And I am too. But, Carol . . ." He pauses. He's said it to her already, in various ways, and it never goes over well. "You have to let her make her own mistakes, you know?"

Carol is quiet. And then, "That's what I did, Sam. That's why she's where she is."

"You can't blame yourself."

"I should have tried to do something. When she had bruises. And we knew it. But I hid from it. And pretended it wasn't happening, even though I knew it was. So now I'm going to do something. Are you going to help me or not?"

"Yes. Of course, I will. You know I'll always help."

"Okay. So. See if you can get any information out of her. Maybe see if she knows anything about that kid Tommy you work with. Whether he's good friends with Ethan or not. And of course, how close they're getting—her and Ethan. You'll do that?"

"Yes."

"You hungry? Wanna come up for mac and cheese? It's all I could manage. I can't bring it down there. My back."

"Maybe."

"I won't be much fun. I'm just on the couch."

"That's all right. I'm fine. I'll see you later."

"Thank you, Sam. I . . . well . . . just thank you."

***

Sam isn't early for visiting hours, but it is taking longer than usual for Garnet to arrive. On the wall is a square where a picture used to be. You wouldn't have known what color the paint was supposed to be without that square. It had been a bright, calming blue, but now it's gray. He figures they must have allowed smoking in here, because a wall couldn't possibly get that dirty on its own. The thought of people's breath yellowing paint makes Sam shudder. On another wall are portraits of Clinton and Gore, both smiling in front of the American flag.

When Garnet is finally allowed in, he gasps at the sight of her. Carol had warned him but he thought she'd been exaggerating. Her arm is in a sling and the skin around her eye is yellow. But it's not just that. She also looks haggard. She's only twenty-one but there is an ancient darkness around her that stuns Sam. She walks straight over and lays her head on his chest; he wraps his arms around her and rubs her back. He looks up to the ceiling, thanks the stars that he is able to have this feeling of being loved and giving comfort. If he could stay here for the rest of his life, he would be happy. Just loving and caring. A tear slides down his cheek, his sadness enhanced by the guilt of having not wanted to come at all. In the long run, he never regrets being generous with his time, but sometimes he forgets to be the person he knows he should be and instead guards his free time too vehemently.

"That's long enough, Prisoner Harlow," comes the guard's voice. "No more touching."

"Is something wrong? Why didn't Mom come?"

"She's fine," Sam reassures her. "Just threw her back out."

Garnet is developing the rigid jaw and tight lips of a person expecting the worst. He is reminded of the way people's faces look when they're stuck in traffic, or when they pick the wrong checkout lane in the supermarket.

As an adolescent, Garnet was bold and often outspoken. He remembers her at swim meets, stepping onto the starting block with her chin jutting out, her shoulders pulled back. She isn't fat, but has a solid, stocky frame. Most of the girls on the team were thin and Sam could tell by watching the way they interacted in line as they waited for their heats that Garnet wasn't popular. Once a girl—yellow hair, blue eyes, like a doll—fanned the air in front of her nose as Garnet mounted the starting block. A group of girls giggled. Garnet didn't notice, thank God, but Sam wondered what other mean things they did to her in the locker room. Some girls—especially at that age—could be so scheming and nasty that they verged on evil. Seeing women at their worst sometimes made him wonder why he felt more comfortable as one of them than as a man.

Carol, sitting next to him on the bleachers at the swim meet, didn't notice the girl making fun of Garnet, or if she did, she didn't let on. But then Carol was an expert at avoidance. She admitted to him once that Garnet's father, Beaver, had cheated on her quite openly, and that everybody knew about his infidelities and his drug use, except for her. It was this talent for avoidance that had also allowed Carol to miss the signs of Garnet's abusive relationship. Back when Sam started wondering why Garnet was wearing frumpy long-sleeved blouses and never inviting Carol or him to come over to the apartment she shared with Ethan, Carol didn't seem to notice anything.

Sam longs to be able to put his arms around Garnet again—to feel useful, nurturing. But touching for more than three seconds is prohibited. He remembers when he first met her, when she was a toddler. He used to spend long afternoons, drinking white Russians with Carol while Garnet played. She grew close to him over time, climbing onto his lap while they watched television, brushing and styling his hair. Playing with his makeup. It was he, in fact, who'd given her an education in femininity. Carol never wore makeup and shunned dresses, but Garnet loved to doll herself up. She used to ask Sam for fashion advice—which skirt went with which top. Would those shoes make her legs look longer? And how would they work with that hemline?

Sam says, "Your mom told me some women don't like that you have a rich boyfriend?" He feels another tear slip down his face and, as though it were contagious, Garnet starts to quietly weep as well. "There, sweetie, there. Okay, listen, let's talk about something else for now. How's your roommate? What's her name?" He blows his nose loudly.

"Shanise."

"That's right."

"She's okay. Actually, she's pregnant. It turns out." Garnet's laugh conveys helplessness and sympathy and a mountain of bad luck shared with her cellmate.

"Oh my dear. Goodness gracious. How did that happen?"

At this, Garnet laughs for real, bringing them both relief. "In the usual way. I thought you knew how it happened!"

Sam puts his hand to his mouth and says, "Ooh. Honey. I know. Oh I do know how it happens."

"Well, anyway. He's married. He's a guard," she whispers. "He's a bit of an ass, you ask me. Pretends he's deep when really it's just that he has nothing to say."

"What will they do?" Sam imagines himself as a character in one of the cheesy soap operas he likes to watch sometimes—the simplicity of the characters is a comfort.

"He got her a pill." She continues to speak in a low whisper and avoids looking at the guard on duty.

"What do you mean? A pill? Aren't those illegal?"

She nods, clears her throat and says, "Tell me what happened to Mom? How'd she throw her back out?"

"Oh at work." Sam hopes it's not obvious that he's lying. "Whoever did this to you," he says. "Will they leave you alone?"

She shakes her head and leans in. "Some girls. They want. Well, I have to do a favor for them. Or they'll do worse."

Sam yelps but quiets down immediately as Garnet gives him a look and a slight nod toward the guard. "Worse? They'll do worse?" he whispers.

"This isn't that bad," she says. "Small crack in the rib. It's almost all healed. I'll be fine."

"Garnet. Sweetheart. It's not right." He is becoming hysterical; his legs are twitching under the table.

"Stop now." She glares at him, her face serious. He stops, takes little breaths through his nose, thinking fleetingly of Poppy's yoga instructions.

"What's the favor?" Sam tries to keep his voice down. "Not that that's what it is. Favors are things people do of their own volition. This is coercion."

"Don't say anything. You have to promise. I won't tell you unless you promise. Really swear."

"Okay, I promise."

"Say lightning will strike me dead if you tell Mom."

"Strike *you* dead? Why?"

"Swear on my life. If you tell her, I'll die. And it will be your fault. And you know, it could happen. So, don't break it."

"Don't say that!"

"I won't tell you."

"Okay, okay. I promise. May you die if I break my promise. Whatever it is, I don't want her knowing anyway. God."

"You know she worries."

"Garnet, tell me. What is it?"

"He had to smuggle some drugs in. Ethan did. They weren't specific, and he brought weed. But now they want more. And they want something stronger. But he can't do it anymore. He did it twice and now he says that his dealer left town or something."

Sam shifts nervously. He isn't sure he wants all this information. He loves gossip, but this is too much. He realizes that his status as father figure but not father has allowed him to be exempt from the difficult parts of parenting. Garnet has always told him things she wouldn't tell her mother, and he never had to shoulder the irrational blame inflicted by her when she was a teenager. He's always toed the line between friend and authority figure. He is ashamed to realize that the reason she trusts him with her confidences is because his role has never required him to discipline her. Now he feels the weight of her secret and doesn't know how to manage it.

Without thinking he says, "Honey, I'll get it for you."

"Where will you get it?" she says. "It's not just pot they want anymore."

He pulls back, but the hopefulness in her expression makes him soldier on. "Just tell me where his usual dealer is. I'll find him."

"Will you? Thank you, Sam."

"Yes. Of course. Where does he get the stuff?"

Garnet looks doubtful again. "I can't ask you to do this."

"If there's any chance I can't pull it off, I won't do it. Just tell me where to go. It's been a long time since I . . . well . . . just tell me where to go. I'll do my best."

"You know the Dairy Queen on Fremont? That's where the guy deals from."

"Dairy Queen?" He laughs but Garnet shushes him. "So much for family dining. Lord. Okay, I'll do it, but in the meantime," he says, "can you keep these . . . brutes . . . away?"

She nods, almost resolutely. She seems stronger than when he came in and he imagines that he is giving her strength, and it makes him proud. "Make sure they know it's not Ethan that's getting it. That weasel. Make sure they know he's out of the picture."

"Sam. If you can get it, it means Ethan is lying to me. I don't blame him, I guess, for not wanting to do this. It's a big risk. But you're right, either way he's letting me down."

"You'll . . . cease contact . . . if he's lying about it?"

"That's a lot to ask. It's not like making me promise to do my homework or something. I'll make up my own mind. You know that."

They sit in silence. Sam decides to tell her about the night he saw Ethan with Tommy. The more information he has about Ethan's current routines, the better.

"It happens I saw Ethan a few nights back. At the Sheraton."

"Really?" She squints doubtfully.

"Yes, he was with this kid Tommy, who works with me at the newspaper. Tommy is my boss's son. I suppose you know all of Ethan's friends . . ."

"I know a lot of them, but I don't know any Tommy."

"Nice kid. He just moved back. I think from Colorado, his dad said."

"Nope. Don't know him. Did you talk to Ethan? You and him never got along."

"He was very mean and nasty, my dear. A complete asshole, actually. Pardon my French. I'm not going to force you to promise you won't see him anymore, because I know you take promises seriously. But I'm telling you this: He's a nasty piece of work."

"Don't you think maybe he's just shy, and maybe was brought up wrong?"

Sam coughs the word "Homophobe."

"I know. I know. I'm thinking about it. I'll do what's right. At least I'll try to."

Sam leans back and crosses his legs, satisfied.

"If there's any chance you're going to be caught, don't do it. Okay? I can handle things in here."

"As much as you promised me, I promise you. Okay, honey?"

As they hug goodbye, Sam strokes her hair. "I'd do anything for you, you know? You're a shining star, Garnet. Don't forget it."

***

Back in Carol's Buick, Sam kneads the rubber bear key chain. He marvels at the changes a day can bring. Now he's as invested as Carol in getting Ethan out of Garnet's life. Well, he can do it all, he thinks. He should have a superhero cape, for he's going to save Garnet, keep her from Ethan, and start a new career in a new city. Why not? Why can't he? A few candy clouds are tacked onto the blue sky and the wind through the open window blows warmly through Sam's hair. He flips through stations, trying to find a song to sing along to, but nothing grabs him.

As he nears home, he begins to feel a little less sure. The logistics start to feel overwhelming. And his promise to Garnet. He hates having to keep secrets, and this one will be especially tough. Truth is, he is a terrible secret keeper. As someone who has always been unable to pretend to be something he isn't, he finds it strange and awkward when people hide things and themselves from others. But he is superstitious and he takes his promise to Garnet seriously. How well she knows him! But, if he doesn't tell Carol, how will he manage to do what Garnet needs him to do?

His dream of moving to the city needs to take a back seat. He'll get this done, and then he'll think about moving. The flattened bags and plastic bottles and orange straws that litter the parking lot behind their building have all dried out with the lack of rain. Their edges lift and tap in the breeze. Sam parks the Buick in Carol's spot. He sits in the car, thinking. He has started to hatch a new plan—a plan that, if he pulls it off, will keep Garnet out of trouble and convince her to stay away from Ethan, as well as help her to keep those threatening inmates off her back. When he can explain all the details to Carol, after the fact, she'll understand and be filled with gratitude. And finally, after he's sorted out this mess, he'll embark on his glorious new career. Carol will make him a big going-away dinner and, when he's gone, will send care packages of Tollhouse cookies and Rice Krispies treats in the mail.

ANOTHER COCKAMAMIE PLAN

Carol

Carol holds her breath and leans on the register.

"Are you okay?" Ron calls from the grill.

"I threw my back out. I thought it was better, but all this standing up . . ."

"What were you doing? The macarena?"

"Friggin' macarena. Yeah, right. It was the limbo I was doing. Don't make me laugh, Ron. It hurts to laugh."

A student pushes a small box of cereal along the counter, and Carol punches in the price with her right hand while grasping the register for stability with her left. "One-fifty." She slides two quarters up the ramp from their compartment and counts out three dollar bills. The student shoves the change into his pocket and glides away. "Shit," she whispers, rubbing her lower back.

Later, as she is wrapping cookies in sticky sheets of plastic pulled from a tattered cardboard dispenser, Ron comes up behind her and puts his hands on her shoulders. She wheels around. He stands back, his hands in the air as though she were pointing a gun at him.

"Sorry," she says. "You scared me."

"Turn. I maybe help."

"You take me by surprise like that, you're gonna make me throw my back out all over again." She turns and leans on the counter.

"Ready?" Ron says. She nods.

"Up here?" he says, his hand between her shoulder blades. "Or down here?" He slides his hand to rest in the small of her back.

"Yup, down there."

"You been upset," he says.

"I don't need psychoanalysis; it's my back."

He places the heels of his hands along her sacrum with his fingertips splayed out toward the edges of her hips and begins moving his thumbs in small circles on the sides of each vertebra.

"That's it," Carol winces. "Oh, that's it. That's good."

"I know you are sad. Your daughter, she gonna get out. She a good girl, I know this."

Carol breathes noisily as he rubs. "You wanna know the truth?" She tries to relax the muscles Ron is massaging. "I am worried about my daughter. She's been having trouble with some of the other girls, women, in the prison there." She remembers the three tough-looking guys who had come to see Ron the other day and says, "I wish there was someone who could protect her." As the words come out of Carol's mouth her forthrightness surprises her. She isn't exactly asking for his help, but she hopes he will offer it.

"Maybe she's smarter than you think?" Ron's voice is soft as he concentrates most of his energy on the work his hands are doing.

"Yeah."

"Maybe she knows what's best for her."

"She's just a kid! And someone hit her. Beat her up. She's the best kid in the world and she doesn't deserve any of this."

"Here?" Ron pushes his thumb into her sacrum.

"Yes. Thanks. That's good." Her disappointment that he hasn't offered to help protect Garnet is eased by the fact that her back is starting to feel better.

"How's it now?" he smooths out her shirt. She stands straight and turns around, takes a couple of steps away from the counter and then back again.

"Good. It feels a little better, actually. Thanks."

He turns to the employees' lockers. "I gotta go, I'll be late."

"You have your other job, huh?"

"Yes." He unbuttons the snaps at the front of his cook's shirt and tosses it onto an overflowing laundry hamper.

"You know it's great, what you're doing."

He turns to face her, his T-shirt bunched around his wrists like a pair of handcuffs. "What am I doing?" He raises his arms and slides the shirt over his head.

"Working two jobs. Going to school." She wraps a cookie, places it in the bin.

"You're a mom," he says, "that's a hard job. The hardest."

"She's not even around." Carol's eyes sting with emotion, and she turns away quickly. She grabs a paper towel from the roll on the wall and wipes her eyes.

They look at each other and the eye contact makes Carol jittery.

"So, about dinner. I still want to cook for you. Maybe this weekend? Or if not, next?"

"Maybe. I'll let you know. Thanks."

He hurries out, through the rust-tiled kitchen, past the registers, around the Formica tables—grey flowers with irregular petals of slouching boys in oversized sweatshirts and girls in shiny tracksuits.

Carol replays their conversation in her head several times. But even more than their conversation, she analyzes Ron's body language. The way he turned to face her in just his undershirt. Is he aware that the sight of his semi-naked torso excites her? She doesn't get the feeling that he enjoys looking at her the way she likes looking at him. And she's sure she wears that admiration on her face. But the touching. His touch. So caring. She can't decipher if it's tender the way a parent's or a friend's touch would be, or if there is something more.

And she wonders if he could actually help Garnet. She assumes he's involved with some shady characters—whatever that even means. All Carol knows about crime she learned on television. Or who knows? The men who came to see him could've been anyone. Maybe they were relatives. If they were dangerous people, then she should be more afraid. But she's not afraid. She assumes her intuition will do its job—and it's telling her not to be afraid. But then, what's her intuition telling her about her crush? She thinks that most likely he's not interested in her; but maybe that's just her insecurity trying to keep her back. She tucks it all away and brings home a tiny hope that maybe he will love her.

*****

It is Carol's day off, and she and Sam embark on plan B. The two of them pull up in front of the Dairy Queen on Fremont.

"We're either brilliant or very stupid," Carol says.

Sam turns the rearview mirror in his direction and pats at his hair. Carol melts into her seat.

"How we're going to get the . . . drugs . . . into Ethan, if you manage to get any. It seems pretty crazy . . . There must be some other way . . ."

"Hey, that's Tommy," Sam interrupts her.

They slide down low in the front seat and watch him go in. Sam takes a deep breath and opens the door. "You stay here," he says.

"Wait a minute. Hold on. I'll go." She grabs his wrist.

"We said I was going to." He looks surprised but there is a touch of relief in his voice.

"We didn't think it through. Look at you."

"Look at you," he fires back. She is determined now and doesn't even notice the insult.

"I should go. It's my daughter. Hell, if I get caught, and I end up in prison, maybe we'll be together." She's not sure why, when they made this plan, she was willing to let Sam take the risk of trying to buy drugs. She realizes now how much more sense it makes for her to do it, and feels courage and strength in some far corner of her consciousness. Overwhelming those feelings, fear tries to talk her out of it.

"Carol. It was my idea. I should be the one."

"It was your idea and it might be stupid or it might not, but this part isn't really that risky. Look. All I'm trying to do is buy drugs. I'm not a dealer. I don't even have anything on me. What's the worst that could happen?"

"But, we said I would," Sam says weakly.

"These kind of people are going to be nicer to me than to you. You know that."

Finally, he agrees. She gets out of the car and crosses the street.

Trying to be nonchalant, she browses the menu behind the counter. The kid in the DQ smock has meaty acne scars, a long nose, and prominent cheekbones. He would be handsome, in a feline sort of way, if it weren't for his complexion.

The kid ordering is Tommy. Carol wouldn't have recognized him if Sam hadn't pointed him out from the car. He's pulling money out, but the guy behind the counter pushes his wallet back toward him and says quietly, "see you out back." Then, in a louder voice, he says, "Blizzard? Just Reese's Pieces? Anything else?" He turns to the ice cream dispenser.

Carol moves up to the counter and says to Tommy, "Oh hey, you know my friend, Sam, right? We met at the Sheraton. That night . . . Britney Spears was supposed to show up? Too bad about that." He looks at her blankly. "I had to leave early because I threw my back out."

"Oh yeah," Tommy laughs but stifles it. "Sorry. Yeah, I'm glad you're better."

"Yeah, all better. Ha ha. Sam. You know, he hears these rumors. About Britney Spears? You never know when they're going to be true. I don't like her music much anyway."

"Me neither. But it would've been dope to see her."

The kid in the smock pushes a buttery heap of ice cream dotted with orange and brown buttons across the counter. Tommy takes it and heads for the door, saying, "nice to see you again." Carol appreciates his politeness, even though she knows it's not sincere. She watches him exit.

The kid behind the counter says, "Can I help you?"

When she turns to him, all courage slides out her feet and she's left speechless.

"Lady? You okay?"

"Yes, yes. Sorry. Um." She looks up at the signage. "I'd like. Dru . . . um. Chicken strips, please."

"Size?"

"Small."

He tells her the price, and she pays. As he heads back into the kitchen, she looks out the plate-glass window, trying to work up her courage. I want to buy drugs, she will say. No. Something more specific. Cocaine. But no one would call it that. Blow. That's what she'll say. Her eyes focus on movement across the street: Sam is jumping up and down and pointing. She goes out, baffled.

"That way," he says, running to meet her. "Tommy went down there, behind. That must be where he deals from."

"And I'm just supposed to go back there?"

"I don't know," Sam says urgently. "Maybe just see if it's true. See if that's where they deal the drugs."

She goes to the opening of a narrow alleyway that leads behind the building. The ground is stained with the ammoniac tang of stale urine. She looks back at Sam, who is retreating to the car, holds her breath, and tiptoes through. At the end, behind the DQ, there is a dumpster, two anemic maple trees, plastic bags suctioned to a chain-link fence by previous winds, cigarette butts, and flies like winged raisins flinging themselves hysterically over several piles of what she hopes is dog shit.

The Blizzard with Reese's Pieces is perched on a cinder block.

She crouches behind the dumpster, out of sight. Her heel is in a clump of half-hardened shit, her back aches, and a branch is stabbing her in the flank, but she remains quiet.

"Just some Mary Jane," Tommy is saying.

"Here. Have some chicken strips. That crazy lady who said she knew you left without them." The kid puts a strongbox about the size of a muffler on top of a milk crate and the two of them sit on either side of it. Carol pictures them in forty years, imagines the box of drugs would then be full of fishing tackle and that it would be early morning and they'd be setting up for a long day of fishing and drinking beer from the can.

"Derbin, where are you?" comes a voice from inside the Dairy Queen.

"Shit, the pipsqueak is back." He pulls a baggie out and shoves Tommy's money into the box.

Tommy laughs, pocketing his weed. "Thought you said the guy was never here."

"He's always over at Starbucks—I think he's trying to get it on with a barista. Whatever." He calls toward the screen door, "I'm out here, just having a break!" To Tommy, he says, "Catch you later." The rasp of Tommy's jeans is close enough that Carol can hear it as he passes. She squeezes her eyes shut and hopes she's better hidden than one of those Chinese pandas she's seen pictures of, thinking they're invisible behind a thin reed of bamboo. Then he is gone.

The manager's face is an orange blur behind the screen. "Derbin, you can hear the bell out here, right? If anyone comes in?" His voice tries for authoritative, but he sounds intimidated.

After the screen door slams, Carol stands up stiffly and goes to the box. She can hear the manager's and Derbin's voices and the sound of water running, dishes clanking. She tries to open the box, but it is locked and there is no key anywhere nearby. "I'll finish in a minute. Would you take care of that guy?" comes Derbin's voice as the bing bong of the electronic bell indicates that the front door is opening.

Carol grabs the box and limps back down the alleyway. She can hear the screen door bounce back against the frame and Derbin kicking the chair it had been on. "Just a fucking minute. I lost something." She dashes across the street, nearly getting flattened by a van that has to slam on its brakes and swerve around her.

"Drive. Quick!" She holds the box on her thighs and slides down the seat nearly to the floor. Sam says nothing, all of his attention on the road.

When they are safely away, Sam says, "Jesus, Carol! What did you do?" Then he sniffs several times. "What's that? Smells like dog shit."

Carol puts her foot onto a wrinkled McDonald's bag and pinches her nose shut. "Holy shit. We're really in it now."

***

Later that evening, in Sam's apartment, the box sits patiently in the middle of the coffee table while Carol and Sam plot. Carol, on the sofa with a pillow under her knees, is doodling in the margins of a book of crosswords. Doodling usually calms her, but she finds her tense pencil will only draw the parallel lines of prison bars and knotty loops of barbed wire. Sam is pacing.

"We can't do much until we get it open," he is saying.

"I don't know what you thought we were going to do with these drugs anyway." She looks up from her doodling to stare at the box as though it were an unwelcome guest. "The plan was cockamamie to start with. Drug him? Why did I even listen to you?"

"It's not cockamamie, whatever that is. And you didn't have to steal the whole box!"

"How are we going to open it? And what if he saw me running?" She snorts. "Running. Me. I didn't even know I had it in me!"

"I can get it open. I'll get it open. Leave it to me." Sam picks up the box, holds it against his hip. "You've done your part. So, I'll do this. Maybe it was a cockamamie plan, but we're in it now. You get some rest. And don't worry. I'll take care of it."

Carol is relieved that he is leaving with the thing, taking it away from her. She considers pressing him on what he plans to do but decides to leave it be, to let him handle it. It was his idea anyway. This is her default behavior, her comfortable place and, while the invigoration of having left that comfortable place remains, she can't deny the calming feeling of letting someone else take control again.

However, she realizes that a small part of her actually liked having the box around, as a physical reminder of her bravery. She replays the events of the afternoon. Hiding behind a dumpster. That was her, a middle-aged mother! What if she'd been caught? Shot at? She still can't believe she wasn't. She feels exhausted, the way she used to when she was a kid after a full day of sledding or swimming. It's delicious.

Finally, her thoughts turn to Ron and the possibility that he will come over this weekend. What will she wear? She resolves to buy something tomorrow, takes a couple of Advils for her back, and goes to bed.

***

On her way to the Dress Barn, Carol passes Va Va Voom. She stops just past the door, checks her watch, makes sure no one is looking, and ducks in. The woman behind the register is as big as Carol, but she is a totally different species, fashion-wise: she wears a silver tank top, shorts, and a flowery scarf draped across her shoulders. "Want to seduce someone?" she asks matter-of-factly, as if it were a garden shop and Carol were buying bulbs. Want to plant some begonias? Carol feels her face get flushed and looks away. Every item her eyes land on makes her shiver with embarrassment.

"It's not really anything," she tries to explain. "Just in case, you know. I guess I'm hoping." The woman chuckles and comes out from behind the counter. She leads Carol to a rack full of silky, stringy items. She pushes them this way and that, finally retrieving an orange bodysuit contraption crosshatched with seams and satiny elastic.

"I have one of these at home, and my husband, he begs me to wear it." Her smile is open and easy. She is like a child showing off a new bike. "Try it on," the woman says, pushing it at Carol.

In the dressing room, Carol slowly pulls at the sleeves of her T-shirt. She hugs herself underneath the fabric and tries to work up the courage to pull it off. She hasn't gotten dressed in front of a mirror in years. She doesn't even own a full-length mirror and doesn't do anything with the small one in the bathroom apart from looking for the gaps between her teeth while flossing and making sure there are no globs of moisturizer in the crevices next to her nose.

Finally, she squeezes her eyes shut and pulls the T-shirt off. At first, she is shocked at her paleness. Her arms and her face are pink, but her stomach and breasts are milky. She is big but, she decides, not overly flabby and, especially after seeing the woman working here, acceptable. She slides her pants off and pulls the lingerie over her underwear. The dissonance between the silky orange G-string and Carol's baggy briefs makes her laugh out loud. Then she laughs even more as she pulls the thing up over her ten-year-old Maidenform bra. She almost takes the bra off to get a feel for how it will look, but decides that would be too much. She likes the feel of the silk next to her skin. She stops herself from imagining Ron's hands on the straps. She takes one last look at herself, spools the thing down her legs and gets dressed.

When she emerges from the dressing room, the woman is busy rearranging dildos in a glass case. "Well?" A blueberry-colored plastic penis dangles from her hand. Carol nods and brings the suit to the counter.

"It's just for . . . you know, I don't have any . . . I mean. Just in case, you know? There is someone. And I'm hoping."

"Listen," the woman says after Carol has run out of steam. "I bet it looks great on you." She puts it into a bag and Carol pays.

"Thanks," she says to the woman. "This is big," she adds, and the woman seems to know what she means.

"You just have fun, hon. Okay?"

Carol rolls the bag into a ball and shoves it into her pocketbook on the way out the door.

***

On Friday morning, Carol watches Ron and starts to feel certain that her attraction is one-sided. He doesn't notice that she's gotten her hair cut and dyed. He isn't looking at her at all.

"Is that soda or iced tea?" Carol asks. The student in front of her indicates that it is iced tea, and Carol punches in the price. "Five fifty-five," she says to the next, and the student shoves a ten-dollar bill at her. She usually plays games to keep herself entertained when she is working, such as giving people the slightly wrong amount of change: She'll give one student five extra cents and then short the next one five cents, just to see if they'll notice. They never do. The only ones who count their change are the adjuncts.

Today, to distract herself, she decides to try to not speak, just to see if anyone will notice. She looks at the next student and points at the green numbers on the register. He gives her a bill, she dumps change in his hand, and off he goes without a word. The next student says thanks but doesn't appear to care whether she answers. She takes money from eight more students before another one thanks her. She nods.

"Have a good one," she whispers.

The student, a girl whose eyes look damp behind thick glasses, says, "You too" and walks away.

It's only a matter of time, she supposes, before jobs like hers are replaced altogether by machines or robots. What is she doing here anyway? Besides making just enough to pay rent and bills? She is about as useful as an aluminum box with a money slot and change dispenser. She imagines a future where rich people live with their robotic slaves in gleaming edifices that soar into the sky while people like her scavenge underground for bugs and roots . . .

She is distracted by her imagination and doesn't notice that the next person in line, sliding a cookie down the counter, is Ron. He grins and she nearly falls off of her chair.

"Take it," she says, her fingers twitching from constant price ringing.

"I get it for fifty percent," he reminds her.

"Yeah, but I won't tell." Her calmness is anxious and studied, and she tries to lighten up. "Go on."

"You okay?" he asks.

"Of course I am," she says. "Are you?" She wants to ask him about Saturday but loses her nerve. He leaves two quarters on the counter and unwraps the cookie as he walks back to the grill. Carol swears at herself under her breath.

The next person in line is Mike Bruss, Garnet's old English teacher. He moves his Nantucket Nectar from one hand to the other, wipes the condensation from his palm onto his pant leg. "I went to visit your daughter," he says.

"Well, I'll be damned. Hello."

"Sorry. Sorry. I always do that. Just blurt out what I'm thinking."

Carol laughs. Imagine me, she thinks, embarrassing a professor. "No, I'm glad. I bet she was happy to see you. And I'm grateful."

He hands her a soggy five, and she makes change.

"She didn't look great."

This description isn't surprising to Carol, but hearing it causes a spear to run through her heart and she becomes overwhelmed with grief and shame. Here she is buying lingerie and living her life, and Garnet . . .

"I'm sorry, I didn't mean to . . ." Professor Bruss is even more awkward than usual.

She shakes her head and looks to the next person in line. Mike Bruss wanders away.

ROBBED OF PAROLE

Garnet's Diary

I got a totally unexpected surprise today.

Guess who came to visit me? Professor Bruss. He's like fifty or something, but I'd marry him if he asked. Oh God, if Ethan ever finds this! I think I sometimes hide things from myself, because if I hide them from myself then Ethan won't ever find them and I don't have to be afraid of him. God, how fucked up is that?

I adore Professor Bruss. But I couldn't ever say that to Ethan. Even though I don't want to have any kind of romantic relationship with him. He's ancient and he's married. But he's kind. I'm realizing that I have to hide too much of my real self when I'm with Ethan. Like I can't talk about things that are important to me, because it could make him mad.

I can't believe he actually visited me! I was nervous when I saw him. Like, he was always there in front of the class, and all us kids would listen and try to say smart things and he was this funny guy who was just incredibly real and intelligent and you never felt threatened and you never felt like what you said was stupid— even though some people did say some stupid things. But he never made them feel stupid. I might have rolled my eyes at them sometimes, but he never would.

Then, there he was in the visiting room. And you know what he said, Diary? He said that he really hoped I would go back to school when all of this blew over. He said he thought I was great! He showed me pictures of his wife and his dog. He said Mom did a good job raising me, and that he knew it was hard to raise a kid when you're on your own, and that his mother had had to do that too. He didn't stay too long, just wanted to make sure I knew that he hoped I got out soon and that mostly he hoped I'd keep studying. I feel happy today. ☺

Fuck. Fuck. Fuck.

E. and M. want more. What gives them the right? Because they're stronger? Shanise was feeling sick and didn't go outside. Of course. She's feeling sick all the time and isn't there for me at all.

Meantime if I don't produce something, I'm going to get beaten up again. I told Shanise when I came in that they were threatening me and she was like, "Gar, they won't. I'll talk to them. Or just get it for them." As helpful as a stone in a flood. Shanise is wrapped up in her own problems. Hasn't taken the pill yet but keeps saying she's going to. Officer Frank was in the yard today and he asked me about it.

"I don't know," I told him, and at first he was angry. "Tell her she takes it or else." And he was moving closer like he would hit me, but then when I turned and started to walk away, he said, "Wait. Tell her I'm asking for her. And I don't want to hurt her."

Then E. and M. cornered me against the fence. Eloise with short dreadlocks around her ears and fingertips dry and white like she'd been digging in cornstarch. Molasses short and stubby and with hair cut right down to her scalp. "You know what happened the last time, Snow White. You don't come through again, things are going to be worse." E. nodding and M. doing the talking. They must be getting something from somewhere else too, because they seemed pretty strung out. M. was scratching at her wrists and E. looked sweaty. She smells like mold. They said I had until the end of the week. It's Tuesday. I don't even know what that means—the end of the week. Is it Saturday or Sunday or Friday? I don't think they know either, but I better get on it. I'm feeling nervous, signing off.

Shanise is sick again and went to the infirmary because she threw up. I'm pretending to be sick too so I don't have to go outside either. When anyone passes, I cover my head with the blanket and moan. E. and M. won't do anything to me when Shanise is there, but when she's not I have to be careful.

I brought it up with Shanise, about her cousin and Molasses demanding more. "Oh, don't worry," she said. "I'll talk to them. They'll leave you alone." She said it but her voice was far-off, like it was traveling through a tunnel to get out of her mouth. And I don't think I believe her. Maybe she just doesn't have any room left for anybody's problems but her own. But isn't a true friend someone who can put their own problems aside and think about yours?

Or, maybe I'm the one who's not being as good a friend as I should? Poor Shanise. She really doesn't want to take that pill. And the longer she waits, the more dangerous it could be.

Things are okay between her and OF because she told him she took it. I heard him come by and whisper to her. I pretended to be asleep but I wasn't.

"Baby? You get it? The thing I got for you? You take it?"

She hummed: Mmm hmm.

He said, "Yes? You did?" and she hummed yes again. "Love you baby," he whispered and then went off. I heard her turn over on her cot and sigh a big long exhale, but I didn't say anything. I know she didn't take it. It's still over on the urinal altar, wrapped up in a chocolate wrapper. Like a poo that Big Bird left there.

I hope Shanise doesn't take the pill. I hope she has the little sesame-seed-fingered thing.

I know it's stupid, and there isn't any future for it. But I can't help thinking that a baby is good no matter what. No matter how much I remind myself that it's not like Shanise and I would be able to bring it up here in our cell (and then it would grow up motherless, and probably end up right here in Stratton Island). But still, I push all that out of my head and think, God, wouldn't it be great to grow a baby inside your body?

Although if I'm completely honest I'd have to say that I don't know if I'd feel as excited about it if it was my baby. I want her to do it, but, could I?

Guards walking by again . . . Ugh.

Here's what happened today.

Shanise and I were avoiding E. and M. and hanging around near the guards. Shanise had promised that if she felt sick she'd try and come out to the yard anyway, to keep me safe. Which is nice. She's feeling a little nauseous, but she came out.

The wind was blowing the dust around the women's feet so if you could've blocked out the guard towers and fences and bleachers and the distant hills on the other side of the river, then you could trick your eyes into thinking that we were all standing on the surface of Mars.

Sometimes it feels like this place could get washed away by the Otis. You can almost imagine the river wearing away the rock that the prison stands on. Like decay under the gumline, the rocks would get so worn down that the whole cement-block structure would just topple off into the river, like an old person's teeth. Women in orange jumpsuits would swarm from the windows and fall like chili flakes into the water.

We made it through rec time without me getting beaten up, and we were back in our cell. I picked up my pen and was about to start writing. My favorite one, the one I'm using now that makes a mousy scratching noise that comforts me, even if I'm rambling on paper, which is what I'm doing because I don't want to think about what happened next. With Warden White.

There I was with my pen and my diary and feeling okay because nobody's beaten me up this week and the guard comes and says, "Prisoner Harlow, warden wants to see you," and he takes me up to the guy's office—the place you don't ever want to have to go when it's not for a parole hearing. Which I was supposed to be having soon.

But Ethan fucked it up for me.

I remember the first and last time I pissed myself—the day I got arrested—and I don't want to ever do it again, especially not here.

I remember that day so clearly. Two cops showed up to my Mom's place—which was where I went after the fight—after I knocked Ethan out with the armoire.

I had called 9-1-1 and left him unconscious, because I was scared. He was breathing, I could tell, and I had managed to shove the armoire off of him, but he wasn't waking up, and I didn't know what to do. I was nervous, so I went to Mom's place. She and Sam talked me down, and we kept calling the hospital to see how Ethan was, but they wouldn't give us any information. Then, after a couple of days of that, there was a pounding on the door. Mom was at work. When I opened it, they nearly rushed me, and I had been on my way to the bathroom and my bladder was full, and they scared me so much.

It was humiliating. They wouldn't leave the room when I got changed out of my pee-soaked jeans, just turned the other way to give me some privacy. I stuck the dirty pants in the hamper, but I have thought often about whether Mom noticed the smell. That was a bad day, but I think today was worse.

Warden White is this pale guy with a thick head of gray hair. And his skin is white but he has yellow teeth—I know because he smiled at me when I came in and smiled at the guard who left, but neither smile was a real smile. There wasn't anything good behind it; it was just his responsibility to perform a task and pulling the corners of his mouth over toward his ears was part of the task.

"Prisoner Harlow, do you know why you're here?" When he talks it sounds like he has too much spit; he makes a kind of smacking noise with his tongue and he also has some white guck in the corners of his mouth.

I shook my head. He pulled a piece of paper toward him from the corner of his desk and looked at it for a long moment, like he was memorizing what was written on it. "It seems you have broken the rules."

I thought he knew we'd gotten stoned out the window and I wondered why I'd been brought there alone, because Shanise was as guilty as me. But no.

"Do you deny having had relations with a man in the ladies' room on May the sixth?" I was trying to think what the date was and what day Ethan and I had done that, and simultaneously working out if relations really meant sex, and also thinking how funny it was that he called that place the "ladies' room." Warden slammed his palm on his ark of a desk. (If the prison does go tumbling over, I'm going to look for that desk and ride it to Canada.)

"Do you deny it?" he demanded and I shook my head. I could hear my brains rattling inside my skull. He wrote something on the paper in front of him, punched a stamp on it, and said, "Parole has been suspended until further notice." So that's it. Parole has been suspended until further notice. Parole has been suspended until further notice. All work and no play makes Garnet a dull girl. My head's about to explode. Over and out.

I have a plan.

Don't tell anybody. Ha ha. I better not write about it. I lock this diary up, but I wouldn't know if anybody was going through my stuff and reading it. Who knows what they do? They're allowed if they want to. I don't have any rights to privacy. Nobody does. They can look up your twat if they want to. They can do whatever they want.

That's why Shanise is so conflicted. Because on the one hand OF is a total weirdo, the way he strokes his goatee trying to look all deep and thoughtful. But on the other hand, he protects Shanise. Hell, he's even protected me because I'm her friend. And he's given her something that it's nearly impossible to get in here—a feeling of power and a tiny bit of dignity. Sex that is consensual. Not like what Ethan and I did that day. I didn't want it, but I went along.

I dated a guy in high school before I met Ethan. Derby.

I don't know why I'm thinking about him. Actually, I do know why I'm thinking of him: Because I'm thinking about respect, dignity, and consensual relationships.

I dated him for a couple of weeks. At first, he was funny and I thought he was nice. He was in my algebra class with Mr. Roper. He was the king of getting Mr. Roper to start talking about the olden days.

"What did you and your friends do during the summer when you were our age?" Derby would ask. Or, "What was it like when Wattsville had the glass factory?"

Mr. Roper would gladly stop talking about quadratic equations and reminisce. I actually really liked that guy. He was spacey and easily distracted but he also kind of got that most of us weren't going to remember much of what he was teaching and so he knew that for a lot of us, it was more useful to have a human interaction than it was to keep trying to pound equations into our brains. I guess what I'm saying is that he didn't have this overblown sense of the importance of his subject, like a lot of teachers.

Anyway, Derby sat a few seats in front of me in the next row. He would turn around and make this face where he pushed his eyebrows down into his eyes and puckered up his lips so he looked like a beanie baby. I didn't really know him before that class, but I was flattered that he liked me. Neither one of us was popular or particularly good looking but it was high school and so we were starting to be able to throw off the condemnation of the popular group and be our own people.

I remember Derby in those first days. I think it might've been the first time I really fell for someone. The bell had just rung and we were squeezing through the door into the hallway, leaving Mr. Roper to shuffle his papers and erase the chalkboard and do whatever it is that teachers do when they don't have any students in the classroom.

"You have plans Friday after school?" Derby said, and I shook my head no. He was taller than me and really skinny. He had hair that stuck straight up from his forehead and he had acne scars, but he was still kind of handsome. At least I thought so. At first. He wore a little gold cross around his neck, which was weird to me. I didn't have any religious friends back then.

On Friday, we hung out near school, walking around. We got coffees and sat on the monument down by Crescent Circle. I still remember I put the gum I was chewing on the plastic cover and the heat of the coffee made it all melty and sticky and I threw the whole cap away and drank the coffee without a lid.

Derby was actually a little bit shy. He gave me a kiss at the door to my apartment building, and it was a sweet, dry kiss, with no expectations.

But then, the next weekend, he asked me to go out again, and some of his friends came with us. This time, we took a bus over to the mall. We did our own things, his friends going off to look for black-light posters and lighters and T-shirts while Derby and I split moo-shu pork at the food court.

But then, everything fell apart on the bus ride home. The two of us were in the back and his friends were about halfway down toward the front, and they kept turning and looking at us and giggling.

And then, Derby became a different person. When I said before that we were growing out of the roles we'd been assigned by the popular kids in the middle school, I really believe that we were—but maybe Derby was still under the influence of all that. Or maybe he was growing into meanness. Or else, he had a split personality. He started kissing me, his tongue trying to reach the back of my throat, and I kept trying to push him away, because when his head moved to the side, I could see his friends getting off on watching. Their elbows were hanging over the back of the seat and they were pushing each other and laughing and they started to call out instructions for what they wanted him to do. "Grab a titty," one of them said. They were complete losers. Obviously. But he did it. His hand went inside my coat and started squeezing my boob like he thought he might get juice out of it.

I jumped off the bus at the next stop and walked the rest of the way. I was giving him and his friends the finger inside my coat pocket. I wish I'd been brave enough to do it to their faces, but I guess that might've landed me in even bigger trouble.

You know what? He never even apologized or anything. It was like it never happened. It was my first experience of the way a guy can make you feel helpless and insignificant. We finished out the year in Mr. Roper's algebra class, the two of us doing everything we could to ignore each other. I think the whole episode helped my grade, because I was working so hard to not pay attention to Derby that I started to actually learn something.

Anyway, that was junior year, and I met Ethan senior year, and the rest is history.

When I'm down, I pull Professor Bruss's visit out of my memory and hold onto it, turn it this way and that in the light. I don't know if he'll ever come back. It's not like we're going to become great friends or anything. I can't imagine confiding in him about Ethan, or about anything else that's happening in here with me, and he didn't ask what happened to my eye, even though there was still a bit of yellow around it. I feel so, I don't know the word, maybe valid is the right one. I feel like a worthwhile human—for my thoughts, not for being a girl or being cute or sweet or a good cook or anything else. What a feeling. I don't know if I've ever really had it before. I mean, Mom and Sam both make me feel good about myself, and they tell me that I should study and be a person who learns stuff and thinks about stuff and does well, but it's like they're talking from the other side of a fence. And they pushed me over that fence, when I started college, and there I was, and Professor Bruss lives in that world, and he thought it was okay that I was there.

So fuck you, Mrs. Thaxter, for always making me feel small and worthless. And Ethan, if you can't get yourself to shape up, then I'll have to say fuck you to you too. I'm happy for some reason, even though I think I shouldn't be, considering.

Inside my head, I nourish my plan like a small life. Like Shanise's baby.

Good night.

DRILL BITS AND A LOCKED BOX

Sam

Sam puts his duffel bag on the floor under the coat hooks. There are towels inside, around the drug dealer's metal box, but still it makes a dull thud when he puts it down.

"Going somewhere?" Larry asks. He's slipping coins into the vending machine.

"What? Oh, yes, I mean, well, not really. I mean, I just have to drop some clothes at the dry cleaners."

"First thing I check when I buy something is that it isn't dry-clean only." Larry takes his Styrofoam cup from the mouth of the coffee machine. Sam, Tommy, Jaime, and Jorge move into position on the line.

Since the Hondurans have been working here, they've been courteous enough to Sam, but they don't seem very comfortable with him. Not the way they are with Tommy, and it makes Sam a little jealous. He watches as they try to communicate with one another. Although they can't say much, they laugh and gesture. Is it because they are heterosexuals, Sam wonders? They have that in common. But Larry isn't gay, and he seems, like Sam, to be an outsider. Well, there is that habit of his. Having a secret seems to have made Larry more empathetic. Sam knows from experience that it could've gone the other way.

Maybe it's because they're young? But the uncle, Jorge, is about Sam's age. Sam thinks about the way you click with certain people but not others, and that train of thought brings him to Carol. He doesn't have a lot in common with her, so why do they seem to click so well? Sam wonders, as he has many times, whether he feels close to her because she doesn't ask much of him. She allows him to be, and she takes care of him. He is grateful for it but worries that he isn't challenging himself enough. Francine and Chloe push him to do more with his life, while Carol wants him to stay with her, watching too much TV, letting herself go. Maybe he is growing away from her, away from Wattsville.

Suddenly he remembers the box of drugs in his overnight bag, and it sends a jolt of nervous energy into his gut. He taps a stack of ads into place and puts it into the hopper.

When break time comes, Sam lingers by the coat hooks, not wanting to let the bag out of his sight. Tommy grabs his hoodie and heads toward the parking lot. "You coming?" he asks.

Jaime and his uncle are chattering in Spanish, and they nod and smile at them on the way past.

"Oh, I, uh, I've been having allergies," Sam says, "so I thought I'd, you know, take my break inside today."

Tommy stares at the vending machine for a long while before saying, "Hey, I saw your friend. That lady. Kind of heavy. The one who was at the Sheraton with you the night Britney Spears was supposed to be there. She was at the Dairy Queen."

"What a coincidence." Sam picks up his jacket. "Actually, let's go out. To hell with allergies. It's too nice to stay in here."

"If you see that lady, ask if she took something."

"What do you mean?"

Tommy shakes his head. "She'll know what I mean. Maybe. My friend who works there, at DQ, he says something's missing, and he thinks I took it. I didn't. I don't know who did. Just ask her, okay?" Sam is edging out the door.

"I'm not sure what you're talking about . . . but I will ask her." Sam's voice is thready.

"Tell her the thing that's missing. It's gonna be blamed on me. Okay? I was the last person there."

Sam can hardly speak, but he manages to say again, "I'll ask her. But she wouldn't ever take anything that wasn't hers. You can trust me on that."

***

After work, Sam ducks out without saying goodbye. He takes the path through the woods, his overnight bag slung over his shoulder. He needs to get the thing open, and he needs to get it back so Tommy won't be blamed.

Leaves have unfurled on fast-forward with the early spring heat wave. Ferns are no longer tight little curlicues but sway gently, their fans of flat leaf reaching toward the path where Sam walks. The zingy blue sky makes the normally mousy Otis appear crisp and clear. Sam breathes in the sultry air, letting it sweep through his nose and expand his chest. He passes a rusted-out car frame and wonders when it will finally be swallowed and digested by the earth around it. The one remaining tire has nearly turned to dust. There is an old storage container as well, its door wedged open slightly so Sam can see some of the things that are inside. It looks like homeless people or partying teenagers have used it as shelter. There are the remains of a campfire, rusted cans, a busted TV, and some other flimsy items that at one time might have held value for someone.

Over by the mill, there is no contractor truck and no noise but the scraping of a single shovel. He picks his way from the path to the parking lot and eases over to the old structure.

"Hi." He leans against the door and speaks softly, so as not to startle him.

Ronaldo turns. Sam admires his compact frame in a sweaty T-shirt, his small, close-set eyes and dark eyebrows, narrow hips hugged by dirty jeans. "Your friends are working out great at the *Chronicle*," Sam says finally.

"Why do I keep seeing you here?"

"Actually, I have a sort of favor to ask." His palm is sweaty where he holds the duffel bag. "The kids who used to work at the *Chronicle* had a bad attitude, not like your friends," Sam says, hoping to remind Ronaldo of the favor he did for Jorge and Jaime. "Where's your boss? Not here?"

"You have a favor to ask? Why should I do it?"

"I'm sorry. I really am. I just . . . I pass by on my way from work. The buses are so unreliable, it's usually faster to walk."

Ronaldo leans his shovel against the wall and crosses his arms.

"Thank you," Sam says. He pulls the strongbox from the overnight bag and puts it on the ground. "I need to open that."

"What's inside?"

"Oh just some personal things. Makeup."

"You bring that all the way here for me to help you and only it has makeup inside?"

"Silly, I know, but you see, it's my favorite foundation. And some other things, you know, that are worth more . . . My grandmother's jewelry. I lost the key."

Ronaldo goes to a toolbox and brings back a drill. "You don't mind the box gets damaged?" he says, pushing a battery pack into the bottom.

"Oh no, I don't mind that." Sam puts his hands over his ears. He squeezes his eyes shut as the drill tears, screeching, into the metal; when he opens them, Ronaldo is wedging open the box. He dashes over and tries to take it from him, but Ronaldo has already seen what's inside.

"Where you get this box?"

"Oh okay! I just found it! You're not going to tell anybody?"

"You didn't find it," Ronaldo puts his hand inside, pulls out a disorderly stack of bills.

"Oh, there's money," Sam says, hovering, reaching his hand tentatively toward it.

Ronaldo stands. "You want to get yourself killed? You steal this from somebody?" He paces across a small slice of ground, muttering: "No. Somebody send you to test me. Somebody send you. It's a test. But why?"

"No, no, no! I came to you because I thought we were friends. Of a sort. I mean, we've been through so much together already, sort of? I'd like to know you better. Wouldn't you like to know me?"

Ronaldo stops pacing. "Ignacio sends you to me as a test. To test loyalty. Why does he do this? Did he tell you? How do you know him?"

"I don't know what you're talking about. I don't know any Ignacio." Sam remembers the car he'd seen Ronaldo get into. The car just like Francine's. "Is he the guy in the Bugatti?"

"You don't know him, how do you know he drives this car?"

"I . . . pass by here. I told you. I saw you get in a car and out again. Remember? You were crying?"

"I think you should just take . . . your grandmother's makeup . . . and go." Ronaldo shoves the box into Sam's hands.

Sam takes some bills and pushes them toward him.

"I don't want money," Ronaldo says. "Not this money."

"I'm so grateful to you for this." Sam picks up the duffel bag and slides the box into it. "Look," he says, noticing a pair of boots on the ground, "someone forgot their shoes."

"Those are mine. I work another job in the mornings. I try to get out of this life I am in. I save money. I go to school. I'm going to be a lawyer. This is why you have to leave me alone. Why you have to go now, quickly."

"A lawyer? How noble."

"Where did you get the box?"

"It's kind of a long story. Who is Ignacio?"

Ronaldo shakes his head. "Ignacio is my boss. Not anymore. He was my boss. I did some very bad things, but not anymore."

"Your boss is Irish."

"That's my other boss. I have a lot of bosses. I work at Wattsville Community College also, in the kitchen."

"You do? You must know Carol!"

"The cashier, yes."

Sam nearly jumps up and down. "That's my friend! Carol."

Ronaldo's smile is quizzical and relieved. "Ignacio didn't send you," he says with finality.

"Of course not." It occurs to Sam to say that fate has brought them together, but he doesn't. He gazes at Ronaldo, unable to recall the details of April in his firefighter calendar—Ronaldo has taken them over. The face in front of him has softened, and a light has been turned on underneath the skin. Ronaldo glows with something childlike and luminous. The trees, the sky, the breeze, they soften and wobble around the two men as recognition pulls them toward each other.

Sam takes a step. Ronaldo looks away but stays still. Sam reaches his hand forward, as though gauging the friendliness of an unknown animal. Ronaldo takes his hand and holds it. He pulls gently and Sam takes a quiet step. The bag drops to the ground. They stay that way, connected through their hands and arms, feeling the earth's molten center working its heat up into them.

"Have you ever done this?" Sam is close enough now that he can feel Ronaldo's breath on his cheek. Ronaldo shakes his head.

They walk together to the back of the structure. "McMaster will come back, but from here we see him first." When they stop, Ronaldo kisses Sam and then pulls back, indicating that he isn't sure what to do. He's never had the courage.

Sam takes the lead, gently.

***

Afterward, Ronaldo tells Sam some of his history and of his predicament. The day Ignacio pulled up in the Bugatti, he brought news. He informed Ronaldo that his sister, who is nineteen, and whom Ronaldo hasn't seen in ten years, is getting married to someone high up in the cartel, and also that his mother had died. Ignacio thought he'd been delivering good news, at least about his sister: Ronaldo no longer had to send money to her. She'd be taken care of. "Ignacio has no heart or soul," Ronaldo concludes.

"I'm so sorry about your mother," Sam says.

"Thank you."

"But why did you leave? Why did you come here? To the United States."

"Many reasons," Ronaldo says. "I tell you one. Emilio. This man was my partner in the organization. We did raids of people the bosses didn't like. Terrible things. I will face God one day, this I know. Emilio, I thought . . . I thought we. Well, like you and me, now. But I was wrong. He wanted to kill me then. So I left. Ignacio maybe knows about that. I'm not sure. He doesn't care because I did a job here that he needs. No more. I quit. He doesn't like it. But I quit."

"How scary," Sam says.

"This box. This will get you into a lot of trouble. Where did you get it?"

"It's a long story." They hear McMaster's truck pulling into the parking lot. "I'll tell you. Later!" Sam shimmies as he pulls his leggings up over his thighs. He crosses the space between them, takes Ronaldo's face between his hands, and kisses him gently. He lifts his shirt and kisses the tattoo above his nipple.

"I won't tell Carol," Sam promises.

"Not anybody," Ronaldo says. "Not anybody," he repeats, looking worried.

Ronaldo takes up his shovel and Sam dashes into the woods, his sneakers in one hand and the duffel bag with the box in the other, until he is far enough away that he can sit down and wiggle his feet into his shoes.

FROM PUEBLO TO WATTSVILLE

Tommy

Tommy Stall's trip to Wattsville was the bomb. He'd been dreading it because it's almost three days from Pueblo to Wattsville, but he met a guy named Henry, a postman who'd recently quit his job and was moving to Brattleboro, just because he could. The bus was mostly empty, except for the stretch between St. Louis and Indianapolis, and Henry and Tommy stretched out across the seats and pooled their liquor and had a party and talked about life.

When Tommy told his friend Hanky about it, he described Henry as a Mr. Miyagi kind of character who'd helped him across the country, from one life to another, inside that Greyhound bus. Of course, he and Hanky had been drunk at the time. They were at the Blue Heron, their local. Marguerite, bartendress extraordinaire, reminding them to take it easy on the booze, and her husband Dom, who'd been sitting at the end of the bar nursing coffees and doing crossword puzzles since he gave up drinking a decade earlier, telling her to let them be, and weren't they grownups now and shouldn't they be taking care of themselves. "Shit, don't they both have mothers already?"

"I might've kept going," Tommy was saying, "with that dude Henry, all the way to Brattleboro. If I wasn't meeting my dad. Henry saw life as a big adventure, the future a frontier."

"Right," Hanky said. "Sounds like a loony tune and you'd have woken up one morning in Brattleboro thinking, *what the fuck am I doing here?* And anyway, you wouldn't have ever known the pleasures of the Blue Heron. Or lived with me."

Hanky and Tommy only had such conversations when their other roommate Derby, a wiry kid who carried himself around like he was Pablo Escobar, wasn't with them. Derby put everybody on edge, but nobody would admit it. Even

Marguerite and Dom seemed to go tight-lipped when Derby came in, and they, presumably, didn't even know that Derby was a dealer.

Lately, Derby had a new sidekick: a rich kid from White Hills named Ethan. Ethan paid for Derby's drinks, bought drugs from him, and in return his cred got bolstered: hanging with someone like Derby was not for the faint of heart. Hanky and Tommy still hung out with them but were about ready to admit to each other that they were better than that.

"That dude Henry had a point," Tommy said, aiming the lip of his Genesee at Hanky.

"Maybe. But then again, who gives a shit where you are? Like we're here in this dumpy bar and what difference would it make if we were in a dumpy bar in Brattleboro? Sorry, Marguerite!"

"Exactly! The dumpy bar in Brattleboro wouldn't have Marguerite! That's my point! It does matter where you are! And the world's fuckin huge, dude."

Marguerite chuckled and brought them two glasses of water.

***

Now Tommy is remembering Henry and seeing a weird kind of parallel between that Greyhound bus and where he is now. Metal, square, big enough for a dozen or two human beings. This box is not moving though, except a bit of a sway when there's a strong wind. No windows, no movement, but still a metal box that will shepherd him from the past into whatever the future will hold. If only Henry were here. Or Hanky. Anyone. But instead, he's lying on his side, his hands bound behind his back. He had to piss so bad and hours have gone by since he was nabbed, so he's pissed himself and now his pants are stiffening. His head is throbbing, his mouth feels like a bag of dust. He knows why he's here, but still it doesn't make sense. Being accused of something you didn't do is bad enough, but it's much worse to be accused and then actually punished for it: kidnapped and locked in a metal box in the woods. (He was blindfolded when they brought him here, but he knows it's the woods because of the sound of the wind in the trees, the chirping of birds, their little scratchy feet hopping about on the roof—or maybe those are squirrels. When the wind is calm, he thinks he can hear the river, so he assumes it is the Otis.)

A chick, Tommy thinks. That would be cool. To be in here with a woman. Not his mom. Maybe Simone. No, not Simone. He doesn't know her well enough. Camille.

***

One morning when he was nine, Tommy's mother woke him up early and brought him to the bus station. His dad was a DJ at the time and was working the overnight hours, so he wasn't home yet. It was the eighties, but Tommy's parents, Larry and Pearl, ever since he could remember, had been stuck in the disco generation. They'd dance in the living room or leave him with a babysitter and go to parties; they'd sleep late on weekend mornings when they were both off of work and emerge from their waterbed after noon to find Tommy watching early-afternoon programs that were too old for him: *Charlie's Angels* or *21 Jump Street*.

Pearl called her husband from a pay phone at a bus station somewhere in the middle of the country. First, she was whisper-yelling, blaming him for whatever had happened between them and then becoming more defensive. She had almost hung up the phone when she remembered Tommy. She pulled him over and handed him the phone. "Mom says we're taking a vacation," he'd said to his father. Larry said he had a cold and Tommy suspected he was crying, but he had no choice but to ignore it and go along with his mom.

A man met them at the bus station in Pueblo and brought them to the house where they lived from then on.

There was a small bedroom made up with a polyester comforter with a design that featured a huge portrait of a man Tommy would learn quickly was Jesus Christ. Tommy dropped his bag on the shag-carpeted floor and asked his mom when they would be going home.

"Soon," Pearl told him. "We're just going to stay a while and see what we think."

Tommy called his dad every few days but, as his mom got more and more annoyed by him asking when they would be going home, he started calling less and less. It's not that he thought about it. He just kind of gave up.

Quinn was a devoted member of Keepers of the Sacred Faith, and Pearl, with Quinn's help, had become convinced of the role of Jesus in her life. There were KOSFaith meetups in different members' houses on Wednesdays and Fridays, and services on Sundays.

Tommy hated it, especially the weirdos that would speak in tongues and fall onto the floor. Luckily his mom never pulled that shit, but Quinn did—regularly. Tommy, seeing through it all, would've been exceedingly lonely but for his best friend Camille. They were both homeschooled and weren't allowed to spend time with anyone who wasn't a member of KOSFaith.

Camille was a master of deception. Tommy knew she'd sneak off and go on dates with different guys—guys outside of KOSFaith—but her parents were delusional and had no idea.

***

One Wednesday night meeting, Camille gave Tommy the secret eye roll that said meet me in the bathroom. Tommy stood up and bowed apologetically to Camille's dad, who was leading that evening's bible discussion, and went up the stairs. Camille's mom crocheted coverings for the extra toilet paper rolls and tissue boxes and had gifted them to every KOSFaith member, so it seemed like every bathroom Tommy and Camille met in was the same bathroom but in different colors. The ones in Camille's bathroom were pink.

"Is the cough safe?" Camille said, sticking her head in the door.

"If the cloth sayeth," Tommy said, giggling. They were always coming up with new names for KOSFaith.

"Thomas," Camille said, closing the door behind her. She was the only one who called him Thomas. Everyone else called him Tommy. He laid the *Old Farmer's Almanac* on the back of the toilet.

"Camille was naughty last night." She often talked about herself in the third person, which Tommy thought was weird but very cute. "She tells the 'rents she's going to save souls downtown, but what does Camille do instead?" She leaned in. "Smoke marijuana!" She did two or three little jumps like a Who in Who-ville on Christmas morning.

"What was it like?" Tommy asked, nervous but excited. He was a couple of years younger than Camille.

"Thomas, it was crazy. I mean, it made things funnier. Wild, relaxing, mind-opening. It's hard to explain, but you can think about things and things make sense for a while."

Tommy's stomach was knotted and he felt like he had to make a bowel movement, but he didn't want to ask Camille to leave.

"It was so easy to fool Dennis and Jeanine." Those were her parents. "I was high as a kite and I told them I was thinking about God and they believed me." Then she got kind of serious. "Actually, I worry about the day they find out the truth. They're so convinced I'm going to be the next Joyce Meyer or something."

"Don't worry," Tommy said. "They might not ever find out."

"Sometimes I envy you," she said, and Tommy thought, *envy me? Really?*

As if he'd said it out loud, she went on, "I mean, sure, your 'rents won't let you do anything, because they know you reject the teachings. I mean, it means you don't have the freedom I get, but at least they're not going to find out anything new."

"Quinn isn't my parent. But yeah," Tommy said thoughtfully. "I guess the thing that would surprise them is if I finally said, 'Yeah, Jesus is my savior. Bring it on.'"

"Poor Quinn and Pearl," Camille said. "But in the long run, it's probably better to be honest."

"You could be," Tommy said.

Camile appeared to think that over for a moment but then said, "Naw. It's too late. But hey, let's get stoned! Before Friday's meeting. I can get us some!"

Now Tommy really got nervous. He looked at the pink tissue cover and imagined that it would grow horns and dance across the back of the toilet if he were stoned. He said he wouldn't do it before meeting, but he agreed to meet her that Saturday. Quinn was going to be out of town on business, "selling soap," Tommy said. "Pearl won't mind. She always falls asleep in the afternoons." Tommy relished calling his mother Pearl. It made him feel cool, and older.

The following Saturday, Tommy told his mother he was going to the skate park but instead headed over to the plaza in front of the Tinseltown Theater, which was a hangout for kids—many of whom seemed to be in some sort of trouble. He wasn't sure, but he suspected some of them were runaways. Camille was sitting on the sidewalk with her legs draped over the lap of a blonde guy. She was dressed in an Indian-print skirt with sandals and socks and a black T-shirt. The outfit would've been acceptable to her parents, except that her socks were dirty and she had several leather bracelets with punk-style spikes. And she was fiddling around with the blonde guy's earlobe, which Tommy had to stop himself from staring at. But the touch between them was like a neon sign that burned his vision.

He sat down on his skateboard and pretended to fit in. After they hung out for a while, Kurt sliding out from under Camille's legs every now and then to sell someone something from his dirty orange fanny pack, Camille stood up and grabbed Tommy's hand. She got onto his skateboard and said, "Give me a ride!"

"Where are we going?" He said, pushing her, touching her waist, which he'd never done before. Touching her like that gave him a crazy feeling. Like he didn't want to touch her there any more than he'd ever want to touch his mom there, but doing it shifted something in him, opened something and closed something at the same time. By the time they arrived at the playground, he already felt off-kilter. They smoked a joint together on a small rusted-out merry-go-round. First sitting up, and then lying down, pushing themselves in circles with their feet.

Then Camille said she had to get back to Kurt. Tommy watched her skirt sashay back and forth as she walked away; he lit up the second joint she'd left him and stared at the sky.

His brain was empty as he walked home, dangling his skateboard in front of him and kicking it rhythmically. He'd thought about plenty of stuff on that merry-go-round, but now none of it really mattered. He just wanted to eat a peanut butter sandwich and lie down.

"How was the skate park?" Pearl said. Her eyes were watering because she'd been cutting onions, and Tommy thought she looked incredibly sad. He almost wanted to hug her, but instead he took his sandwich and went upstairs to lie down on Jesus Christ's face.

***

Tommy didn't look back after that first time getting stoned. It was an escape that made his life bearable and also more interesting, even if it meant he was beginning to deceive his mom and Quinn almost as much as Camille did.

The two of them did get stoned a few times out the bathroom window of whoever's house they were in, but neither of them liked it very much and they resolved to meet on as many Saturdays as they could, telling the 'rents that they were volunteering at a soup kitchen or passing out flyers. They'd hang with Kurt and some others down at the Tinseltown, skate or walk the few blocks to the playground, get stoned and come back.

Quinn and Pearl were delighted that he was hanging out with Camille, who everyone believed was especially holy, as she made a habit of falling around and blubbering when the spirit entered her.

But then came the end of that era.

Camille wasn't involved, luckily. Tommy was skating around the plaza by the Tinseltown when Kurt asked him to do a favor.

"I gotta piss like a racehorse, dude, but there's a guy who's supposed to show up any minute. Here," he said. "Take this and when the guy, his name is Steve, shows up, just hand it over. It's already paid for. Thanks, dude."

Tommy shoved the baggie into his pocket and stood in Kurt's spot, in the boarded-up doorway of a derelict Chinese takeout place. Just as Kurt reached the end of the block, two cops came out of nowhere, grabbed him, and then ran toward Tommy. He tried to run but his hand was stuck into the front pocket of his jeans because he'd wanted to ditch what was in there. He didn't make it far, and the two cops brought both him and Kurt downtown.

Quinn's brother was a cop and, even though they didn't get along because his brother wasn't a member of KOSFaith, the brother did Quinn a favor and got Tommy off. But that was it. Quinn was beside himself and booked him a bus ticket.

"Anywhere he wants to go," Quinn said. "Anywhere. But he's out of this house."

Pearl was sniffling, her face and her eyes red. "Tommy," she kept saying. "How could you? I thought you were with Camille?" Tommy kept his mouth shut about Camille, and they all agreed he'd go back to Wattsville. His dad could get him a job inserting at the *Wattsville Chronicle*.

So that was how it was decided.

***

Now Tommy is locked away in a storage container and nobody, not Pearl, not Larry, not anyone, knows where he is. He tries to melt into the birdsong outside. He imagines the sky, which he thinks is still blue because there are gashes of bright light worming in through the corners of this rusted-out box. But night should be coming soon. He wonders how cold it will be and whether he'll be able to sleep with his hands tied up. Whatever those guys used to bind his wrists, it's starting to feel like knives and there are pains shooting up and down his arms.

He rolls onto his other side, worms his way toward an old pile of newspapers and rests his head on them, supporting his neck and bringing a measure of comfort. He is the handsome guy in the Posturepedic ad. He'd been in charge of Posturepedic sometimes on the line at work. That guy, asleep. The woman cuddled into his arm. Their heads cradled by fluffy white pillows, a comforter tossed messily across their partially clad bodies. The circulars, flying into the newspapers, made the mattress a magic carpet, a blur of cleanliness and bliss.

Ever since he met Simone, just a couple of weeks ago, he can't stop imagining her head on his arm like that. At first, she'd reminded him of Camille—they had similar wavy long hair and heart-shaped faces with small chins. But Simone is softer, and a little bit less troubled.

He remembers the first, no the second time he saw her. The first time had been at the Wagonwheel, where she is a waitress. They'd all been ogling her—Tommy, Hanky, Derby and Ethan. But they'd left suddenly, following Ethan to his red Volkswagen—one of the new ones that are kind of space-age the way they're shaped like a shiny pod. So that was the first time, and the second time was the next morning, when she'd appeared in their apartment.

Tommy and Hanky, hungover, watching re-runs and she'd emerged from Derby's bedroom, her hair messy and her lips swollen. Gorgeous and pink like an over-loved stuffed bunny. She looked mystified, guilty, like she needed someone to take care of her. Tommy knew she didn't really care about Derby and wasn't sure why she'd gone home with him, though he suspected it was because Derby had whatever drugs you wanted.

"Do you know where the bus stop is?" Simone said. She was clutching a big suede purse with a macrame cord dangling from the zipper.

"Sure," Tommy said. He looked at Hanky, who had fallen asleep. Tommy got up, slid the remote from Hanky's hand, and silenced the Gilligan's Island theme song. "I can show you."

Simone had started rifling around the depths of her suede purse but wasn't having any luck. "Cigarette?" she said. Tommy grabbed one from the coffee table and lit it for her by the door.

At the bus stop, Simone smashed the butt into the sidewalk with her toe and reached around inside her bag. Tommy watched her rummage and wished he were a cigarette pack in the bottom of that big sack. "You don't have any?" she asked.

"Sorry," he said, indicating that he'd left his pack in the apartment.

"It's just, it makes the bus come faster." She looked away, toward where the bus would be coming from. Her hair was shiny, and Tommy imagined that if he could touch it, it would feel like feathers.

"How does that work?" he said.

"Murphy's law," she said. If you light a cigarette, that's when the bus will come."

"Murphy, yeah? Never heard of him."

Simone laughed and explained that if things can go wrong, they will.

"Right," Tommy said. "That's what happened to me in Pueblo. Now I know who's to blame. It wasn't my fault, it was Murphy."

"What are you even talking about," Simone said, laughing.

"Never mind, it's a long story. But I see what you're saying. Murphy has a lot to answer for, that's the truth."

When the bus finally came and she climbed on board, he sat for a long time, watching it disappear down Market Street.

***

Tommy manages to sleep for an hour, maybe two. He is woken by a bright light, which it takes him a while to realize is daylight. The door has been opened and there's someone standing over him. He blinks and tries to rub his eyes with his shoulder, which turns out to be physically impossible, and finally he can see that the person standing over him is Derby. There are voices chattering in Spanish outside, but they're faint and calm, like maybe they're discussing the weather or football. Derby's got a knife and he's coming toward Tommy and he looks like the grim reaper. Tommy shakes and chatters and squirms around on the floor and Derby grabs him by the shoulder and turns him over and cuts the cord that had been binding his wrists.

"You smell like shit," Derby observes. Tommy considers what to do now that his arms are free, but he can't seem to get them to move. The arm that's on top of him feels dead like it's one of those pebble-filled stuffed snakes you can win at the carnival. Tommy remembers going to a carnival with his parents when they were together and wanting one of those stuffed snakes—its head diamond shaped with a red felt tongue sticking out of its black mouth. A typical example of how famine makes the most paltry dish appetizing. Those snakes, he realized later, were garbage.

He can't think of anything to say, and doesn't think his voice will work anyway because his mouth is so dry. Derby starts talking, but Tommy starts to cry, to blubber, tears running down his face. His arms scream with pain and stay floppy but stiff, attached at the shoulder but otherwise not a part of his body.

Derby gets fed up, leaves, and the door gets locked again.

Tommy sleeps. When he wakes, he sees that there is a pair of sweatpants and a plastic bucket. Also, a camp lantern, so he can see better. There is a gallon of water and a loaf of Country Pride bread. Tommy gets the bottle open and drinks a third of it. Then he works the bread bag out of the little plastic tag that cinches it, and eats. He takes off his jeans and puts on the sweatpants. He pees in the bucket, which he figures is what it's there for.

"Hey Derby!" he yells. There's no sound, just the faintest swishing that could be the river but might also just be wind. Something motorized—a motorcycle or dirt bike—goes by. He yells but it doesn't stop. Then it's quiet again.

CITY, CAPITAL C, AND JOHNNY WITH A P

Sam

"It should be small," Sam calls from the bathroom. He is brushing his hair in the mirror. "We want him to eat it all at once."

"We're sure it won't kill him, right? Much as I'd like to see him dead, I'd hate to get locked up for murder."

Sam puts the hairbrush down and comes out of the bathroom. He is wearing pink satin pajamas with spaghetti straps. Looking at the plastic baggie full of white powder on the table, he says, "No, that won't kill him, just make him wired and then sick."

"You're positive it's cocaine ? I've only done it the once; you're sure it's not something else? Crack?"

Sam sits on the edge of the sofa, his hands on his knees. "Even if it is crack, what's the difference? It'll just make him sick enough to keep him out of the picture. Maybe get him addicted. Maybe get his parents involved."

Carol shifts the pillow under her knees and sips from a can of Diet Coke. "Or at least they'll take his car away and he won't be able to get out to Stratton Island."

"I think it's brilliant, darling. We may just be geniuses." He stretches his arms over his head. "So, I was thinking, about Tommy's father," he says, sing-songy. "The handsome Larry. You know I think he likes you. He was asking about you."

"At a time like this, you wanna try and fix me up? Why do you always want me to go through the same roller coaster you keep getting yourself on?"

"Who says I'm on a roller coaster?"

"You think I don't know you? You're in that funny mood you get in when you've slept with someone."

"What makes you think that?" Sam feels stupidly transparent. "Okay, so there is a certain someone. Not my usual type. In fact, he's closeted still."

"Oh, oh, oh, well that's no good. Who is he?"

"You're just avoiding the topic of Larry, who, I might add, is a really great guy. We've become friends, you know, and you two would be perfect for each other."

"Well okay, it so happens that there's someone else." Carol's mouth is a flat line, and Sam can tell she's nervous and excited.

Sam's eyes widen. He's tried suggesting possible love interests for Carol, and she nearly always rebuffs them, but she has hardly ever admitted to liking anyone on her own.

"Honey, do tell!"

"A guy at work. South American, actually. I never dated a Latino guy before."

"A what?" he sits down slowly. "What's . . . what's his name?"

"Why does that matter?"

"It doesn't, I guess. Well, good for you . . . You, ah, you have a date with him or something? Does he know you like him?"

"I think so. He's friendly to me. We haven't really, you know."

It's been so long since she's expressed a romantic interest in anyone that he wants to feel happy for her even though he suspects that the person she's talking about is Ronaldo.

"Well, if it doesn't work out, I think you should keep Larry in mind as a backup."

"Backup, ha! Imagine that. When it rains it pours, right?" Carol half-laughs. "This guy, he's just so nice. You know I always choose assholes. He sends money home to his mother in South America. Still takes care of some brothers and sisters. Anyway, you're probably right that he's not interested. He's just a nice guy."

"I didn't say that, honey. He might like you. But Larry is nice, too."

"I'm sure he is." Carol lowers her legs over the side of the couch and stands up stiffly, her hands on her lower back. "Now let's get this thing baked."

***

"It really is big," Sam says. "I do think we should've made it smaller."

The cake is in a box from a popular bakery with a small sticker that says, "Thanks for all your help. From Garnet." They are parked outside of the house where Ethan has moved back in with his parents: a gigantic peach-colored mansion in White Hills. The houses in this area generally aren't visible because they're hidden behind gates and mini-forests, and Carol and Sam can only make out a sliver of the house from where they are parked near the end of the driveway.

"I had to make it fit the box, to make it look professional, or he'd be suspicious."

"Well, I guess it has to look as good as I'm sure it tastes, the cocaine notwithstanding." Sam laughs anxiously.

"You know I think the drugs worked a little bit like baking powder. The thing rose like twice the size of a normal cake."

"What if he feeds it to his parents? To that cow-faced mother of his?" They both start to laugh, a little hysterically.

"Ooh, stop. My back." Carol clutches the steering wheel and pulls herself up straighter. "Hey," she says, "how come every normal person has a regular number, but all these rich folks feel the need to write it out in penmanship? And they name their houses, too. Can you imagine naming a house?"

"I'm going to put a plaque on our building. 'Casa de sexy women,'" Sam says, doing a little dance with his shoulders.

They look up at where *seventy-seven* and *The Pines* are written in curlicue script over the entrance to the driveway. "Well. Looks like it's show time," Sam says.

The super-polished quartz-stone driveway makes a hollow clacking under their feet as they creep toward the front door. There are no cars, except for a trailer belonging to a landscaping company, and they can see as they approach that there are several Latino men trimming hedges and blowing cut grass into a pile.

"Oh Jesus," Carol grabs Sam's arm, nearly tipping the cake box onto the ground. "Imagine if Ron was here. He works another job. I don't know what it is."

Hearing Ronaldo's name spoken out loud, confirming his fears, releases a jolt of electricity into Sam's gut, but luckily, under their tense circumstances, Carol doesn't notice. They move from tree to tree, any noise they are making camouflaged by the racket of the landscapers' motorized equipment. Finally, Sam places the box on the mat and shuffles back behind the bush where Carol is waiting. "Well. That's that. Mission accomplished."

Carol grips his arm. "You're sure it couldn't kill him, right?" she says again.

Sam puts his arm around her shoulder. "The world would probably be better off if we did just kill him, but don't worry. I'm sure he'll be fine." They move across the manicured lawn. Carol catches up to Sam next to a dogwood in full bloom—a riot of pink blossoms.

"God, look at that," Sam says, gazing up through the flowers.

"Come on, Sam, we gotta get out of—" She is interrupted by a red Volkswagen beetle crunching over the driveway.

"Get down," Sam grabs Carol's arm, and they sink behind a decorative boulder next to a plot of pansies. Ethan gets out of the car and, without acknowledging the landscapers or noticing the intruders in the front yard, opens the side door to the house, letting a spotted cocker spaniel out. The dog bounds gleefully back and forth across the yard a few times before heading straight for the cake at front door.

Sam's and Carol's heads peek over the top of the boulder like two clumps of moss as they watch the dog take a corner of the box in her teeth and fling it around until the cake has tumbled out in a heap, and then gobble it up with voracious abandon. The side door opens again, and they hear Ethan call the dog, whose name is Sunshine; when the dog doesn't come, he lets the door click gently closed.

Sunshine starts to waggle her head back and forth with a ferociousness that makes Carol and Sam hold each other in fear. She growls and paws at the ground, and then with a quiet squeal that sounds like the air being let out of a wet tire, she collapses.

Carol and Sam run stealthily—Carol with one hand on her lower back and hobbling—to where the dog is lying, panting, her tongue folded into a heap on the ground next to her mouth. Her eye is rolling back into her head and white foam spills over her wet, pink lip. The formerly square cake box is like a mobile home after a hurricane—frosting smears and chocolate crumbs, the rubble of splintered furniture.

They hover over the dog as it takes a final, shuddering breath and then lays quiet. Carol swoons and leans against the front of the house, inadvertently pressing the doorbell with her shoulder. Inside they can hear it gong like a cathedral.

"Run!" Sam says. He picks up the soggy box and they dash back behind the boulder, crouching just as the front door opens. Ethan's face is blurry behind the screen. He mutters something and then goes back inside without seeing Sunshine, dead on the welcome mat.

***

It's ten o'clock and Sam is in his pajamas, praying like his mother taught him to. On his bedside table is a small altar with an assortment of items representing his various intentions, hopes, and wishes. Next to a wax statue of a fatly sitting Buddha and a pair of his mother's costume earrings, he places a picture that he drew of Sunshine—a Hershey's-Kiss-shaped body, banana tail, and rectangle ears. "I didn't mean it," he whispers. "It wasn't your fault you belonged to those . . . people." He closes his eyes and pictures the sweet, frolicsome cocker spaniel covered in white light and feeling nothing but pure bliss as she (or he?) floats to heaven or rejoins the cosmos, or whatever may happen.

His gaze moves to a faded and cracked photo of his grandmother. She was a spiritual person, but she would never leave the house without lipstick. He likes to think he inherited his sense of style and grace from her, though sometimes, living in Wattsville, it all seems so pointless. He might as well take up dairy farming or something. His thoughts turn to his friends' suggestion that he move to the city— where his talents would be appreciated.

Just as he has the thought, Chloe calls, affirming his sense of communion with the universe.

"Darling, I've gotten you an audition. At the Hungry I. It would be a regular gig and a good one. Johnny P., we've told you before, books them and he has a last-minute opening. He's agreed to meet you. Tomorrow." Sam's hand nearly loses the power to hold the phone, and he tucks it between his ear and his shoulder.

"I don't know what to say."

"Sam, I believe in you, and you're my friend. Why wouldn't I? But Johnny P. has a very full schedule. I've told him you can be at the venue at four o'clock tomorrow afternoon. I hope it suits. Well, it has to suit, doesn't it? You can stay here, after."

The gears in Sam's brain begin to tick and whirl. "I have to work until 2:00. I think the bus leaves at—"

"That's too late. You'll have to skip work, or else leave early."

"I don't know. I have to ask my boss. He might let me go early. But I can't stay long. I have to work on Saturday too."

"Darling! Johnny P. is an important man! You just have to be here. I don't care how. I told him you would."

"Well, couldn't you check with me first?" Sam asks, feeling cornered.

"I've done something nice for you. I don't see why you're talking to me like that."

"I'm sorry," Sam concedes. "You're right. I know my job is minimum wage crap. It's this once. Okay, okay. I'll see you tomorrow."

After he hangs up, he picks up the picture of his grandmother and presses it to his heart. Then he holds it at arm's length where he can see it clearly.

"Nana, did you do this for me?" He hugs it to his chest once more before putting it back on the table.

He remembers what he'd promised to do for Garnet. He won't let her down, he tells himself. He'll bring the drugs to her in a couple of days. And he'll return the box of drugs and money, so Tommy won't get into any trouble. Soon. Life might not give him this chance again.

***

It's getting close to midmorning. Sam is nervous. He picks up a can of Coke and, like a fish that slides from the grip of an inexperienced fisherman, it flops onto the floor and bleeds sticky liquid into a puddle.

"Oh shit." He kneels to retrieve it.

"It's the way the hands get," Larry says, approaching with a bouquet of paper towels. Inserting makes the men's hands turn black and dry out, becoming as smooth and slippery as patent leather. Sam mops up the mess. They are in the break room, fluorescent lit with scuffed linoleum tiles. Styrofoam coffee cups and soda cans and wrappers and foil bags overflow from the opening of a gum-pocked aluminum trash barrel. Sam pushes the paper towels into it. Larry looks at his watch, again. Tommy hasn't shown up yet.

"Is Tommy sick?"

"He never called. Um. We. He. Last night—" Larry is interrupted by Jorge and Jaime coming indoors. "He'll probably be in soon."

Sam had planned on asking Larry if he could leave early but with Tommy out he can't bring himself to do it. If two people are missing on the line, things slow down to the point where the remaining inserters won't finish until almost three. It's quarter-to-ten, and the next bus is at ten-thirty. If he doesn't catch that, there won't be another until one. He'd have to leave early to catch it, and even then, he might miss the audition.

As the machine rumbles to life, Sam understands that this moment is a crossroads that will define what will happen with the rest of his life. He can forget his career; forget the opportunity life is giving him; forget finally being recognized for his talent and his style; forget downright blossoming for the first time in his life—something his mother and his grandmother would have applauded. Or he can choose to be loyal to this menial job.

He begins to feel resentful toward Larry, as though it were his fault that Sam is stuck in this dead-end corner of nowhere. But, of course, it isn't Larry's fault. Larry, Sam becomes certain, will understand. He will visit him in the city, meet new people. In fact, Sam isn't just doing this for himself. He's doing it for Larry, too! Larry enjoyed spending time with Chloe and Francine. Sam will get him into fantastic nightclubs and introduce him to wonderful people. He'll finally be able to let his hair down, in a place with no judgment. Larry will completely understand. He'll even thank him! Sam clutches his stomach and moans.

"Oh, I feel sick. Wait. Don't."

Larry's hand hovers at the lever. "What is it? Are you okay?"

"I ate fajitas last night. I think I'm going to . . ." He runs to the bathroom and slams the door. His fake retches sound like seagulls fighting over a sandwich. He finishes by coughing and flushing the toilet, then splashes water on his face. In the mirror, he looks deep into his own eyes and mouths, "Say yes! To life!"

"Gosh, I hope you feel better," Larry says as Sam picks up his bag, pouts apologetically, and leaves.

***

On the Greyhound, Sam feels adventurous and, as the bus moves farther from Wattsville, he feels less guilty and becomes more excited. He can't concentrate on the book he brought with him.

"I should have brought something with a plot," he says to the woman next to him. He stuffs *You Can Heal Yourself* into his bag. The woman says, "Hmmm" with taut lips and leans into the narrow corridor to look out through the windshield. Sam rolls his eyes and tries to sleep.

At the Port Authority, he wakes with an erection after dreaming of Ronaldo.

He limps through the bus station, trying not to breathe. He had bound his penis and it is painful; he has to either get to a bathroom and rip the tape off or stay still until he goes soft again. He sits on a stool at a red Formica counter and orders watery coffee in a Styrofoam cup, amazed by the lack of hostile and disgusted looks he receives. Among the riffraff of the Port Authority, he is relatively run-of-the-mill. It might have felt heavenly if not for the suffocating stink of piss and garbage.

***

Sam arrives at Chloe's apartment before 3:00.

"I'm just about to do a little waxing," she says, opening the door. "Just a little touchup. I'd hoped to do it earlier but you know the way the day gets away from you."

Sam drops his overnight bag on the floor and sits at the table. Chloe's apartment is cluttered and messy and much smaller than Sam's in Wattsville. He pushes a pile of papers away so he can rest his elbow on the table and prop up his head. Chloe is in the bathroom; Sam watches her moving around in the sliver of mirror that he can see through the gap where she's left the door ajar. "How was the bus ride? I'm glad you were able to get off work," she calls.

"Well, I managed." He wonders where Ronaldo is right now. Maybe still at the college. Maybe talking to Carol. Maybe leading her on. From Carol his thoughts make a beeline to Sunshine, and he gets anxious. He has a lot of business half-finished. He pushes that thought away and focuses on this new job opportunity, this possible new life.

Sam moves to the sofa, where he can lie back. An orange cat springs from behind a cushion and begins nuzzling its tiny wet nose into his neck.

"I forgot you have a cat."

"Mmm hmm."

He shifts away from the cat, and, when it comes closer again, nudging his shoulder, he pushes it onto the floor where it contents itself by rubbing along the soles of his boots. He can hear the thweep of wax strips being pulled. Chloe makes a muffled noise that sounds like, Be done in a sec. Sam pulls his boots off and tosses them lightly at the cat, making it scramble.

"Francine's meeting us later," Chloe says as she emerges from the bathroom, her five o'clock shadow replaced by a raw, pink chin. "Francine can afford electrolysis, but I'm on a budget. You wax too, right?" Sam nods, rolling his eyes. Her skin has a thick polyurethane shine to it, as though she's applied some kind of oil. "It's hard work being a girl," Chloe says, pulling her dressing gown tight and going to the kitchen—a counter space along one wall with a microwave, a small dirty stove, and a sink—and fills a glass with water. "You want one?" she says to Sam, holding up the glass.

"No thanks."

"So. Any news in your life?"

Like one of those children's toy binoculars clicking through an assortment of scenes, Sam pictures all of the events that have taken place in the last few days. Each scene gives him a short burst of related emotion: fear and guilt over what might happen to Tommy if he's blamed for the missing box; sadness over poor, dead Sunshine; anxiety over Garnet's situation in prison; Carol's crush on Ronaldo. Ronaldo! Sam puts the back of his hand to his mouth. "I met someone," he says finally.

Chloe pulls a chair from the table and sits down. "Tell me. What's he like?"

Sam looks at the ceiling and rocks his feet from side to side like windshield wipers. "Very nice. Very, very nice. So ... naive, in a way."

"Uh oh. Newbies can be tough."

"I think he likes men," Sam concedes, finally speaking a part of what's been worrying him. "I'm afraid I'll be the intermediate. You know—oh screw it anyway—if they're straight we're not womanly enough, if they're gay, we're not manly enough. But you know I think he may be different."

Chloe clucks. "You'd better not fall for him, honey. Don't let yourself in for heartache."

Suddenly Sam regrets having opened up to her. And he hasn't even mentioned anything about the fact that his love interest is, or has been, involved in drug trafficking. Or that apparently, he's been flirting with Carol. He hugs himself and watches Chloe's words turn to arrows that shoot down his fantastic love balloon, turning it gray and making it clunk onto the floor.

"You ready to go?" Chloe is at the closet, shimmying her torso into a red dress. "You want to change?"

"No. I'm okay." He stands and brushes cat fur from his pantsuit.

"Oh honey. We're not going to be walking that far." Chloe looks pointedly at the flat sandals he's pulled on, a curly look of disgust on her lips. "The boots with a mini would be nicer. You have a mini? Don't you think?"

"Oh, I suppose so," Sam says, shrugging out of his short-waisted purple blazer. "I'm just, oh, I guess I'm tired." He toes off the sandals and unzips his bag. He pulls out a short skirt and goes into the litter-box-scented bathroom to change. Chloe sighs and sits down to wait for him. The cat bounds immediately onto her lap, and she begins to coo and he to purr.

Sam emerges.

"Much better, darling." Chloe puts the cat gently onto the sofa behind her. "Pants suits are nice and elegant for the traveling woman, but to go out on the town? And those sandals . . ."

***

At the club, they order a drink and wait for Johnny P. The waitress informs them that he is running late but will be in shortly.

"Why do you call him Johnny P., instead of just Johnny?" Sam says, twirling the straw in his soda. Chloe and Francine have always talked about him in tones that indicate he's a very busy and important man, but Sam never thought to ask why they always include the initial P. when referring to him.

Before Chloe can answer, Sam's phone rings. He squints at it, holds it away from his face. "Honey, can you see that?"

Chloe puts her hand on the phone and snaps it shut. "Here he comes," she says. "Maybe you should power it down." Sam turns off the phone and slips it into his purse.

I say yes to life, Sam thinks. I say yes to life.

"Sam, this is Johnny. Johnny, this is Sam."

"I've heard so much about you," Sam says, stretching his hand toward the small man. He has longish brown hair that he wears slicked away from his face and a thin necktie. He looks like a kid trying to appear grown-up so he can get into a twenty-one-and-over UB40 concert.

"Yes, I heard about you too." His voice is tiny and high-pitched. "It's nice to finally meet you," he squeaks. Sam leans in, to hear him better.

"Oh, nice to meet you. Sorry, it's a little loud in here."

"So, you are ready to show me your stuff?" Johnny P. asks. His voice is like one of the Chipmunks'.

"Yes. Sure," Sam says. They stand in silence as Johnny P. shows his finger to the bartender, who knows what he means and starts to mix his drink. Sam looks to Chloe, hoping she will make some conversation, but she is sipping her drink.

"So," Sam says, "What does the P. stand for?"

"What P.?"

"Johnny P. What's the P. stand for?" Chloe takes a sudden and intense interest in her own fingernails, and Johnny P. clears his throat.

"My last name's Hughes," he says, frowning. "Hughes with an H." He rocks back and forth on his toes a few times and glares at Chloe. "I'm not sure I have time today, actually," he says, "I've got things to do." He turns and weaves through the crowd that has started to form. Sam grabs the edge of the bar to keep from sinking to the ground.

"Why didn't you tell me?" he says, not sure whether to laugh or cry. "About the P. thing? Shit."

"Oh, I never thought . . . you'd ask him that." Chloe starts giggling. "I guess I should've told you," she sputters. "About his ... size. Oh, dear!"

"And his voice?" Sam says, starting to laugh, too. "Is he a grown-up?"

"Yes. He's forty-three. We don't call him . . . pee . . . to his face! Pee wee. Puny. Oh, the poor thing."

"He's not what I expected. That's for sure," Sam says.

"Oh don't worry. He's used to that kind of thing. God knows I didn't make up the nickname. He'll get over it."

"With you," Sam says. "But maybe not with me!"

"Oh, Sam, dear. Don't worry. With a voice like yours, when he hears you, he'll forget all about it. You'll fill the house, and that's all he cares about."

"But when will I get the chance?" Sam pouts. "After all the trouble I took to get here."

"Let's enjoy ourselves anyway. You're here so let's have some fun! Cosmo!" she calls to the bartender.

"What the hell," Sam says. "Make it two!"

***

The bus ride will surely kill him. He'll never make it back to Wattsville; what he needs is to be emergency airlifted. He sweats and breathes into a paper bag. It's a full bus and a healthy-looking woman, whose muscular buttocks remind Sam of Poppy from his yoga video, pushes past him and into the window seat.

He makes at least five trips to the back, each time thinking that the cavernous steel tank's sloshing stew of blue lumpy liquid is going to be the last thing he'll see in this life. He heaves until there's nothing left in his gut but stink and guilt and then slinks back to his seat. The woman scoots as close as possible to the window and holds the inner spine of her book so close to her nose that she can't possibly be reading it.

Finally, by some miracle, the bus pulls into Wattsville and sighs as the engine ticks to a stop. Sam drags his overnight bag behind him and wastes money he can't afford on a taxi home. He can't bring himself to call Carol, not after he's fallen so spectacularly off the wagon.

Last night, he'd shirked his conscience and ordered drink after drink, not sure if he were celebrating or drowning his sorrows. "I met somebody," he'd called to the ceiling of whatever bar they were in, and ordered another. Or he'd yell, "I just ruined my career. Don't know whether to laugh or cry! Johnny P.!" and again, order another. He only remembers a few short flashes: kissing a bachelor-party groom at the request of his friends. Climbing on top of a bar—there was foreign money shellacked onto the dark wood—and belting out a compilation of songs from *Jesus Christ Superstar*. Getting stuck in a bathroom stall and slithering out underneath the door. Telling Francine off. Arriving at Chloe's apartment? No, he can't remember that. He'd woken there, still drunk, and thrown up in the kitchen sink, not remembering exactly where the bathroom was. He'd tried to clean up the mess before slipping out, but was pretty sure that when Chloe eventually emerged from her room, she was going to find bits of the dinner they'd eaten—Thai noodles and pea pods—stuck in the kitchen drain. Chloe's cat sat primly on the kitchen table, staring him down and then retreated, disgusted, back into Chloe's bedroom. In the taxi, he'd had to roll the window down for air and had managed to hold himself together as the driver wove along one of the avenues, crossed town to Forty-Second Street, and pulled up in front of the Port Authority. Someone had already thrown up on the sidewalk in front of the side entrance, which gave him some solace, and he managed to make it to a trash barrel before heaving whatever was still in his stomach.

Finally, he slides onto the bed and covers his head with a pillow before falling into a guilt-ridden, miserable sleep.

When he wakes, it is late afternoon and there is a metallic blue sky between his building and the one next to it. It should be overcast to match his mood, but there it is, compounding his guilt. He tries to sit up, but his head is filled with gravel. When he used to drink a lot, he'd kept a bottle of Advil on the nightstand and a case of Gatorade under the bed, but he is out of the habit now and, since back in February he'd spring-cleaned the whole apartment and finally put the pain relievers into the bathroom cabinet, he has to roll from the bed and shuffle, head hanging, to retrieve them. He uses his cupped palm to drink water from the tap and swallow the pills.

The answering machine winks angrily, but he ignores it.

He fell off the wagon. He missed work without calling in. He slept through visiting hours at Stratton Island. He has a stolen box of drugs and money on the top shelf of the closet. He killed a dog . . .

He goes back to bed for several hours. Finally, after dark, he makes his way to the answering machine and pushes play.

First is the operator. "Collect from Garnet, will you accept?" He can hear her voice behind the operator's: "Sam, I need some help, remember that thing we talked about, well—" and the operator cut her off. She tried again, "Collect call from Garnet, will you accept? Sam, call me! I really need it so if—" and she gets cut off again.

By the end of the message, Sam is sitting straight up on the edge of the sofa. He is going to have to try and smuggle in something, and soon—and if he gets caught? Sam's thoughts are cut short by the next message.

"Uh hello. It's Larry. From the *Chronicle*. You're supposed to be here? I hope you're feeling better? Uh, I hate to ask it, but if you are feeling better, it would be great if you could come in. Tommy's not here again so we're a little short-handed. Give me a call if you can. I'm actually starting to get worried. I don't know what's happened to him, well, or to you, but I . . . I need to talk to you. I hope the stomach thing wasn't bad. I hope you're better. Gosh, I hope you're better. Anyway, if you can. Okay, bye."

Sam stares at the box of drugs and money on the top shelf of the closet and feels a giant fist squeeze his organs. Could Tommy's disappearance actually be his fault? Tommy was the last to be seen behind DQ with the box. The kid at the DQ must have a boss. Sam follows the trail of his thoughts as it leads to Ignacio—the bigwig in the Bugatti. But if he is Derby's boss, then Ronaldo might know Derby too. And Ronaldo knows that Sam has the box . . .

Sam goes to the bathroom for another three Advil.

The next message is from Carol: "Hey, it's me. I don't know where you are, but listen. I can't stop thinking about the dog. I'm, um. I'm not okay. I don't know how you are. I just wish you would pick up. I tried your cell . . ."

He takes the box down and looks through it again. There is a pile of cash, probably more than a thousand dollars, a dozen baggies filled with white powder, a couple of bags of weed, and six or seven rolled joints. Sam takes one of the joints and lights it. He needs to loosen the grip that all of this is having on him in order to be able to think. He looks at the VHS sitting on top of the television. Poppy. Yoga. He tries to slow his breathing, calm his mind. But he can't.

He smokes one of the joints, unplugs the phone, and pours himself back onto the bed.

RECKLESS LOVE

Carol

Sam didn't come home last night and Carol is worried. And she can't stop seeing the foamy mouth of the dead dog. She's not sure why it is the dog's mouth, specifically, that appears in her waking nightmares. Death. She hasn't seen much of it, but the foam, and the lip that fell away from the creature's teeth, haunts her, and the fact that she is responsible for that death has made her feel as though she were underwater, unable to breathe.

She remembers the days previous: she'd been feeling frisky and courageous and, for one of the only times in her life, as if she were taking action. Being brave. She was saving her daughter. She was flirting with her coworker. She had felt good. Now that stubborn superstition that's been anchored in her brain since adolescence—that her emotional life must maintain a steady balance between happiness and despair—is affirmed: being happy only means that she will have farther to fall when her emotional seismograph rights itself. She fears happiness. She is determined not to let it happen again.

Over at the grill, Ron is laying strips of cooked bacon onto one side of a grilled cheese. The murmur of voices echoes through the cafeteria like weather. A student approaches with a yogurt and Carol tells her the price. Her face feels carved in cement; the lines of her frown draw her cheeks south. Her guilt has enshrined her in a posture of misery. And then here is Professor Bruss, with his usual Nantucket Nectar and a bagel. His brightness is an affront to the rock she's made herself into.

"Hello, Carol," he says. "How are you?"

She tries to smile but can't. A switch has been thrown in her brain that obliterates both compassion and logic. "Okay."

"How is Garnet doing?"

"Shitty." He looks shocked. She wants to hurt something. "Well, how do you think she's doing?"

"I'm sorry. I didn't mean. I just was wondering."

Is he for real? "Why are you so interested? She's too young for you, if that's what you're getting at."

"No," he says, sliding change into his pants pocket with a shaking hand.

She feels guilty, but she's dug her hole and she can't get out: "Just mind your own business. Garnet has enough trouble without you putting ideas into her head."

He takes the bagel and the Nantucket Nectar and leaves. Usually, he sits and eats under the windows, but today, he takes his food out of there—back to an office, maybe, or classroom. She doesn't even know what the academic departments look like . . .

The outburst has buoyed her, oddly enough. She'd felt badly for him while it was happening, but now it seems that inflicting pain has eased her own a little. She's less regretful than she is reckless. She wants to tear things down.

Is this how criminals start out? They are perfectly nice people until they make a mistake and then they can only identify with the mistake they made? They forget who they used to be and develop a need to perpetuate their own badness? No, guilt is creeping back in. Such a nice man. Did she really think that he was giving Garnet false ideas? No. She didn't. So why did she say it? What other crazy thing might she say or do?

Ron is lowering a tray into the steam bath. He looks preoccupied, too. As usual, he smiles at the students as he slops mashed potatoes and hamburgers onto plates, but something seems different about him. Or is she just imagining it? No. It's in his eyes. The brows stay flat when he smiles and his smile is smaller, more serious. You can't see as much of his teeth. For a moment she wonders if he's become so Americanized that he's suddenly embarrassed of the way his mouth looks. Carol finds it attractive, with the couple of gaps and the teeth less-than-white. It shows character. She's musing about how a woman would never be found more attractive due to missing teeth when there it is again, the mouth of the dog. The pointy teeth. The pink gums. The foam. She squeezes her eyes shut and wipes down the counter, rings in more orders; she focuses on the food as it is pushed by.

After the lunch rush dies down, Carol pours herself a cup of ginger ale and goes into the kitchen where Ron is wrapping leftovers in their square stainless-steel boxes. She leans against the counter and watches him.

"Are you okay, Ron?"

He doesn't stop working but says, "I'm okay."

She stares into the middle distance for a long time before letting the tears that have been on reserve behind her eyes march like two small armies down her face. She grabs a paper towel and wipes them away. "I'm not," she says.

Ron abandons the box of plastic wrap and puts his arms around her as she cries. At first, Carol leans her head on his shoulder, her hand holding the paper towels to her face. Then her other hand makes its way around his back. She'd been shorter than him when she was leaning against the counter, but as she stands, filling in the distance between their two bodies, she is almost the same height. Inside her head there is nothing but static and disbelief.

Here he is. So close. She turns her head as her hand goes up his back to the side of his face. His lips are so near to hers. The distance is nothing. She starts to lean toward them, her lips loose and ready. His breath smells sweet, like melons.

Just as she makes contact, he turns his head and pushes her gently away.

"I'm sorry," she says.

He stands back, aims his eyes in the direction of the walk-in door to her left, and says, "Things are hard for you right now. I know."

She starts to wonder if she actually did try to kiss him. He's acting as though it was a simple hug.

"I'm sorry," she says again.

"For what? You're upset."

She wants to yell, For trying to kiss you, you idiot! "You have to go to your other job," she says, turning away and throwing the rest of her ginger ale into the sink. She starts her cleanup tasks and they work together in silence.

She is busily wiping down surfaces when she notices that Ron has stopped working. The sudden knowledge that he might be looking at her, that he might be admiring her, that maybe he's changed his mind, ignites a fiery blush under her skin and she stops and turns. He is in fact looking at her, but not with any trace of lust.

"Sam," he says. He looks cold, shivery, even though it is warm. Carol is mystified. She waits.

"Your friend, Sam. I know him."

"Sam? You know him? The same one? My one who . . . ?" She mimics long hair and a dress.

"Yes. That one. I uh. We uh."

Her face changes from mystification to recognition; her eyes widen.

"You what?" she shrieks and suddenly cannot help laughing. "What? You? How did you? What? You guys? You're a thing?"

He doesn't laugh with her but glances nervously out of the kitchen to the cafeteria. Finally, she calms down. The humor is wearing off, and mortification is settling in.

"Well. Okay. I understand now." She sees fear in his face. "I won't judge you," she says quickly. "You must know that I would never judge."

She goes slowly to the register; there is someone there with a bag of chips.

This is it, she thinks. Now I know. The chapter has ended. And a slow-moving melancholy settles itself around her. Ron gets changed and grabs his threadbare backpack from the hook. Even though he's broken her heart, she can't stand to see him go.

"I can give you a ride," she says.

He seems serious and thoughtful. "You know what?" he says. She waits, shakes her head meekly. "You know my name?"

"Um. Ron. Right? Is it a joke?"

"It's Ronaldo. Nobody want to say the whole thing. Americans, they like things short and easy."

"Gosh, Ron. I can call you that. Ronaldo. You prefer it?"

"Nah," he says, smiling. "I don't mind. Just thought I'd tell you. Because we're friends."

"I can leave a little early if you can wait a bit," Carol says. "To give you a ride." She's surprised she wants to stay near him. She should be humiliated, but still, she wants to be near him. She hasn't even begun to think about how the whole thing makes her feel toward Sam, who kept it a secret from her. She tucks that away to mull over later.

"Thank you, Carol," Ron says. "I wait for you." He goes to a table and sits by himself. He takes a book from his backpack and starts reading, taking notes. Carol waits for a few students to choose drinks or chips and then finally pulls the grate down. She brings the cash tray around the back, into the kitchen, where she deposits it in the safe.

When she comes out, Ron is talking to the same two men who'd come in the other day. She stops and watches, afraid to move closer. The two strangers look mad. Ron shrugs, as if to say he can't help them, but she can tell he's uncomfortable. When he talks to these men it's like he's a completely different person—no wacky-toothed smile, no high-fives, no curious kind eyes. Then they all walk out together. She is hidden behind the pillar where the condiment counter is. But she realizes that Ron hadn't even remembered her. Ronaldo. He hadn't even glanced back to see if she were there before leaving without her. She goes to the door, but they are gone. Is he going to come back? Should she wait? She walks the periphery of the cafeteria, but he doesn't come back.

***

Carol is early for visiting hours, and it takes them ages to bring her daughter. With every second she's kept waiting, scenes from the last couple of days weigh on her like bricks on a balloon. She would pop if the air weren't already seeping out. She is flattening. The dog. Lashing out at Professor Bruss. Sam: Where is he? And Ronaldo. With Sam? Together?

Finally, Garnet is led in; seeing her daughter inflates her a bit.

They sit across from each other. There is no other human being in the world that Carol can look at like this—unflinching and frank. But Carol is afraid her daughter will sense the darkness around her so she looks away.

"Everything okay?" Garnet asks.

"Fine," she lies. "You good? You look good." Garnet nods, pushes a strand of hair behind her ear.

Carol asks about parole. Garnet's face crunches up, and she looks at the ceiling. "Nope, it was cancelled."

Carol puts her hands together in front of her face like she's praying, her elbows on the table. Her nose slides down her forearms, and she squeezes her eyes shut. She thinks about Garnet as a baby, as a toddler, her chubby hands cradling Carol's cheeks as they sat together on the BarcaLounger. Her baby. Her everything. She is crushed—not just for Garnet's sake but for her own.

"It's okay, Mom. I'm fine. Mom. I'm fine." Garnet is talking quietly, trying to calm her mother without making a scene. Finally, Carol does calm down, stares at the vending machine as though it could anchor her to the planet.

Carol thinks to ask her daughter why she lost parole, but she doesn't care, and she doesn't want to talk about it. What's done is done.

"Did Sam come yesterday?" she asks finally.

"No, but I figured . . . well, I figured he just couldn't make it. Is everything all right? Where is he?"

"I'm not sure. His phone must've been out of battery. He didn't tell me anything. But you know him. He could've gone anywhere on a whim."

144

Garnet's jaw starts to wiggle back and forth and she looks cagey, like there is sand inside her clothes.

"What?" Carol says. "What is it? What happened?"

Garnet shakes her head.

"Garnet." It is a strain for Carol to keep her voice low. "What?"

"I didn't want you to know," Garnet begins. Carol waits for more. "Sam was going to . . . do me a favor. I had to get something, get something brought to me here. Ethan did it once, and I had to do it again."

"What? Why?" The guard at the desk hushes her loudly. Carol shows him her palm in compliance. "Sorry," she says. "What? Why?" she whispers this time.

"Something . . . illegal. For . . . I was . . . in some trouble . . . with some of the girls in here . . . they were threatening me. You know about that."

"You told me that was nothing, a misunderstanding and that it was all resolved, it was all over."

"Well. It wasn't. Okay. Sam. He might have . . ." Garnet starts to cry. "He might have gotten caught. With the stuff. What can we do? Can we call someone?"

"I'll think of something," Carol says, remembering their antics at the Dairy Queen. She didn't know that Sam had other reasons for doing it. But . . . he has the box . . . Where is he? Why didn't he show up if he said he was going to? And why is he keeping so many secrets?

As if she can hear her mother's thoughts, Garnet says, "I made him promise, Mom. I made him promise he wouldn't tell you."

Carol reaches across the table and grasps her daughter's hands. She wishes she could pull with all her might, pull Garnet to freedom like this prison was a car wreck.

"Mom," Garnet says. "Please don't worry too much. I'm going to get out of here. I promise."

Carol holds onto her daughter's hands and looks into her daughter's eyes. It is like looking into a mirror.

***

Carol's apartment is usually spotless, but when she gets home she throws her coat onto the couch, kicks her shoes across the room, and lets her pocketbook drop onto the living room floor. She sits heavily, changes her mind and goes to the kitchen for a package of Chips Ahoy, returns and starts to eat as she thinks through all that has happened. All that is going to happen.

Nothing has worked. She and Sam have tried to do what is best for Garnet, and they've failed again and again. Garnet had attempted to rise above her lot: raised by a single mother, broke, and against the odds, she had been excelling in college. But the forces-that-be have conspired over and over to keep her, to keep them all, down. The need for revenge buoys Carol, gives her strength.

But then despondency rears its head again. The dog. And Ronaldo had been . . . with . . . Sam. This she still can't get her head around. She wishes she'd been able to give Ronaldo a ride so that she could have asked him more. She imagines confronting Sam about it. The betrayal she felt has petered away, giving way to wonder at how on earth Sam had managed to even meet Ronaldo, let alone have . . . relations . . . with him. And for them to put it together, that she knows them both? Her thoughts run to loneliness. She has been left out. Sam is her best friend, and he's grown close to someone that she has known for longer. It's always this way, and she feels inadequate and hopeless. And forgotten.

At work, Ronaldo is friendly with so many teachers and students, while she is always alone. In fact, she reminds herself painfully, she'd probably just severed from her life the first person she'd started to develop a friendship with in a long time: Mike Bruss, Garnet's teacher. Sam has his friends from the city, Francine and Chloe, and now he has Ronaldo, too.

The cookies are gone, and Carol is pouring herself a glass of orange juice when the doorbell rings. She rushes to open it, thinking it must be Sam, whom, above all—beyond his betrayal and dishonesty—she is worried about. And she misses.

She swings the door open, one hand on her hip, ready to pull him in and read him the riot act for a) making her worry and b) not telling her about his relationship with Ronaldo. But it isn't Sam. It is Larry, Sam's boss.

"Is everything okay?" she says.

"I'm not sure."

Carol opens the door wider, and he enters. He stands for an awkward moment just inside and she leads him to the kitchen, pulls a chair out for him.

"How did you find me?" she asks.

"I was looking for Sam. Your name's on the mailbox."

"You tried his bell?" Carol says.

"Not home."

"Did you call the police?" she says, thinking of the crime that she and Sam committed. They have exiled themselves into the shady world of criminals, undeserving of police protection. She is relieved when he says no.

"I bet he fell off the wagon," she says, "done something stupid." She prays he wasn't arrested trying to smuggle drugs into Stratton Island. But no, he would've been granted one phone call . . .

"He seemed so responsible."

"I don't know. He is. Usually."

Larry coughs. "Can I get a glass of water?" Carol fills a glass from the tap and hands it to him.

"You're a thoughtful boss. Coming out here to find him."

"I was going to be in the neighborhood anyway," Larry says defensively.

"I mean it," Carol says quickly. "I think it's nice that you're worried. I mean, I know, you probably need him at work. But still, nobody does that, you know?"

Larry blushes a little. "Well, my son lives nearby and, to be honest, he missed work too, and I don't know where he is either." He finishes the water and puts the glass into the sink. "I'm worried. I also wanted to talk to Sam about something that happened. He, my son, might be angry at me."

Carol waits for him to say more, but he doesn't. "Okay. Well, I have a key to Sam's place. Let's see if he's been home at least. There might be some clues."

Carol grabs the key from a drawer and follows Larry to the front door. As they are waiting for the elevator, she picks a red feather from a fold in his sleeve.

"Hey, looks like you've been wrestling with one of the Muppets," she jokes. It reminds her of the merchandise in Va Va Voom, so she assumes he's got a girlfriend. He takes it in two fingers and laughs nervously.

"Must have come out of my comforter." He rolls it into a ball and puts it into his pants pocket.

Carol rings the bell several times and then puts the key into the lock. They peer into the apartment. There is the usual disarray, which Larry thinks is the result of a break-in. He looks alarmed.

"Don't worry, this is the way it always is," she says. "Sam?" She goes to the kitchen, calls again, and then to the bathroom. At the door of the bedroom, she stops. There is a body on the bed, and it isn't moving. She takes a step closer, and there is Sam's hair in a snarly mess on the pillow.

"He was sick," Larry says as he comes up behind her. "He threw up when he left work the other day. Sam?"

Sam groans and Carol sits on the edge of the bed. "Oh thank God. Jesus Christ, I thought you were dead. What the hell? Where were you?"

Sam rolls over. "I was sick. I'm fine, though. I'm fine." Carol knows he's lying. Any time he's sick he calls her. She can tell from the clothes that are crumpled up at the end of the bed and from the overnight bag that remains unpacked that he's been partying, and she figures he went to the city.

She sits on the edge of the bed. "I visited Garnet," she says. There is a long pause as the two of them wait for Larry to take the hint.

"Where's the bathroom?" Larry says finally. Sam points. He goes in and closes the door.

"She needs the stuff," Carol whispers. "Why didn't you bring it to her?"

"I will." He rolls over, his forearm draped across his eyes.

Larry comes back, wiping his hands on his pants. "There's no towel," he says.

Her anger simmers because she knows that Sam must have lied to Larry to get out of work. She doesn't want to erupt with Larry here, so she takes her fury—he is so thoughtless, to tell Garnet he'd do that horrible favor for her and then to blow it off, to fall off the wagon after lecturing Carol about staying on it, to have relations with Ronaldo, who is so sweet, and then to go off drinking and, most of all, to have abandoned her in the midst of her troubles—and goes out, slamming the door.

She leaves Larry with him, and hopes, for both of their sakes, that Sam comes clean with him and doesn't lie. If he loses his job, so be it.

Back in her apartment, she is overwhelmingly lonely. Sam acts selfish, but at least he has people who love him. She thinks harshly that he doesn't deserve all the good people in his life. While she, who thinks so often of others, is alone. With Garnet in prison, her world is cut in half. If something were to happen to Carol, Sam probably wouldn't notice, because he's so caught up in his own life—except until he gets hungry or wants to watch something on HBO. She tries to contain her resentment, but it grows like a virus. It overtakes her the way her unfounded anger at Mike Bruss did, unreasonably, like her desire for a drink when she was drinking. An illness, a physical compulsion. It is the pure energy of despair.

She lets her mind float toward Garnet's cell. And Garnet's troubles. And what Carol can do to help. All around the prison is brown water. She imagines climbing into that water and letting it swallow her until she becomes a part of the riverbed and all of her pain is erased. The line between life and death would be a painful one to cross, but once on the other side, everything would be gone. Everything. She is immensely comforted by the thought of nothingness.

THE SMELL OF LIFE

Tommy

When Tommy thinks back to his childhood, before his mom took him to Pueblo, every memory seems to have Hanky O'Malley in it. Hanging at Hanky's house, Hanky's dad fingernailing the label off of bottle after bottle of Budweiser and pouring whiskey into the glass he'd brought from Ireland before he was married. It was nothing special but God help the kid who tried to drink juice out of it in the O'Malley's kitchen.

After Mr. O'Malley died, Hanky's mom actually seemed nicer and happier. Tommy hadn't thought about that before, but now he has time and silence, and it could be hours and hours before anything happens, and it's obviously nighttime because the gashes of sunlight have disappeared and the lantern that Derby brought flickers calmly. How could that guy, Mr. O'Malley, make his family so unhappy? So unhappy that they were actually better off after he'd died?

Marguerite at the Blue Heron said it to Tommy once when he was in there after work by himself, having a couple of bottles of Genesee and a roast beef sandwich.

"You know alcoholism runs in both your families, yours and Hanky's, but Hanky's dad had the darkness in him," she said. "I hope Hanky didn't inherit that darkness. I know your dad, and he had a problem, but he didn't have the darkness. I don't think Hanky has it, he's such a nice kid, and I don't think you have it either, but sometimes you don't know until it comes out, and then you can't drink anymore, isn't that right, Dom? Dom has the darkness, don't you Dom? That's why he doesn't drink." Dom flicked his newspaper out in front of him and kept on reading. "That's why Hanky's dad was like that, he wouldn't give up drinking. Thank God you stopped, right, Dom?" Dom grunted and went to the restroom.

Tommy knows that Hanky is the other side of the coin from his dad: loyal, even-tempered, chill in the extreme. He wonders whether he's informed the police or if he even knows that Tommy is missing. Unfortunately, probably not. There's a good chance that Hanky thinks Tommy is with Simone.

***

The day after Derby's stash disappeared, Hanky was dozing on the couch in front of the TV when Tommy came home from work.

"Dude, Derby is losing his shit," Hanky said, rousing himself. "What the fuck. Whatever happened yesterday, he's gonna fucking kill you."

"I didn't do anything," Tommy said, shaking some weed onto an album cover propped on his knees.

"He's a fucking maniac, dude. Like he's gonna rip your head off."

Tommy rolled a joint and lit it, took a long drag and passed it to Hanky.

"You wanna go to the movies? I wanna see *The Perfect Storm*."

"You saw that already," Hanky said.

"Yeah. But I'll go again. Come on. You want to?"

"Naw. Fuck that. Hey, let's go to the Blue Heron."

Tommy sank into the cushions until they'd smoked the whole joint. "You know what? If Derby is gonna kill me, I think we should go to the Wagonwheel. Anyway, the first place he'd look for me is the Blue Heron."

"The fucking Wagonwheel? Really? It's a haul, man."

"If Derby's losing his shit, I wanna be as far from here as possible."

"Okay," Hanky said. "But let's jump in there and grab a quick shot and a beer first. I'm parched."

"Fine," Tommy said. "Just let's get the hell out of here. What time's Derby get home, any idea?"

Hanky looked at his wrist, which didn't have a watch on it, and said, "Nope. But anytime is a good time for a Genesse."

"Yeah, and any time is a good time to not get killed," Tommy added.

The Blue Heron's door has a small window, the size of a toaster, through which you can see very little. Stained by years of smoke on the inside and exhaust and grime on the outside, it's not good for much.

"Wait." Tommy stopped Hanky's hand from grabbing the handle. "What if he's here?"

"He won't be." Hanky cupped his hands around his eyes and put his face up to the window. "Fuck, I don't know. There's some people in there, but I can't tell. Wait a minute. Actually, shit, run!"

They took off around the corner.

"Was it him?" Tommy said, catching his breath at the bus stop.

"Yeah, I think it was."

"Wagonwheel," Tommy said. "There's the bus now."

"Fuck," Hanky dug into his pocket for bus fare. "I hate the bus."

***

"Dude, I think it might be that gay karaoke night," Hanky said as they crossed the road in front of the Sheraton's parking lot. "Either I'm really stoned, or I think that lady has a mustache."

"Entertainment is entertainment, and besides, at least we know Derby wouldn't—"

"What is it?" Hanky put his hand on Tommy's shoulder, to try and shake him out of whatever trance he'd entered. Then he looked at what Tommy was looking at. "Is that—?"

"Yes," Tommy said.

Father and son stood twenty paces from each other for what felt like hours. Larry was dressed in a Marcel Marceau style striped dress, a red boa and purple Peter Pan boots with fringe at the ankles. On his ears were big fake pearls.

"Um, hi Mr. Stall," Hanky said. "Um, so, I'll see you in there? Tom? Okay."

Tommy didn't answer, but Hanky went into the bar. The next to speak was Larry. "Hi. What are you doing here?" He was fidgeting, and looked like a cartoon character caught without clothes on the way he was trying to kind of cover himself with his hands.

Tommy was stoned and couldn't find his voice to respond, so his Dad went back to the car he'd just gotten out of, started it up and drove away. Tommy watched him go, lit a cigarette and smoked it before joining Hanky in the bar.

Simone was standing next to Hanky's bar stool, her hand over her mouth, and Hanky was getting animated. Tommy could see he was telling her about what had just happened. As he approached, Simone took a few steps toward him and enveloped him in a hug. Tommy, who hadn't really been feeling anything, relaxed into her embrace and started to giggle a bit. He pulled up a stool next to Hanky; Simone said she had to wait on some tables.

"Wait. Are we friends with Simone, now?" Tommy said after she'd gone.

"That's what you want to talk about after what we just saw? He'll have one, too," Hanky told the bartender, who was sliding a bottle of beer in front of him.

"She knew I was your friend," Hanky said. "I think she's been hanging with Derby a bit, actually. But, wait. Your dad?"

"My dad's okay though," Tommy said. "I mean, whatever. Who cares if he wants to put on a dress?"

Simone came back. "It's slow tonight," she said, sitting next to Tommy and putting her hand on his knee. The noise from karaoke buzzed in the background, but the bar was far enough away from the action that they could talk.

She sat with them for a while, listening more than talking, until the bartender gave her a look that said get back to work. She carried a round tray and had a bunch of ones and fives folded lengthwise and looped over her middle finger. She went and took an order, came back to tell the guy behind the bar what she needed. The bartender was a body builder; a tattoo of a tiger flexed with his bicep, making it look like it was running through the jungle, on the hunt. Simone smiled at Tommy while she waited.

After she'd brought the drinks over to the people who'd ordered them, she came back and sat with Hanky and Tommy again, and listened to their conversation.

"We're all like Marky Mark, floating there. You should see it, dude." Tommy was describing *The Perfect Storm*. "I know it's fucked up, but it made me want to go out on the ocean. I think my dad feels like that, and I feel like that. We're all like that, we're all alone."

"I don't like the ocean," Hanky said. "We're land animals. We're supposed to be on the land. Right Simone?"

"What? I don't know. I guess." The two boys waited to see if she would elaborate, but she turned to Tommy and said, "So, how do you feel? About your dad?"

Tommy didn't like being dragged out of a conversation that he was enjoying. They'd had a couple of shots by then, and a couple of beers, and he wasn't sure he'd remember what they were talking about if he got off topic.

"It was a shock, but to be honest, I don't care what he does on his own time."

"You're really open-minded," Simone said. "I like that."

"Hey, Murphy's law, right? That I showed up at the same time as him."

Simone pointed a finger at him, as if to say he was a good student.

The night wore on like that: Simone going back and forth between them and her job, putting her hand on Tommy's knee whenever she sat next to him. Thoughts of everything else—his dad in a dress, the fact that Derby was out to get him—all faded from Tommy's mind, and he found that the only thing in the world that mattered was Simone's hand on his leg.

Finally, she tossed her tray on the bar and said, "That's it, I'm done for the night." She called to the bartender: "Screwdriver, Henry!"

Hanky leaned into Tommy and said, "I'm outta here, dude. I got a third-wheel feeling, and anyway, I have stuff to do in the morning."

They did the toned-down version of their special handshake, a finger flick and a bump of shoulders, and Hanky left.

As the lights went off on the stage and the karaoke guy was packing up, Simone led Tommy outside. It was a warm evening, and she brought him down a wooden walkway at the edge of the parking lot that leads to a dock with a couple of small boats tied to it.

They sat at the edge of the dock with their feet dangling, at first talking, and then kissing. Soon they were making out like the world was going to end the next day, Tommy's and Simone's bodies smashed and rolled into each other like two different colors of Play-Doh.

***

It's morning. Tommy can tell from the light that's beginning to show through some of the cracks. He gets up and moves around the storage container. There are old newspapers on the floor. Moldy and practically disintegrated, but Tommy takes a shit on one, wraps it up and stuffs it in the corner. His nose is pretty much accustomed to the smell in here by now; he understands it is the smell of life, really, when you get down to it, which beats the smell of death. Sometimes, a breeze will squeeze through the cracks, bringing him a welcome whiff of something beautiful. He sits down, finishes the last two pieces of Country Pride and turns the flickering lantern off.

After a while, a motor approaches. He can tell it's a car, and not one of the motorcycles or ATVs that have passed periodically, because it is quieter and kind of ticks when it comes to a stop. Three doors slam. The padlock is opened, and the door squeaks open. Tommy's eyes burn with sudden light and three figures clomp in, jabbering in Spanish. It's obvious they're complaining about the smell, and one points to the bowl of pee and orders another to go empty it. Their features are coming into focus. One guy emerges as the head honcho: he has a folding chair that he unsnaps in front of where Tommy is panned out on the floor and sits down, hands dangling between his knees. He looks at him for a long time before speaking. "You would tell us if you stole this thing, true?"

The guy comes back in with the empty bowl and tosses it; it lands with a thin clunk and rattles around for a while. A third guy is leaning against the wall smoking a cigarette. Head Honcho sees Tommy looking, pulls a pack from his pocket and offers him one. It is delicious at first but then it makes Tommy dizzy, and he feels like puking. It's a connection to the world, though, and he cherishes it between his fingers; he feels as though, if he didn't have it, he would dissolve.

"I have no idea what happened to the stuff. You can check my room, everywhere. I swear to God I don't have it."

"You religious?" Head Honcho asks after Tommy swears to God.

Tommy nods and a tear slides down his cheek. "Praise be," he says.

Head Honcho says something to the guy against the wall, who goes out and comes back with a McDonald's bag. The smell is heavenly. Head honcho takes the bag and pulls a burger out, waves it in front of Tommy's face. "We think maybe you didn't do it."

"I didn't. I didn't. I didn't do anything."

"And also, your friend Derbin, he was stupid to leave the stuff outside, where it gets stolen. If it turns out you didn't do this thing, there are going to be consequences."

At first Tommy thinks he means Derby is a stupid piece of shit and will be punished, but then he realizes that he, too, has probably seen too much now. It sears into him, the knowledge that he'll probably never get out of this alive.

Head Honcho throws the burger into Tommy's lap and he picks it up and eats it. The cigarette is smoldering in his fingers and, with some remote part of his brain, he wishes he could have had one and then the other—food and cigarette—to make it all last. He inhales most of the burger and gets back to the cig. Head Honcho slips a gun out from behind him and fondles it, turning it over and over. Tommy smashes the filter into the ground. It was down to the end, so his last drag tasted like fiberglass.

The guy pushes a fresh gallon of water toward Tommy and he drinks, never taking his eyes off the gun. Head Honcho is casually holding it with the barrel pointed in Tommy's direction.

"I'm a man of God," Head Honcho says, which makes Tommy want to laugh. "You think I'm funny?" he says, which gives Tommy a jolt, because he hadn't laughed out loud.

"No," Tommy says. "I'm a member of the Keepers of the Sacred Faith. Praise be."

"Praise be," Head Honcho echoes. "Okay, my brother. Listen. If you lie to me about what happened, I kill you."

"I didn't take anything." Tommy cries. Suddenly Head Honcho is on his feet so fast that the chair he'd been sitting on collapses. Both minions just stand there, neither one seeming to notice their boss's temper tantrum. He starts pacing, waving the gun at Tommy; Tommy is cowering like a beaten dog, with his hands in front of his face as if he'd be able to block a bullet.

"I'm giving you some more time to think," he says, finally. "I got stuff to do anyway and it's Sunday. I never kill a person on a Sunday." He's thoughtful for a minute and then amends what he's just said, as though it were important for him to be as truthful as possible. "Unless I have to."

Then they're gone. The door slams. The lock gets put back on. The hamburger has given Tommy strength he thought he would never feel again and he's on his feet, fingertips like the legs of a centipede looking for the edge of the door. He finds it, and it moves slightly, but not enough and his fingers get pinched.

Then he throws his shoulder against the door, and it feels really good to do something even though somewhere in his brain he knows it doesn't help at all. He hurls himself against another wall, and another. When he quiets down, he hears laughter and car doors slamming. The car starts and another engine revs—a motorcycle or something. Then it's quiet again. Tommy paces for awhile, until his energy gives out and he lies down.

NO RELATION TO LEVI STRAUSS

Garnet's Diary

Sunshine died. They found her on the doormat. Ethan was upset, understandably. He loved that dog. I loved her, too, more than any other member of his family! They suspect foul play and fired the landscapers, who were the only ones home at the time. I guess maybe she ate some fertilizer or something. I've been crying about Sunshine. It's easy to cry. For Sunshine. For the danger I'm in if I don't get drugs. For Shanise. For the fact that Ethan has pretty much abandoned me. Everything just feels totally fucked right now.

Ethan is going to visit his friend Levi out in California. His mom is sending him in a couple of weeks so he can have some time to get over Sunshine. Imagine that? Being sent on a California vacation because your dog died? (Did Ethan kill Sunshine?!? Ha ha.) So that's it. Sunshine is dead and I'm going to be dead or nearly dead if I can't get Eloise and Molasses anything. Ethan says he can't do it for me. He won't do it.

Levi, by the way, is such an asshole. I only met the guy once. "No relation to Levi Strauss," he said when Ethan introduced us the first time and I laughed, thinking it was funny, but it wasn't long before I realized that it was basically his only joke. He tried to make other jokes, but they weren't funny.

Levi is Ethan's friend from B-squared and he's at some college out in Los Angeles. Pepperville or something. He showed us some pictures of the campus, and it looks like a golf course right on the ocean. He showed us pictures of his car— so shiny—and his girlfriend, also shiny, who, he made sure to mention (several times) "does some modeling on the side." Then he said, "At least you got a girlfriend, Ethan." Trying to be funny I guess, but I'm not sure what was supposed to be funny about it. Ethan managed to get one but she's not so great? And Ethan laughed! It was an insult to him as much as it was to me. Never mind he wouldn't stand up for me, but he wouldn't even stand up for himself. I just sat there for the rest of the night, glaring at Ethan and ignoring Levi, who was too drunk to notice. Actually, they were both too drunk to notice. I should have left. But I didn't.

That night, in bed, Ethan and I had sex. But he was rough and kept his eyes closed and I felt like a prostitute. I didn't even want to do it in the first place, but that didn't matter. I'm sure he was taking it out on me because Levi had made him feel small. It was a hate-fuck. I felt like shit after and turned to face the wall and if he could hear me crying, he didn't say anything.

We talked about it the next day and he admitted that Levi is an asshole. He apologized and said he'd talk to him about it. But he never did. I asked a couple times and first he kept saying he would, until finally he was saying, "Oh, it happened so long ago now that the dude probably won't even remember what I'm talking about. Anyway, he was drunk." As if that's an excuse.

I swallowed it. Learned to forget about it. But it was a betrayal, and now, where's he going? To visit Levi. And you know what else? He's probably barely even going to have a good time because he feels inadequate that he's only at Holbrook, not golf-course university, and his girlfriend is fat and low class and definitely hasn't done any modeling on the side. In fact, she's in prison, and when she gets the hell out of here she'll be an ex-con. A loser for the rest of her life.

Good night.

E. and M. want more. Always more. I told them that I wouldn't call Ethan because we broke up. And I think we did too, even though we haven't said it. They said I'd better get them something or else. Sam won't answer my calls. I don't know what I'm going to do. And here's the other thing: Shanise is going to be found out.

The other day. We were out at the dust bowl for rec time and Shanise and I were walking circles, ignoring E. and M., but every time we passed by the bleachers where E. and M. were sitting, we'd catch some pretty nasty vibes. It got nastier and nastier so we decided to stop walking and just stay over near the Butcher, who was by the fence. So, we're just hanging there, and I'm talking to Shanise—she was telling me about a prize that her little sister won at a science fair. God, I love it when she tells me stuff like that. It's like they're getting to live in that world where there are Professor Brusses who will make them feel worthwhile. And I love when Shanise and I can be outside in the sunshine and talking like that, about good things, and forget for a little while all the shit we're in.

I feel like I know all of Shanise's siblings, she tells me so much about them. It was Bella who'd won the prize—Shanise is so proud of her. While she was talking, I was listening but I was also noticing something about that fence. There's an area where it's curling up and it looks like some kind of animal might have been going back and forth under it. Probably to get the leftover crumbs of whatever snacks we prisoners might have dropped on the ground. Whatever that animal was, it's been digging a pretty good-size hole. A human might fit through it, if she dug it out a little bit more. I'd been looking for something like that, but I hadn't ever noticed it. After I saw it, I felt this weird electric charge, like the kind that makes your insides knot up, but in a good way?

Anyway, we were chatting and didn't notice the Butcher get called away somewhere and before we knew it, E. and M. were on top of us, backing us into the fence. My foot slid a little down that hole. But they didn't notice.

Eloise would be pretty if she wasn't so mean. I used to think she was really pretty—before she started pulling all this shit with me. She's got good teeth and full lips and high cheekbones that are like spatulas under the skin below her eyes. Molasses was never pretty. Her features are kind of square and her face is the shape of an egg on its side.

"Everything okay?" Eloise said, but she said it like she knows something, not like she was asking a question. She's looking Shanise up and down and I hadn't really noticed it, but it's actually becoming pretty obvious that Shanise is pregnant. I mean, if you didn't know, you might think she's just a little fat around the belly, but her body refuses to put on weight anywhere else. I don't know how OF hasn't noticed it. I guess he's not expecting it because he thinks she took the pill and also, he's all wrapped up in his own stuff. And, to be honest, he's not all that intelligent.

"Little cousin, I'm starting to think you've got yourself into trouble."

"I don't know what you're talking about," Shanise says. We start to walk away, but they block us. It's us two with our backs against the chain link and them two pushing in close to us—threatening.

Then Molasses chimed in: "Eloise and me, we were talking. We think we have some understanding about your situation. And we think we can help you, but you're going to have to help us out first."

"What do you think you can do?" Shanise asked, which was basically admitting that they were right. She's Eloise's cousin, so it's not surprising that she still wants to trust her, though she won't anymore! Drugs ruin everything, I'm convinced!

They said there was a big favor they were going to do for her. And they drew it out, like it was going to be some great thing. But all they're going to do—if they choose to—is not tell anybody. That will buy Shanise a bit of time I guess, but people are going to find out soon, one way or another. They have to. I mean, you can't hide it when a baby drops out of the bottom of you. So, if we get them drugs, they won't kill me and they won't rat on Shanise. What a bargain.

Later, in our room, I was feeling kind of mad at her. I mean, what was she doing, just ignoring the whole situation as if it would go away on its own? Like a stupid little kid closing her eyes and thinking she's hiding.

"So now we have to get them drugs or else they're going to tell the warden, the guards, whoever, and your mom too, that you're pregnant." I was mad but I was still whispering.

"Gar, what would you have done? Huh? Don't get mad at me like the same thing couldn't happen to you. What would you do if you'd gotten pregnant that last time with Ethan? You think you'd have done something different?"

I thought about it and I had to admit she was right. There are times when you just have to hope the world makes things right for you. When the only real choice offered is no choice at all, so you forget about it and hand the reins of your life over to chance.

Unless there is some other way: Some choice that nobody offered, but that still exists. You just have to be able to see it. And then be brave enough to make it.

We sat for a long time. It felt like the end of the world was coming.

Sam came through.

I can't believe it. He had it in his boot—he wasn't even sure what it was. It's cocaine. When I got back and told Shanise, she said we should try some to make sure it's not just baking soda or something. I reminded her about the baby and she was like, "Oh, yeah. The baby." Sometimes I wonder about her—she's so cool and understanding most of the time and then other times she does and says things that I don't understand. How on earth could she even think about doing cocaine? I mean, not to mention the fact that Sam risked everything to get it to me. Imagine I just snorted it with Shanise! And her pregnant! What kind of person would I be?

I rubbed a tiny bit on my gums and it was the real thing.

I can't believe the risk he took. He really lucked out that nobody made him take off his shoes. They often do. And with the way he was looking, I'm surprised they didn't immediately suspect him of using. He was shaky and pale, and after we hugged, he confessed that he'd fallen off the wagon and gone out all night in the city, that he'd gotten sick all the way home and missed work.

He tried his best to keep it together, but I could see that he was really upset.

"My problems aren't anything compared to yours, my dear. I just hope that . . . this," he jiggled his boot at me, "will help keep you safe." It started to dawn on me that he was saying he'd gotten me something for Eloise and Molasses and he goes, "It's hard to imagine that . . . it . . . could keep you safe. I mean, how ironic is that?"

I was super scared. More than with Ethan. Being rich and white and straight means that Ethan gets away with a lot. Plus, Ethan only brought pot. If he got caught, he'd get off with a slap on the wrist, I'm sure. I kept thinking, how did my life come to this? And then I kept thinking that Sam must really love me to do this. It's awful to think what might have happened if he'd gotten caught.

Sam risked everything and Ethan is going on vacation. Because his dog died. I'm sad about Sunshine too, but I could have been killed. It happens. There was a lady who got on E. and M.'s bad side, and she ended up dead. They said she committed suicide, but around here, in whispers that I'm sure E. and M. want people to believe, lots of ladies say they killed her. I have no idea what to think, but I know E. and M. both thrive on people being afraid of them, so when people think they killed that lady, it gives them credibility.

I'm trying to picture Sam going into the DQ and buying drugs. I'm amazed that he did that for me. Speaking of DQ. I'd kill for a Blizzard. No. That's not true. I'd kill to be able to go and buy myself a Blizzard. I don't care if I'd get to eat the thing or not.

Fuck.

I gave the stuff to E. and M. and at first they seemed like that was great, they weren't going to hassle me anymore. But I don't think twenty-four hours went by and they came back at me. Eloise looked especially terrible: her cheeks shriveled into her face so that her cheekbones would poke her in the eyes if her eyes hadn't also shrunken so far back into her head. With Molasses you couldn't really tell the difference. Maybe Eloise did the whole thing and now they need more for Molasses. Who knows what happens with the two of them when they're alone in their cell. (You'd think the warden would separate them, but I guess everyone's too scared to complain, so things just keep going the way they are.)

"*Snow White, you didn't get enough, you see that's the problem. The quality wasn't bad, was it, Molasses?*" Molasses nodded and sniffed. Eloise went on, strung out like she hadn't slept at all. "*So you see if you want everything to be cool, you're going to have to ante up.*"

I don't even know what ante up means, but that's what she said.

"*Twice what you got us. Got it? Get to work.*" And the two of them turned and walked away, Eloise like the spine of an umbrella that's come apart in the wind and Molasses like a big tin can next to her. Shanise had been hanging around at the side of the yard with Officer Frank and she came over.

"*What was Eloise saying?*" she asked and I told her.

"*Well, shit,*" she said, "*can your friend get you some more?*"

"*No, he can't,*" I said. "*I'm sick of this. I can't do it. Okay?*" I started feeling really mad—at E. and M., at Ethan, even at Shanise. "*Okay, it was one thing when I was with Ethan, and I can even understand why people would resent him. Hell, I even resent him. And I can understand too that people would resent me for being with him. I guess. But we're broken up. And it wasn't him who did me the favor this time. It was Sam, and for him to do that for me . . . I won't ask him to do it again. That's for sure.*" I must have been yelling at this point because Officer Frank came over to see what was going on. Shanise told him it was nothing, just a discussion between girls on the rag, and I said, no, it's not, and I told him that Eloise and Molasses had been threatening me.

After OF left, she turned on me.

"*Okay, she's far from perfect, but she's still my cousin. And now her mom will tell my mom and it's all going to come down on me . . . Us,*" she said, and she started to cry and stomped away.

Now that I'm writing about it, I know that it's just that she was freaked out about what's happening to her so she's taking it out on me.

OF came back to ask what was going on, all mad because I'd upset Shanise. Like those two were on The Love Boat and didn't have a care in the world. I was so tempted to tell him that she never took the pill—just to even the playing field, because it felt like I was the one getting all the shit. I told him that E. and M. should be in solitary, both of them, but he just laughed. He laughed! Fuck him.

Before he went back over to his romantic little scene with Shanise, he said this: "*That friend of yours. Just so you know, was arrested. He, or she, I don't know, whatever it is, had illegal drugs on him.*"

"*That's impossible!*" I cried. "*I saw him. He visited me.*"

"It was on the way out. Arrested. You have some bad friends, Prisoner Harlow."

So that's how it is now. We're fucked.

Finally, I shared my plan with Shanise. It was as much about her and the baby as it ever was about me anyway.

Neither of us sees any other way out.

THE MAN IS GAY

Sam

Sam holds himself erect in the very middle of the back seat, sure that the armrests are covered in germs. Even though he's in the back seat of a cruiser, he is giddy that he didn't get caught for the actual crime he'd committed—slipping the powder-filled baggie under the table to Garnet—and instead is being brought in for something he knows isn't a crime. He'd forgotten about the joint that was tucked into the lining of his purse. So long as they don't find anything else, they'll have to let him go; possession of a small amount of marijuana isn't a criminal offense.

But Tommy is missing, which is really worrying him. Larry thinks it's because he saw him in a dress: he thinks his son fled in an adolescent huff. This version of things comforts Sam, who is anxious that he and Carol have landed his coworker in a heap of trouble.

***

"I don't know where he went," Larry had told him. "And it's worse than that. I think it's my fault."

This was last night. Sam was in bed, recovering from a spectacular hangover. Carol had marched off, slamming the door behind her, leaving Larry—who was more sympathetic—standing awkwardly in the bedroom. He leaned on one leg and then the other, his hands on his hips and then in his pockets and then smoothing his hair, his mustache. He didn't understand that Sam, still under the covers, badly needed to pee.

"Tommy saw me. In the dress." Larry sat down on the chair in the corner of the room. It was covered in clothes, but he perched on the edge of the seat.

"Careful, that one's delicate," Sam said, pointing at a sequined article on the arm.

Larry moved it. "Pretty," he said absently.

"Larry," Sam interrupted. "Go to the kitchen, will you? Make some tea. Or coffee. I have to . . . relieve myself."

"Sorry, sorry." Larry bowed on his way out.

When Sam got to the kitchen, Larry was standing by the window.

"You know what? I'm sorry. I actually came here because I wanted to make sure you were okay. And now I've laid all my problems on you. I don't know what I'm doing."

"Not at all," Sam said, trying to grasp what was going on. He'd spent the last twenty-four hours in bed, ignoring the world. Now Larry was apologizing to him, after Sam had lied to him and then missed work for a second time without calling. He wasn't sure he could trust his good fortune.

"I'd better go. I'm glad to know you're alive, though. I really am. You'll be at work in the morning?"

Sam finished tying the belt of his bathrobe. He put on his favorite smile—the one he used on stage to make the crowd love him. "For the best boss in the world? Of course I'll be there!"

***

But now he might miss work, because he's in the back seat of this cruiser, and he knows that they might very well keep him for days.

Sam hopes Larry is right, that Tommy was upset with his dad, or that he was on a simple bender and blew off work. He prays that the kid hasn't gotten into trouble with the Dairy Queen dealers. He needs to get that box to its rightful owner, and fast. But first there is the immediate problem. The two police officers seem amused, and Sam is on his best behavior. The one in the passenger seat is a redheaded woman. Sam expresses admiration for her hair color and she smirks at her partner—a handsome Black man who smiles back at her and Sam can tell, from the way her smirk is halfway to a smile, that she actually liked the compliment.

They arrive at the station and Sam is relieved to stand up and have the handcuffs removed. His hair had been hanging in front of his face and finally he can push it back. When they lock him up, he paces, seeing himself and his problems as though he were a character in a movie—here he is, in a jail cell, pacing, worrying, hoping to make up for his bad deeds.

He's not there for long, thank God. The redheaded woman unlocks the cell and tells him he's free to go.

"It's Clairol," she whispers as she relocks the cell behind them.

He puts his hand on her forearm. "Honey, it looks one-hundred-percent natural. I kid you not."

Back in his apartment, Sam pulls the box down from the shelf in the closet and surveys the contents one more time: bags of powder, marijuana, some rolled joints, and cash. He thinks the right thing to do would be to pay for the drugs he took—which is what he and Carol had gone to the Dairy Queen to do in the first place. But it's not like the kid from the DQ had been doing an honest day's work. It's not like he'd been digging potatoes and Sam and Carol were stealing them from him. And besides, he and Carol had to work so hard to get the thing . . . and get it open.

He's thinking about crime and risk. Don't criminals deserve to make a lot of money? Look at the risks they take every day! He could use a little extra cash, and he feels as though he's earned it. He slips two twenties into his wallet and then takes two more—for Carol—and closes the box as best he can. He feels a little guilty for that, too—ruining the box with Ronaldo's power tool. Ronaldo! Sam feels suddenly lighter and imagines spending the forty dollars on a nice meal for the two of them. He slips the money into his pocket and heads up to Carol's apartment.

He rushes in when she opens the door, trying his best to diffuse her anger by sparking past her into the living room.

"Well, such an afternoon I've had, let me tell you." He sits on the armchair, puts his flowered duffel bag on the floor. Carol remains standing. "Carol, I'm sorry. I fucked up." He says this looking directly at her, and expects her to unleash some fury or at least some guilt, but she just gazes into the distance. "I'd love some soda. Do you have any?" She nods and goes to the kitchen. He calls to her while she pours. "I did it, Carol. I brought the stuff to Garnet. She should be fine."

When Carol comes back with his glass of Coke, there are tears in her eyes. "She'll be fine? But for how long?"

Sam takes the glass she offers him. "But I did it, honey. I did what I was supposed to. I brought cocaine into the prison, and I smuggled it to her under the table, and now she's going to be fine."

Carol sits on the sofa, shoves her hands between her knees as though she is cold. Sam notices that the slope of her shoulders appears to be solidifying—where before she just slouched, now the curve in her spine seems to have become permanent. He pulls his own shoulders back and takes a sip.

"It's not going to be good enough. You know? What are we—are we going to have to keep breaking the law because they can't keep her safe in there? We couldn't keep her safe from Ethan, and we can't keep her safe now. Maybe the world doesn't want her. Maybe it doesn't want any of us."

"Carol, love." Sam puts his glass on the coffee table and moves around to sit next to her. "Don't go thinking that. Hey! I didn't tell you. I got arrested!" He waits for her to express surprise, laughter, anything, but she doesn't. He goes on, tells her the story. Whenever she looks as though she might cry, because she's barely listening to him, he doubles down, embellishes: the officers were actually in love with each other; the woman wrote down the name of the color she uses on her hair; he paced for hours in the cell; he even invented a dangerous cellmate, who, luckily, didn't beat him up, or Sam would probably be dead now.

"Honey?" he says, as he runs out of story to tell. "Carol, what? What's wrong?"

"Nothing," she says, obviously lying. They sit in silence for a while.

"Larry's son is missing," Sam says. "He saw Larry in a dress." Carol looks mildly interested, but not enough to ask any follow-up questions.

"Anyway," Sam says, "I have to get that box back to the Dairy Queen. I'm not sure how, but we got what we needed and now we have to get it back."

"I disagree," Carol says. "What if she needs more? What if we have to get her something else?"

"Honey, I am not going back there with any illegal substances. Didn't I just tell you I got arrested? They'll be searching me very thoroughly from now on. Not that they didn't before. It was a dangerous thing for me to do. Extremely."

"Give it to me, then. I'll keep it in case she needs more."

"I can't! I have to bring it back! You know that. Larry's kid, Tommy. He said he was being blamed for the thing, and he hasn't been at work. Carol. What if something happened to him? What if he's going to get hurt?"

Carol slides away from Sam, putting several inches between them. She stares straight ahead. "You're not going to give it to me?"

Sam stands up. He has a tepid temper but is feeling as fiery as he ever has. "If you were so worried, why didn't you go get the box yourself and smuggle it in?

Huh? Carol? Why did you wait for me to do it? You knew where it was. Why didn't you come up to my apartment and take it and bring it to her?"

"I don't have an answer for that," Carol says mechanically. "I don't have an answer."

"Oh snap out of it!" Sam says. "You have to stop worrying so much and making people feel guilty! Even Garnet says you're making her life harder, with all your worrying, the pressure."

"When were you going to tell me about Ronaldo?" she says.

"What?" Sam squeaks. "What do you mean? What does that have to do with the price of milk in China?"

"We're friends, or so I thought." Carol is moving now, across the living room. There is a low table with framed photographs on it and she picks up one of her and Garnet, when Garnet was in fifth grade. Sam took it when the three of them went for a day trip to see the Statue of Liberty. Mother and daughter have the same hair, but Garnet has her father's flat nose and blue eyes. She was leaning into her mother against the wall at the top of the torch, the sky was blue, the city a mottled palette of red brick, cement, and glass. Carol had her arms around her daughter and was squeezing tight. She had confessed as they'd ridden the elevator back down to ground level that she'd been more frightened than Garnet; she was pretending to keep her daughter safe, but what she was really doing was clinging on to her for her own dear life.

"Just another thing I've lost to you," Carol says acidly. Sam thinks she's talking about Ronaldo, but she's staring at the picture of Garnet. Sam throws both hands up in a gesture of frustration. He isn't going to feel guilty for having an affair with Ronaldo. The man is gay, so Carol didn't have a chance. That isn't his fault, is it? Besides, she didn't tell him anything about her crush. And he hadn't told her about Ronaldo yet, which doesn't mean he wasn't going to tell her. He hadn't gotten around to it, that's all. And if she were talking about Garnet, well, that was ridiculous. It's her daughter, and if she thinks she's losing her to someone, well, then she's got a serious problem. "You know what?" he says. "I'm done talking to you. Good luck."

Soon after he slams the door, his anger starts to dissipate. He feels sorry for her. But that's not a basis for a friendship. He needs friends he can respect. Maybe his friendship with Carol has reached its end. If she's going to deny him happiness because it hurts her feelings, well then, maybe it's time to let it fizzle. Maybe it's time to really move to the city.

Back in his apartment, he puts Carol out of his head and takes the box down. "Shit," he says as he dumps the clothes from his duffel bag and puts in the box. "Now I have to take the bus."

SIMONE TOLD ME

Tommy

When he wakes up, it is to the sound of the padlock being unhinged and the door squeaking open. Tommy shuffles his feet around, trying to push into a sitting position and block the gash of light from his eyes with both hands. The two minions are dragging a bag of something. Concrete? No, he can see it's not a bag of something, it's a bag of someone. There are arms hanging to each side. The person is not moving. Dead? Unconscious?

They leave the person in a heap and go off again, pulling the door closed. Tommy lights the lantern, and he can see, as he moves closer, that the unconscious person is Derby. Tommy puts his hand under his nose, and there is a slight warmness coming from his nostrils. He is alive. Tommy slides as far away from him as he can.

There's nothing left to eat or drink besides about an eighth of the gallon of water and Tommy imagines that the South Americans are going to starve them until one kills the other. And eats him. He looks around the place for something to defend himself with. Neither of them is especially buff, but Tommy is certain that if it came down to it, Derby would be able to knock him silly.

Tommy is wearing the sweatpants that Derby brought—before they decided he might be the one responsible—and his pee-stiffened jeans are crumpled in the corner. He thinks maybe he could use them to tie Derby's wrists. He grabs them but gags when the smell wafts up. It's like they're frozen, even though it's not cold, which makes him think about what kind of salts and minerals must be in urine.

He scans the place in the glow of the lamp: a few piles of old newspapers. Charred wood from homeless people building fires. The carcass of a television. There are some rusted, bent nails around the floor. They are weakened with age, lumpy and orange, and when he puts pressure on them, they snap. A picture frame with no picture. He picks it up and it breaks into several pieces. The TV is his best bet. He pulls the back away from the front. It's so old and decrepit that it comes apart easily. He clutches the silvery screen in its plastic frame. This is all that stands between Derby and him. He will smash it over Derby's head if he tries anything. He sits against the wall and waits. Something about the wholeness of the TV screen in the midst of the wreckage of this container calms him. He likes the fact that it's smooth and square—not jagged or rusty.

Finally, Derby starts to groan and move.

When he comes to, the first thing he says is, "My fucking head. Oh, shit my fucking head."

Tommy realizes with relief that when a person is knocked unconscious, they don't just pop up like they do in the movies and jump back into the fight. Derby is hurting. He's shivering, so Tommy takes his sweatshirt and lays it over his shoulders. Derby opens his eyes but doesn't seem to recognize him at first. Finally, he squints and says, "You asshole."

"I'm an asshole?" Tommy says. "I didn't even do anything, and these assholes have had me locked up for . . . How the fuck am I the asshole? Asshole."

But Derby has fallen back to sleep. Tommy is so tired that nothing really hurts anymore, and his body is like a sponge that hasn't been used yet. Just airy and stiff. And he doesn't think about anything for a while.

After a long time, Derby rolls onto his side and yawns.

"How's Hanky?" Tommy says, trying to act like there's nothing wrong here.

"Fuck if I know. Probably watching TV. You know Hanky. Probably doesn't even notice we're both gone."

"Derb. We gotta get outta here," Tommy says, without much energy.

"Dude. I couldn't give a shit if you get out of here or not."

"They must think you took the stuff yourself, or they wouldn't have thrown you in here with me. Right?"

"Naw. They just want to punish me for letting you get away with it. It's cool. It's a test for me."

"So. You still think I took it."

"I know you took it."

By this point, Derby is starting to come back to life a little.

"They could've killed you, you know," Tommy says. "And anyway, why are you gonna be such an asshole to me when I didn't do a thing?"

"Tom. You were the last one there. It had to be you."

"What about the lady? The one who didn't eat her chicken strips. She was there too. Did you go find her? Maybe she took it."

At this Derby's body starts to shake a bit, because he's laughing. His laugh is snorty and sarcastic. He gets up and pisses in a corner.

"Dude, the bucket," Tommy says, but Derby ignores him.

"I wish we had a TV," Derby says. Tommy makes a shadow rabbit out of his hand and opens and closes the jaw against the TV screen. Derby doesn't even smile. In the light of the flickering lantern, their two faces wink like a couple of Halloween pumpkins.

And then the lantern dies. It's nighttime now and it's pitch dark. Tommy takes out a lighter, but the little flame doesn't do much and his thumb quickly gets hot. "Don't waste that," Derby says. "We don't need to see nothing. We both know there's nothing in here but us and a heap of garbage."

"I never asked you," Tommy said, trying to keep him talking. "You got any brothers or sisters?"

"Yeah."

"Which one?"

"Sisters."

"What're you gonna do when we get out of here?"

"Get laid, first thing."

"Yeah? But what about long-term? You're not gonna work at DQ your whole life."

"That's a very mature question," he says. "Most dudes don't even think about that shit."

"Well, I do."

"Me too. I think about it a lot. But you might've noticed that I'm more mature than most."

Tommy smirks in the dark. "You're not going to have your job, though? I mean . . . dealing? You'll be at the DQ, assuming we survive, but you won't work for those guys, right? Not after this."

"They'll get over it." Derby rolls over and sighs. "It's not the first time they've roughed me up."

"Jesus."

"Yeah, well. I'm proving myself, that's all. They're probably testing me. These guys are more big-time than you know."

"So, they want to test you or something, what are they going to do with me?"

"They'll probably have to kill you. That's why I'm telling you things I shouldn't. You shouldn't even know who they are."

"I don't know who they are," Tommy says. "Tell them I have no idea who they are. I couldn't identify any of them if I tried."

Derby stays quiet. Tommy can make out his silhouette. He's like a little hill in moonlight. After some time, he starts to snore.

Tommy sleeps.

In the morning, they are woken by a sudden wind that throws rocks and sticks against the side of the container. There's a flash for an instant and almost simultaneously thunder shakes everything, rolls away like gigantic boulders down a rocky mountain.

"What the fuck?" Derby says.

"Thunder," Tommy says, rubbing his eyes.

Another flash is accompanied by a deafening crack. Tommy scrambles to his feet. The rain starts—like God is dumping a watering can half the size of Lake Erie over the forest.

"If it hits this box, we'll be electrocuted," Tommy yells, putting the TV screen on the ground and balancing on top of it, hoping that glass doesn't conduct electricity. This keeps up for about six or seven cracks of thunder. Tommy is trying not to touch the walls and he's perched on the TV glass; he feels like one of those toys—the ones with wooden joints that are bound together with string and when you push the bottom the doll collapses.

In the flashes, he can see Derby is still lying on the floor.

Another flash, but the thunder a few seconds behind it.

"I think it's getting farther away," Derby yells above the sound of the deluge. Thunderstorms are loud anyway, but in a metal box, the sound is amplified and it's as though there are people on the roof using jackhammers to dig up pavement. Rain washes over the box; the wind and the water seem to make it wobble like it's floating. Water is streaming down some of the walls, making soggy puddles on the floor. The shit that Tommy left in the corner starts to smell worse.

One Mississippi, two Mississippi, three . . . then it's five seconds away, then the thunder comes from miles away and Tommy isn't sure if it was even attached to a flash of lightning anymore. Then, finally, the rain and wind die down.

"Derb?"

From the other side of the container comes Derby's voice, and he's laughing.

"You're feeling better?" Tommy says. "Your head feels better?"

"Naw. Not really." He stops laughing and is completely quiet.

"Derb? You okay?" Tommy says.

"Fine. I'm just fucking with you."

"Derby, did they tell you to kill me?" Tommy's voice is meek.

"Maybe," he says. "Maybe not."

"Well, if you're going to kill me, why not tell me some stuff first. Satisfy my curiosity. Plus, if I'm dead, you'll be locked in here with a dead person. That won't be any fun for you."

"You're right, Tom. I don't want to sit here with you dead. But maybe I can get out when I want."

"You can get out when you want?"

"Maybe."

"How?"

"Maybe I got a key in my pocket?"

"You got a key in your pocket?"

"Yeah."

"The lock is on the outside. And anyway. What the fuck?"

"You're a bug, and I'm pulling your legs off one at a time." Derby's voice is kind of hollow, like it's coming straight out of his lungs and up his windpipe without making any kind of a pit stop at his brain.

"Derb."

He chuckles. Teh, heh, heh.

"Why the fuck do you have it in for me?" Tommy pulls the lighter out of his pocket and lights it. He sees Derby more clearly, and the expression on his face is fear. Like a little kid. But then he gets control and arranges his features into a sinister mask.

Tommy lets the lighter go out and slides down with his back against the wall until he's sitting with his knees pulled up. "Derb," he says. "Cut the shit. There's no key and you know it."

"You don't know nothing," Derby says. "You don't know shit, and I know everything."

Tommy starts to giggle because Derby sounds like such a little kid. Like what the fuck is that supposed to mean? Does he really think that Tommy knows nothing and he knows everything?

"Okay," Tommy says. "If I know nothing and you know everything, why don't you tell me some stuff?"

"What do you want to know?"

"Well, first of all, Why do you have it in for me? You've always acted like a dick to me, and I'm wondering if you're jealous of me and Hanky." Derby makes sounds like a wild cat. But Tommy goes on, suddenly giddy with the power to really piss him off. "Like, do you think you're . . . you know . . . that you're hot for Hanky?"

Derby comes thrashing and lands on Tommy, his hands crawling up Tommy's chest until they find his neck and fasten around it, and Tommy realizes that this is what he wanted. To have it out. To take him on. Fuck him and his bullying fucking Pablo Escobar act. Fuck them all.

Derby isn't as strong as Tommy thought he would be, because of the concussion probably, but Tommy isn't that strong either, and it's like they're two eighty-year-old men rolling over and over each other. Tommy knocks one of Derby's hands off his neck but he gets it back; Tommy's fingers are on Derby's face, prowling for his eyeballs. His palm finds Derby's nose and pushes it up and away but Derby shakes him off—they're both getting slippery with sweat— Derby's hands tighten on Tommy's neck and he doesn't have the strength to get them off and he can't breathe and all the fear that had gone has come back, double strength.

Tommy starts to black out, so he stops struggling, and when he does, his airway gets opened for a second and he gets some breath, comes back to life, and Derby has relaxed his grip enough—probably because he thought he'd won—that Tommy manages finally to throw him off.

They are both panting. Finally, Tommy pulls out his lighter. Derby is in a ball on his side.

"Derby."

"Fuck off."

"What the fuck. You tried to kill me."

"Naw. If I'd wanted to I would've." But his voice is muffled, weak. Tommy lets the flame go out, and it is dark again.

"Listen. We might both be killed. I don't want to live my last moments being an asshole, and I'm sure you don't either."

"Right, Gandhi. I see what you're saying." Tommy can hear Derby push himself into a sitting position.

"Seriously."

"Yeah, seriously. But nobody's going to die, except, maybe, you."

"Right. What makes you so sure they're going to let you live?"

"Whatever. I've been working for them for a long time. I can handle them."

"We need to work together to try and get out of here—that's what we have to do."

"Oh okay. So, you seem to know everything. You're just a fucking freak with a freak for a father."

Tommy goes cold. If he weren't sitting already, he'd fall over. "What did you say?"

"I said your father's queer."

Before he can begin to reason with himself, to shuffle through ways Derby might have found out about his dad, he's on his feet and flying across the space between them. He gets his hands around Derby's neck and is trying to smother the life out of him. But neither of them has any energy, and they both flop onto their backs.

Tommy is panting. "That thing you said about my father. What did you mean?"

"I mean Simone told me about him."

Simone told him. The words might as well be bullets because that thing Tommy had been keeping himself alive for is gone, just like that, in three words: Simone. Told. Me.

Tommy pictures her, with him, telling him Tommy's secret. The thing that made them connect. The thing that she promised she wouldn't tell. Tommy may be crying, he's not sure. He may be keening over the death of the last little bit of goodness that he thought he might live for. He has nothing left to say. So he doesn't say anything.

ANGORA TENTACLES

Sam

The bus stops down the block and across the street from DQ. Sam wonders what he should order and whether he should hand the dealer the box out in the open or tell him that he has it and ask him to meet him outside. There's probably a camera trained on the counter, in case of robbery. He imagines himself from above, on flickering black-and-white film.

Or maybe he should just go down that alley, where Carol followed Tommy, and put the box on the ground. He approaches slowly, pretends to read a flyer taped to the outside of the window. There aren't any customers inside, so he pulls the glass door, cradling the duffel bag.

The dealer is in the back but approaches slowly when the bell rings. He is shorter than Sam would have imagined him, with a shaggy but well-kept head of hair. He wears a tie and looks a boyish thirtysomething.

"Good afternoon," he says.

"Good afternoon," Sam responds. He stares at the man who waits for his order.

"Can I help you?"

Sam switches the duffel bag to his other hand, wipes the sweat off the one that had been holding it. He looks at the corners of the ceiling but doesn't see any cameras. "I, uh. I think I have something of yours."

The man seems to be looking for something under the counter with his hand, without taking his eyes off of Sam.

"I don't think so. Do I know you?"

"You're missing something, aren't you?"

"No. I don't think I am."

"You're not missing something? You're sure? Something you had out back?"

"Sorry ma'am. I'm not sure . . . did you want to order something?"

"Well. No. I mean maybe . . ."

The man takes his hand out from under the countertop, and there is a cell phone in it. "There is a police station a block away," he says. "I have them on speed dial."

***

Back on the bus, Sam wonders if Carol is right. Maybe they should keep the box. If that was the drug dealer, then he must have either forgotten about the missing box or decided it wasn't worth his while getting it back. But maybe that was just a guy who works there. Maybe the DQ isn't actually a drug mart, but just one guy . . . And Sam doesn't know who that guy is because it was Carol who'd gone in looking for drugs and Carol who had ultimately stolen them. He could ask Carol to come with him, but he doesn't think she'd come, and besides, he can't go crawling back asking for help after the fight they just had. He gets off on Hawthorne and changes buses.

***

The sun is getting low as Sam approaches the old mill. The contractor's van isn't there. Nobody is there, and the demoed building is all cleaned out. Sam sits down on a rock to consider what's going on inside his heart. He's not sure what's making him more upset: that Ronaldo might reject him, or that he doesn't seem to have any hope of returning the box to its rightful owner. Well, he thinks, at least he can find Ronaldo—at Wattsville Community College. Even though the weight of the duffel bag is starting to strain his shoulder, Sam doesn't want to get on another city bus and decides to walk home. The light is becoming orange and slanted and picks out the colors of the forest like a magnet to metal, making them zing. He makes his way across the parking lot and over to the trail that follows the Otis toward home.

"Oh for God's sake, you must be kidding me." A guy on an ATV comes racing down the trail from the other direction, and Sam tries to hide behind a tree. The ATV slows down as it approaches and comes to a stop.

"Hey lady," the guy has a Latin American accent. Sam steps away from the tree, straightening his clothes. "You shouldn't be walking these woods, you know? These woods are dangerous."

"Oh, thanks. Yes, it's just shorter than taking the road. And Route 22 is so ugly."

"You should get out of here," he says. "Walk on the street."

"Okay. Okay, thanks," Sam says, backing up. The man revs the engine but doesn't move.

"Hey!" Sam says, "Do you know Jorge and Jaime? They're friends of mine. From Honduras?"

It's a silly question, he knows. Just the first thing that popped into his head.

The man ignores the question. "What you got in the bag?"

"Oh this? Nothing. Just my makeup and a couple of other things."

The man revs the engine again and takes off, tipping his sunglasses back down onto his nose.

***

The next morning, Sam prays that Tommy will be at work. If Tommy is at work, Sam will give the box to him and he can do with it whatever he likes. But Tommy doesn't show up, and Larry has to fill in on the line. Again. Jorge and Jaime don't seem to notice the strained silence of their two coworkers. Larry looks worried as hell and Sam casts sidelong glances at the door, hoping Tommy will come in, and at Larry, feeling his anxiety over his missing son.

At break time, Larry goes to his desk and sits quietly. A storm passed through in the early-morning hours while they were working, but they hadn't heard it over the sound of the machinery. There are sudden puddles on the pavement and the mulch is soggy. Jorge goes in and grabs extras of yesterday's newspapers; the men layer them on the benches before sitting.

"Ronaldo?" Sam says to Jorge and Jaime. "You know where Ronaldo works?"

Jorge nods and says, "Community College."

"Yes, yes, but with McMaster?"

Jorge shakes his head and takes a bite of the sandwich he's pulled out of a paper bag. Sam sits in silence until Larry comes and sits down; he doesn't notice that the wood is damp.

"I called my ex-wife," Larry says. "It wasn't a good idea."

"Does she know anything?" Sam asks. "Is he there?"

"No. And now I've got her on my case because she thinks I'm a bad parent. Because I'm depraved. Maybe she's right. Maybe she was right. To leave. Jesus."

"Larry, I'm sorry. He'll turn up. I know he will!"

Larry looks doubtful. "I called the police," he says, and his eyes fill with tears. He wipes them roughly with a handkerchief and blows his nose. Jorge and Jaime reduce their conversation to whispers and cast sidelong, sympathetic glances.

"They'll be coming around here." Larry motions in the direction of the Hondurans. "They'll have to be gone. Otherwise, the cops will start asking questions. So I have to fire them too."

"No!" Sam says. "No! Oh, Larry, he'll turn up! I'm sure of it!"

"But I don't care," Larry says, ignoring Sam. "I don't give a damn about anything. At all. This job. Nothing. If something has happened to him."

"Have you gone to his apartment?"

"Of course I have. Hanky—that's his roommate—says that their other roommate has disappeared too. That they're probably together and so not to worry."

Sam slaps the table with his palm. "See! Exactly! They're together! So, you shouldn't worry."

Larry shakes his head. "I don't trust that kid at all. The couple times I've met him. He works at the Dairy Queen but has all these fancy video game consoles and expensive sneakers. No. I don't trust that kid at all. If Tommy's with him, it can't be good."

Break time is long over, but Larry doesn't move. Sam is putting it together. Dairy Queen. It's Tommy's roommate. But why would he be missing, too? It doesn't make any sense.

"I'll have to tell them today," Larry says, meaning Jorge and Jaime. "I'll have to let them go. At least for the time being. To protect them. And me. The temp agency will send workers."

Sam puts his arm around Larry's shoulder and gives him a squeeze. "I'll be here for you, okay?" he says, feeling the sting of tears in his own eyes. "I'll be here. Now, come on. Let's get those ads inserted."

***

After work Sam takes the bus to Wattsville Community College. He descends the stairs to the cafeteria. It's lunchtime and there are a lot of people milling, in line to get their lunches. Neither Ronaldo, cooking behind the counter, nor Carol, on her seat at the register, sees him at first. He tries to be nonchalant, holds the duffel bag under his arm as though it were a stack of library books. As he slides into a seat at the table closest to the kitchen entrance, three girls who are on the other side of the table seem startled. Their conversation becomes cardboard and static: "Yeah, so like I was saying, I really like the class. You like the class?" And the other two nod, trying not to stare. Sam slides off his seat and pushes open the door that says Employees Only. He can hear the girls shushing each other and giggling.

Ronaldo, when he sees him in the kitchen, grabs him by both shoulders. "Where were you? Jesus. You have that?" he grabs the duffel bag like he's going to take it, but leaves it in Sam's hands.

"I looked for you at the mill, but you weren't there."

"No, we finished that job. Wait here." Ronaldo goes back to the grill, flips a burger and slides a sandwich onto a plate.

"That's not mine," a kid says, sliding the sandwich down the metal rails to another kid.

"Do you mind cooking it?" says another after Ronaldo puts a nearly raw burger on a bun and pushes it across. Behind him, smoke is beginning to thicken above a chicken cutlet.

Carol looks up from the cash register; she stops ringing orders, her hand hovering over the keys. Ronaldo waves at her. "No problem! Just a chicken. No problem." She can't see Sam behind the grill area, sitting on an overturned milk crate next to the walk-in freezer. He is clutching the duffel bag and shaking—he's not sure if it's fear or if it's excitement at being so close to Ronaldo. Either way, he can feel that he is made up of cells that have an electrical charge. They are shivering, bumping into one another and making him feel supremely, magnetically alive.

He doesn't want Carol to know he's here, of course. She wants to keep the box, and why wouldn't she? They got away with stealing it. Nobody suspects them. But she has no idea that Ronaldo is also involved—that it is his boss who will be exacting revenge on whoever he thinks took it. That other kid—Tommy's roommate—is missing, too, and Sam couldn't live with his conscience if anything were to happen to either one of those kids. Finally, after what feels like hours but is actually less than five minutes, Ronaldo crouches in front of him.

His eyes are a shade of brown that verges on orange and, when he trains them on Sam, Sam feels like he could melt, dissolve in diamond-shaped sections through the milk crate he is sitting on.

"We have to get this back," Ronaldo says, putting his hand on the duffel bag, sliding open the zipper. "It is better if I do it. You should just give it to me."

The thought makes Sam limp. All of that excitement—of being with Ronaldo, of doing the right thing to help Tommy—would be gone if he just handed over the box. He holds on; he doesn't want to let Ronaldo take it away. Someone says, "Hello?" and Ronaldo stands up and goes back to the grill. "Chicken nuggets?" The fryolator sounds like a sudden rainstorm. Then Ronaldo is back.

"I took it," Sam says. "I can't let you get blamed for it. I'll give it back. I tried to bring it to the Dairy Queen. But where should I take it?"

Ronaldo puts his palm on the side of Sam's face. "I can't let you get hurt," he says. "I mean, they would for sure hurt you."

Ronaldo is a treasure. Sam can't believe his luck. To think this amazing man is willing to risk himself to save Sam . . .

He takes Ronaldo by the shoulders and pulls him into an embrace. Ronaldo is on his knees, leaning into Sam. Sam is sweating. He is breathing hard, his exhales coming long and slow. And then, "Hey! My nuggets are burning!" The words enter their consciousness slowly, like language from another planet. They don't know what to make of it. "Can I have my chicken nuggets?" Before it can dawn on them, Carol crashes through the kitchen door.

"What the—? Sam? Ron? Jesus." She goes to the fryolator, pulls out the metal basket full of smoking brown nuggets, dumps them into a red-checked paper boat, and pushes them across the counter.

"Take them. They're free," she says.

Ronaldo is mute, standing in the opening between the kitchen and the grill, watching her. She slams the wire basket onto the counter, launching strings of white lettuce and watery tomato slices out of their plastic boxes.

Back in the kitchen, she can't reach her pocketbook. It is on a high shelf that she normally uses the milk crate to get to, but Sam is still sitting on it. "I need that," she says, pointing at it. Sam jumps up.

"I see you have the box," she says, looking at the duffel bag.

"Carol. I can explain."

"Okay," she says. "Just get me my pocketbook first."

He stands on the milk crate and pulls it down. Then, before he can start to explain why he is here, she storms out. Sam follows her as far as the door, watches her go. There are students in line at the cash register, but she ignores them.

"Wait here," Ronaldo says to Sam. Sam can't hear what he says to the kids in line, but they all murmur and laugh and smile and shuffle off to tables without paying. Ronaldo takes the cash drawer out, puts it on the top shelf—where Carol had kept her pocketbook—and pulls the grate down in front of the grill.

At the bus stop, they are both nervous. Ronaldo gets on first and walks to the back. When Sam follows, he motions to a seat further toward the front, away from him. Sam understands and sits, the duffel bag on his lap. At first Sam thinks it is because Ronaldo is ashamed to be near him but realizes quickly that Ronaldo wants to protect him from whoever the bad men are who are looking for the box.

***

"I still don't get what we're doing here," Sam says as the bus pulls away. "The job is finished. I was just here, looking for you yesterday, and there wasn't anybody."

Ronaldo leads Sam into the cleaned-out mill structure. He gives Sam a quick kiss before wiggling a stone from the wall and pulling out a small gun. The sight of the gun gives Sam an urgent need to go to the bathroom. Number two. He leans against the wall and clutches his stomach until the feeling passes.

"You stay here," Ronaldo says as he tucks the gun into the back of his waistband.

"No," Sam says, "I'm sticking with you." He follows closely behind, his eyes trained on the bottom of Ronaldo's T-shirt, where the fabric is pushed out by the square shape of the gun's handle.

Sam has passed the rusted-out storage container a million times, but now, as they approach, he can see that the door is closed and that there is padlock on the outside. Ronaldo puts his arm out to keep Sam from coming any closer, pulls the gun from his pants and shoots off the lock.

At the noise, voices awaken inside the container. Ronaldo scrapes open the door, and there they are.

"Tommy!" Sam says. "Oh my God! Thank God you're okay! You are okay?"

"Jesus. What the fuck are you doing here?" Tommy says, pushing himself to his feet. He looks haggard, as though he were sixty years old, not twenty. His hair has a layer of gray dust matted over it, and there are streaks of dirt on his skin and his clothes. "You fucking asshole. You have the box! I knew it! I knew it was you and your friend." Sam winces at Tommy's harsh words, but Tommy is weak and, as his eyes adjust to the light, he realizes he is being set free. He walks, or rather limps, toward Route 22. The other kid is slower to move. He is standing in front of Ronaldo, staring with hard eyes.

"You go too," Ronaldo says.

"Where's Ignacio?"

"He'll be in touch."

Sam looks back and forth between them, and at Tommy, who is hobbling toward the road.

"He's going to tell someone," the kid says. "You shouldn't let him go."

Ronaldo trains the gun on the kid's head and then moves it like he can brush the kid away. "Go," he says. "And leave the kid alone. He won't tell anyone."

Derby looks suspicious. As he edges past Sam, he mutters "freak" under his breath. "Fucking freak."

Ronaldo hears him and fires a shot into the sky, causing him to jump and, when he realizes that he hasn't been hit, run away.

After both boys have gone, Ronaldo puts the box inside the container, along with the gun, then pushes the door closed. The sound of the scraping door bleeds into another sound. An ATV. The revving gets louder as it crests a hill on the path in the woods and comes barreling toward them.

"*Mierda*," Ronaldo says. "Run!"

Sam heads along the path but doesn't know if Ronaldo is behind him. He keeps running, and can hear the ATV coming upon him quickly. He dodges into the woods, breaking through branches and over rocks, and wades into the river. The sound has stopped, and he looks back. The driver has dismounted and is pointing his gun at Sam.

Sam dives under and swims with all his might, kicking loose his cowboy boots. Fleetingly he wonders if he'll be able to come back and find them later. They are his favorites. He swims out into the river, but before he can reach the quickening current, pain blasts through his right calf. He touches it and feels a stream of what he understands is his blood seeping from a hole.

Everything starts to go dark. He thinks he will sink, but he treads water, slides out of the angora sweater that had swelled and stretched like tentacles around his arms. Another shot is fired, and Sam sees the man on the path wilt and fall to the ground. He thinks he can hear the thud of the man's body as it lands, but the rush of water would make hearing that impossible. He must be outside his body, because he is hovering over the man who now lies still on the ground. Yet Sam is still in the water. It is entering his ears. The pain is fading. Is there a solar eclipse? Sam sees, through a vague foggy tunnel, like the ending of the Looney Tunes cartoons he used to watch as a child—D-d-d-d-dat's all folks!—Ronaldo, diving head first after him.

THE RIVER IS JUST

Carol

Carol remembers dimly that she didn't take the money from the cash register and lock it in the safe before leaving. That detail gets plopped into the brew of nervous tension roiling around inside her and she forgets about it, but not until after it has added to her angst.

She drives erratically, her foot pecking back and forth between the gas and the brake and a couple of cars honk and pass. She is eating a packet of Chips Ahoy, and there is melted chocolate on the steering wheel. One driver gives her the finger, which makes her burst out laughing, but there are tears coming down her cheeks as well.

Finally, she pulls over near the Route 22 bridge, onto a little-used shoulder, the tires crunching over the gravel. The car jerks when she hits the brake. She pulls as far off the main road as she can and eats a couple more cookies. Then she curls up the package and puts it on top of a bag of snacks that is on the floor in front of the passenger seat.

She can make out Stratton Island in the distance—a gray rock sticking up out of the river like a giant tumor in the earth's bloodstream. She twiddles her key chain for a bit, squeezing the tummy of the rubber bear. She opens the glove compartment and takes out her passport. She got it three years ago, when Garnet and she had been talking about taking a vacation to Mexico—which they never did. She flips through the pages, empty of stamps, and examines the photo. She looked good that day. The picture was taken at Walgreens, and the guy got her to smile. She puts passport and car keys on top of a pile of ancient maps and oil-change receipts in the glove compartment. Then she gets out and clicks the door closed.

She wipes her hands on her pants, but the chocolate is smeared into her fingernails and she feels sticky. She thinks of Sam. He has as much reason to be mad at her as she has to be mad at him, but she tries to nurse her anger anyway. Anger is fortifying, whereas heartbreak is debilitating. She tries not to but she can't help thinking of Ronaldo, and she tries to say his name with the rolling R: Dronaldo. Thronaldo. It sounds like the flowing water. She repeats his name out loud as she makes her way to the smooth rocks that lead to the river.

She made a complete fool of herself. Boy, he and Sam must have laughed over her foolishness. Or maybe they feel sorry for her, which is even worse.

The rocks are warm from the sun; the heat feels good on her butt as she scooches down. She puts her shoes on a rock, parked neatly next to each other; the water is frigid on her bare feet. She leans her hands toward the water, but can't reach it. She scoots down further, the water now creeping up past her knees, so she can get her hands in. She rubs them together, washing the chocolate away.

She used to swim as a kid, which is why she'd signed Garnet up for classes at the Y. All those years of mothering Garnet, watching Garnet swim, watching her compete, and Carol didn't once venture into the water with her. This water is frigid, but she senses that it will empty her head and cleanse her in some deep way, so she continues to slide in. It creeps up the fabric of her pants. Her thighs. Her waist. Below her breasts. She leans back, looking into the sky. There is a single cloud, directly overhead. It is shaped like a goat and it starts to edge out the sun. She closes her eyes and leans back, floating.

Something grabs her arm. Strangely, it doesn't surprise her, because she'd always suspected this river to be home to some mystical creatures. It is the perfect place for monsters to hide because you can't see the bottom. She opens her eyes, expecting to see a gigantic octopus-like creature or a diaphanous man with a flowing beard. Or Garnet.

But it is Larry. Sam's boss. From the *Chronicle*. She blinks several times, and it seems like hours pass as they look at each other, the freezing water caressing them both. Finally, she allows him to lead her to the rocky shore.

"What are you doing here?" she asks, after they've been sitting on a wide rock for a while, both of them shivering and leaning into each other for warmth.

"I . . . I followed you. For some reason." Larry is wet to his armpits; his legs are stretched in front of him. "I was following Sam. I just. Well, Sam was acting suspicious. To be honest, I thought he was in the car with you. But you got out and you were alone. I was going to go back, to find him. He's been acting weird, and my son . . . Oh my God, it's a long story. I saw you, sliding down. Doing what you were doing. And I couldn't let you."

Carol is silent, her brain working out what Larry thought she was doing. She doesn't want to deceive him but, instead of telling him that she'd just been taking a dip, in her clothes, which is crazy, she lets him believe that she had been trying to drown herself. She accepts his care and the warmth of the jacket he pulls from his trunk and wraps around her. She can't believe how good it feels to have someone take care of her.

"Are you able to drive?" he asks as they make their way back to the road.

She looks at the Buick, full of gas and junk food, and shakes her head. "Could you give me a ride?"

COMING HOME

Tommy

Tommy is tired, but he knows better than to hang around. Seeing guns and hearing gunshots can do that to you. Derby is on the loose—somewhere.

Tommy plans on fleeing, but he needs clothes. He tornadoes across the living room into his bedroom, whips a few things into a backpack, and then realizes he doesn't have any money. His wallet was in the jeans he took off in that container, not that there was a whole lot of cash in there anyway.

"What the fuck happened," Hanky says. "Derby was all fucked-up looking. And, Jesus. The cops came by. I told them you were with Simone. Were you with Simone?"

"Is he here?" Tommy stops him.

Hanky mouths the word "fuck!" and points to Derby's door.

"Money?" Tommy says.

Derby yells from his room, "Yo, Hanky! Is that dirtbag here? Tommy?"

Hanky opens his wallet, gives Tommy everything he has: twenty-seven dollars. "Go, I'll cover for you! No, he's not here," he yells to Derby. "I'll wake you up when he comes!"

Tommy flies out the door and waits at the bus stop. Twenty-seven dollars isn't enough to get to Pueblo, but it will get him to New York City. He decides that he'll call Pearl from there and ask her to pay for a ticket.

The Greyhound station is just past the Wagonwheel Pub and, as the bus passes, he catches a glimpse of Simone walking out the door and into the parking lot. Before he can think about it, he stumbles to the front of the bus and gets off a stop early. He walks back slowly, measuring how he feels with each step. She fucked me over, he tells himself. But there she is, on the dock, smoking a cigarette, chewing at her fingernails between puffs, and looking sad. He almost changes his mind, but she sees him and the cigarette-holding hand drops to her side as he approaches. Without saying anything, they hug. She says, "You look terrible! What happened?"

"I'm leaving Wattsville," he tells her. "I've had enough of this place."

"Where are you going?"

He thinks about telling her that he'd felt more for her than he'd felt for any girl in a really long time, maybe ever, and that he was heartbroken and angry because she'd deceived him. But instead, he says, "I'll call." She watches him as he turns to leave, her hand rising to her mouth again, with her cigarette.

Tommy is careful not to look back.

**

At the Port Authority, chewing an Egg McMuffin, he calls Pearl.

"Hey Mom."

"Tommy. Is everything okay?"

"Yeah, everything's fine."

"Thank God. You're safe? You're not in any trouble?"

"I'm not in any trouble."

"Thank God. Praise be. Your father called me. I was worried. I prayed."

"Dad likes to wear dresses. Did you know that?"

She's quiet, and then she starts to laugh. Her laugh is wheezy from years of smoking. "Yes, dear. I did know that."

"You think he's going to hell."

"I don't know that for sure."

"But you think so."

"All I do know is that he's not going to the heaven that I'm going to. That Quinn is going to. That you are going to, please God, if you straighten yourself out."

He can picture her. On the couch. Drinking coffee. Not far from an ashtray. Christian romance novel splayed on the table. She loves them. Dog eared, with Victorian or old-West lovelies on the cover. She trades them in at the used bookstore every couple of weeks.

"I don't know if I'm going to that heaven, Mom."

"Tommy. Of course you are. You're a good boy. I just know you're not going to end up like Camille, straying so far afield."

"What? What about Camille?"

"God save her." There is a long pause. He hears a lighter and the hollow noise of her inhale. He pictures the glowing ember flaring with the air she sucks past it, the smoke racing through the filter and into her lungs. It makes him want to smoke, but he doesn't have any cigarettes. "They found her body in the Arkansas River."

Pearl doesn't know how close Tommy and Camille were. If she knew, he's sure she would have picked a better way to tell him. The Egg McMuffin slips from his hand and lands on top of his sneaker. He's staring hard at it, as if with enough concentration he can stop time, shut down the world. Pearl's voice on the phone is saying, "Tommy. Honey. I'm sorry. We're all trying to help Dennis and Jeanine as much as possible. Oh God, I can't imagine what they're going through. They thought the world of her . . . and she does this . . ."

He puts the phone down gently while his mother is talking and slides onto the floor.

Maybe if he hadn't left, Camille would be okay. He should have asked her to come along to Wattsville. He didn't because she was older and she was the one who knew the rules, who made the rules. But he could've asked anyway. He could have been strong, instead of always letting Camille take the lead. Maybe if he hadn't left, she'd still be alive. Maybe, he berates himself, he was the only one she could be real with, the only one who understood what it's like to live in two different worlds simultaneously. The only one who knows what it's like to live in the Twilight Zone, where your parents are nuts but they don't know it, and everybody around you is nuts in one way or another, but they don't know it. You feel like Marky Mark on the big wave, about ready to drown.

When he finally moves from that spot under the pay phone, he stomps on what's left of the McMuffin, grinding it into the floor. He can't bring himself to call Pearl back. He was lukewarm about going back to Pueblo anyway, but now with Camille gone . . .

Eventually he falls asleep on the floor of the Port Authority. He gets moved occasionally by cops or yelled at by crazies, so he stumbles along to some other grubby-tiled corner of hell. He has about three dollars in his pocket.

In the morning, he is sitting on the floor, exhausted, hungry, and sad—about Camille but also about Simone. He's watching people go by, wondering what to do and not wanting to do anything at all. A lady comes over with a small carton of orange juice and a hot dog. She works in one of those little convenience places: sweating hot dogs somersaulting under a heat lamp and wilted cheese danishes.

"You hungry?" she asks, and he nods. She gives him the food, no questions asked. She's probably sixty, and she looks like she's from India. She has on one of those sparkly dresses that are like one big scarf that's wrapped around and around so it covers her whole body, right down to her flat sandals, and she has a red dot drawn in between her eyebrows. Her kindness makes Tommy feel like crying.

Then he thinks about his father, and misses him. Eventually, he goes to the ticket counter. He explains his predicament to a surly dude who is in no mood to be helpful. "If there's an extra seat," Tommy says, "that nobody else is going to use anyway." The guy is smirking so Tommy says: "I just found out that my friend . . ." But he can't get the word *died* to come out of his mouth. The guy waves for the next person in line.

It's not that it doesn't occur to him to call Larry, but he wants to do things for himself, and besides, he's not really used to even having a father—at least not one who cares, who does things for him. He gets a paper cup from a donut place and starts begging. It's not as bad as he thought it would be. It's not exactly an efficient way to make money, but some change starts to accumulate in there. People throw in a nickel or a dime or a few pennies. Some give him a whole dollar and by the time night rolls around he has enough for either half of a ticket, or for a burger. He's starved, so he goes for the burger. Plus, he's wondering what's going to happen when he gets back to Wattsville and whether Derby will still want to kill him.

After he wears out his welcome at Manhattan Burger on Ninth Avenue, he heads back to the Port Authority and puts his cup in front of him on the floor.

A girl approaches. She's been living rough, it's obvious. She has long black hair like Camille's, so black you aren't sure if she dyes it or not, but it's straight, not feathery and wavy like both Camille's and Simone's. She sits down next to him. She has a mangled cardboard sign that says, "Please help. Trying to get to college."

"Hey." Tommy nods at her and smiles, and she says "hey" back. "You really trying to get to college?"

"Sure. Maybe." She looks into his cup and says, "You're doing all right." He thinks she's trying to get him to give her his money, so he pulls the cup closer.

"Yeah, I'm trying to get a bus ticket."

"Where you headed?"

"Wattsville."

She laughs. "What do you want to go there for?"

"Yeah, I guess it's a long story. Where are you going?"

"I'm not going anywhere. Just living." In a flash, she reminds him of Henry, the Mr. Miyagi guy he met on the bus, and she also reminds him of Camille. He's embarrassed that he'd thought she wanted to take his money. People like Simone and Derby will do that to you: make you think that everybody is just out for themselves.

But that's not true.

It's like this girl is all the cool people he's ever met who are trying to live their own lives without anyone telling them what to do. Good people who would help you if you asked.

They sit for a while, watching people go by.

"You need some money?" Tommy pushes his cup toward her and she just looks at it.

"No. You keep it. Get your bus ticket."

"You sure?" he says.

"Yeah. I just wanted to tell you that you can shower at the Y on Fifty-Eighth if you get there first thing in the morning."

And then she gets up and wanders away. He's mad at himself that he didn't get her to stay longer, and he's embarrassed that he must look and smell like ass if a homeless person is telling him to go take a shower. But mostly, he feels like it was somehow Camille, mixed with Henry, coming to tell him to get on with things. Not like it was a ghost or anything, just a message. The universe is weird, Tommy thinks.

At about four the next morning, after another night tucked up against the wall, Tommy makes his way over to the Y for a shower.

Then he calls the apartment, praying that Hanky answers, not Derby. He does. And this is what he says:

"I was on the couch, chilling, when there was banging on the door. They must've had a picture of Derby because they didn't say much to me, or think I was him. They go, 'We're looking for Derbin,' and so I told em, 'He's in his room,' and the next thing, I followed them to Derby's room, and it was locked, so they had to break it, but it wasn't any big deal for those dudes, with their big boots and stuff, so one of them kicked in the door and Derby was trying to climb out the fucking window."

The local news has been going haywire, Hanky tells him. A drug ring busted up and now Derby's in jail, awaiting trial.

"It's been a crazy couple of days," he says. "Some lady broke out of Stratton Island as well. They figure she died in the river, but they're still putting her picture all over the news, in case anyone sees her. Come on home, dude," Hanky says. Then he adds, "We'll have to get a new roommate."

After Tommy hangs up, he goes to the ticket window, hoping someone will have mercy and give him a discounted ticket, since he's still about ten bucks short. It's a different guy this time—a dead ringer for Eddie Murphy. After Tommy tells him his story, he looks around to make sure no one will see him. The guy winks and shoves a ticket under the glass. "I'm quitting this dump next week." Tommy tries to give him the dollar bills like moth wings and stony coins that he'd begged for, but the man shakes his head and shoves it all back.

He sits down at a Friday's and eats a burger with mushrooms, onions, cheese, and bacon, and then he gets on the bus.

***

Tommy calls his dad from the station, and Larry shows up wearing a peach-colored polo shirt and khaki shorts. Tommy thinks he'd look like a yuppie if he had a different face and less of a potbelly. He wonders for the first time if he's gay.

"You hungry?" His dad says and Tommy nods. "Where you wanna go?"

"I don't know. Not the Sheraton."

"The Blue Heron is on the way. You ever go in there?"

Tommy laughs and says, "Yeah, once in a while."

"Marguerite still there?"

"Yeah, she is."

"She used to make a mean sandwich."

***

Marguerite comes out from behind the bar and gives Larry a hug. She puts her hand on Tommy's shoulder and leads them to a booth. "Well, well. Haven't seen you, Larry, in, what's it gotta be now? Years."

Larry sits down on the vinyl bench across from Tommy. He looks proud and embarrassed at the same time.

"This is my son."

"I know." She has a thick laugh, like steak. "Hanky brings him in here all the time. I've seen him a hell of a lot more than I've seen you, isn't that right, Dom?"

Dom puts the newspaper down and comes over to where they're sitting. He shakes Larry's hand and says, "Good to see you, Larry." Tommy can't believe it. It's the first time he's ever seen Dom get off his stool and talk to someone.

"How've you been, Dom?" Dom starts to tell Larry how he's been, but Marguerite keeps interrupting to correct him or add details, and Dom shrugs and says, "She sure hasn't changed," and Larry and Dom laugh while Marguerite takes out her pad and readies herself for their order. Tommy wonders if it makes his dad feel lonely to see the two of them together, still married after however many years.

"We're not doing soups anymore, but we still have all the same sandwiches. Let. Me. See. Tuna melt, right?"

"And a Buckler, if you have one."

Marguerite nods and turns to Tommy.

"I'll have roast beef and a Genesee."

When Marguerite and Dom have gone back to their stations, Larry and Tommy don't have a whole lot to talk about, because they're avoiding the important stuff.

"Your roommate," Larry finally says and then coughs or laughs, it's hard to tell which.

"I'm glad he's gone," Tommy says, which makes Larry relax a bit.

"We don't have to talk about it," Larry says, "if you don't want. I'm just glad you're okay."

Tommy is exhausted and tells Larry he'll fill him in on all the details tomorrow, at work. Larry nods in a way that Tommy knows means he can take the day off if he needs to, but Tommy says he'll be there.

Marguerite brings their sandwiches, which are really good. Just the right amount of fillings and not too much mayo. The food gives them something to do and also to talk about. Sure is delicious, they agree. "Delicious," Larry calls to Marguerite.

"Six letter word," Dom says, "Like an emblem. Blank blank M blank O blank. Any ideas?"

"Famous," Marguerite tries.

"Nope. Doesn't make sense anyway. And it doesn't fit."

"Symbol," Larry says and Dom writes it in there, clucking approvingly.

Marguerite takes their plates away. Tommy would like another beer, but is too self-conscious to order one. Larry has coffee, so Tommy does too.

"Tom, I don't want to be an embarrassment," Larry says, looking around, talking quietly, so Marguerite and Dom can't hear him. "Are you okay?"

"Of course I'm fine," Tommy says, kind of mad that his dad would even worry about it. "There's no problem. There's nothing to say." Tommy is thinking of all the worse things a person can do than put on a dress.

"It's just. I missed you when you left . . . and I'm really glad you're back."

"Dad, It's okay. It's okay."

He looks so grateful. Tommy feels uncomfortable, because he's not sure he loves his dad as much as his dad obviously loves him. He figures that's the way of the world, and it's pretty comforting when you get down to it. All he had to do was be born, and this guy loves him so much for it. Tommy hopes that he will merit that love, someday.

Larry asks if he wants a ride, but Tommy tells him no and that he'll see him in the morning. He feels like walking home, and it's only a couple of blocks.

A DAMN GOOD SWIMMER

Garnet's New Diary

Hello! New friend. Only friend. That's what it feels like sometimes. It's not the first time I've felt like my only friend is a book full of empty pages. First things first. Getting a job was the first thing. Which was easier than I thought. All under the table. Ha! Once a criminal always a criminal! When the rules are dumb then the rules are dumb, and they need to be broken. So, I did what I had to do and I filled out applications and finally, I got a job. It's shitty, but who cares? Coming from where I'm coming from.

I haven't been keeping a diary until now, but I've been writing letters to Mom. She was smart and got a PO box. I hadn't even thought of that, but it was a smart thing to do.

I didn't think I'd actually make it. But I did and here I am. And now, things have cooled off enough that Mom is going to come visit. I can't think of anything in the world that could make me happier. She's coming with . . . drum roll please . . . her . . . boyfriend! Some guy Sam used to work with when he was at the newspaper. She and Sam both say he's super kind. She deserves it. Apparently, he's going to bring his son when they come, for the road trip. His name's Tommy and she says he's nice. So, it'll be a real family reunion, I guess!

Mom and I write letters all the time. One of our favorite topics is what name she's going to call herself when they come visit. My roommates think I'm Carol, so it'll be pretty weird if Mom is Carol too. We've settled on Ariel. That's what I'll introduce her as. I'm Carol Harlow and she's the little mermaid. Ha!

I think sometimes about Shanise's advice for relationships: if your mother doesn't like him, then drop him quick. We'll see if it works in reverse: I'm going to give my mom's new guy a thorough examination, to make sure he deserves her.

Mom forwarded a letter from Professor Bruss. It was in her last care package. That was the best day ever. Mom's homemade brownies and a letter reminding me that I'm worth something.

What else? Sam moved to the city! He's singing his heart out to packed audiences, apparently. I'm happy for him. He lives in a tiny studio in Queens and he shares it with his new boyfriend, a guy that Mom says is also really nice. He's from Colombia. They don't have room for visitors, but I can't think about traveling over the border yet anyway. What a kick: Mom and Sam both got hooked up with new boyfriends! Must be something in the water down there!

Talking about relationships. I think about Ethan a lot. Not that I miss him, but I learned a lot from being with him. I feel like I've cried more tears over that man than he ever warranted, and it's getting easier to forget about him—especially since I'm so busy now, working and getting used to my new life.

Mom says she still goes into Stratton Island sometimes—to visit Shanise now. She says she got so used to the routine, driving out there, and she'd heard so much about Shanise that she felt like she knew her. So, one day she showed up at visiting hours and now she goes every week. The best news is that Shanise will be up for parole soon. She's still seeing Officer Frank, and he's promised to leave his wife. Huh. I'll believe that when Shanise sends me an invitation to their wedding! I miss being able to talk to her, but someday, when the cops calm down and start putting their efforts into finding real criminals, they'll forget about me, hopefully. Or I'll get another identity somewhere. Mom and I can't share hers forever.

It was a blow to Stratton Island, losing a prisoner. It was in some of the American papers. It would've been a bigger deal but some big drug ring got busted around the same time, so I got a little bit forgotten about. That was good luck for me.

What have I lost? Living here? Away from everybody I love? Everything, Diary. Everything.

I lost my diary—the only thing I wanted to bring with me. Like I said. That book felt like my only friend at times.

But I've gained things too. I've got a view that's not bad; I can see the top of a McDonald's M. No bars on the windows. My roommates. Leticia is from Brazil and she works all the time, cleaning houses during the day and waiting tables at night in the same place where I'm washing dishes. She's been teaching me some dance moves. I'm not up for going dancing with her yet, but as I get more comfortable and less scared of being caught, maybe I will. And Domenica. She's from Poland and her daughter, Ivy, is here too. Ivy is four and I'm not bragging but she totally adores me. We bake together when I'm not working—cookies and seven-layer bars and you name it. She's so sweet and it feels nice to have a little kid here—I'd gotten used to the thought that if we'd succeeded in breaking out, I'd have been helping Shanise bring up her baby, and I was excited for that. So, for the moment anyway, I get to help Domenica with Ivy.

I never thought sharing one bathroom with three other people would feel like luxury, but when you can close the door and have some privacy, it's pretty sweet.

And I like Toronto. Of course, we'll see what happens when the winter comes. It's going to be even colder than Wattsville.

You know something, Diary? You'd never believe it but escaping was actually sort of easy, even though the original plan got pretty messed up. Me and Shanise were going to do it together. And her unborn baby. We had everything ready— hair product mixed with shaving cream, toilet paper, and Rice Krispies treats in a perfect concoction, the perfect consistency. I'd been messing with the formula, and curing it like cheese, until I had something that would harden. It was great too, hard as cement. Every night the cell doors are open for almost a full minute before sliding across. Ours wouldn't have locked because of the paste we were going to put into it.

But I ended up not needing it.

Because she took the pill, after all. And the pain and the bleeding and her moaning and a fever set in. It was Officer Frank who came, picked her up, and took her away. He carried her out of our cell and she grabbed me as she passed, her head hanging over Officer Frank's arm.

"Sorry," she whispered. "But I can't swim anyway."

Can you imagine that, Diary? She couldn't even swim! All the planning and we were going to make it: past the guard, who always fell asleep at his post. We were going to slide open the cell door, tiptoe out, make a break for the hole in the fence, down to the river . . .

But she took the pill. She didn't tell me because she wanted me to think she was going to come; she knew I'd bail on the plan if I had to do it alone.

I really had been looking forward to having her here with me. And the baby.

But she took it. Officer Frank came and he carried her away and I didn't even have to see whether the hair-mousse lock-filler was going to work because he didn't close the door when he left! In the chaos, I slipped out, got under the fence, and made it to the river.

And Mom came through with the car and the passport. Just like she promised. And plenty of snacks for the trip.

What have I learned? Lots of things, but the most important is this: I've learned how important it is to be able to swim. I'm a damn good swimmer, Diary. Thank God, I'm a damn good swimmer. ☺

THE VERY, VERY END

Larry Stall told the Hondurans he'd hire them back, after his son was found, but landscaping pays better and they enjoy being outside, especially as the weather has been so nice. They are towing a trailer, large and rickety, with leaf blowers and mowers, back into Wattsville proper from the White Hills neighborhood.

Jorge notices a red Volkswagen behind them. One of the new Beetles, shiny-shelled like the insect they're named after. He recognizes the car: they'd been trimming hedges at that family's house—the Thaxters—and the kid's in a rush, has been following practically on top of their trailer, swerving out into the middle of the road, looking for a place to pass. But Jorge has to drive slowly because of all the equipment they are towing; the trailer is loaded with grass cuttings destined for the city dump.

"*Ve más despacio,*" Jorge says into the side mirror, to the kid, who is driving erratically.

"*Qué pasa?*" asks Jaime, turning to look behind them.

They are on the Route 22 Bridge. The Thaxter kid decides he can't wait any longer, he's late for a flight to California, so he swerves, guns the engine and gives the finger to the pair of unmoved Hondurans as he passes. He veers in front of them, but is going too fast and loses control. The car flips over the guardrail. Jorge and Jaime are astounded at how graceful it seems, the car vaulting like a gymnast.

They pull over and climb onto the guardrail, ready to dive in and help if they need to. The car floats on the surface of the river for a moment before sinking in a chorus of watery burps.

ACKNOWLEDGEMENTS

I don't know if I got it at all right, but for a sense of life in a women's prison, *A World Apart* by Christina Rathbone was my favorite resource. The city of Troy, NY, was my inspiration for Wattsville, but I only passed through and don't claim to know it well. It seemed to have a heart and soul. At a certain point, novel writing becomes a team effort, and I am lucky to have a solid, encouraging, and very smart team in my corner. I'm very grateful to those who read and critiqued early drafts of this novel: Lisa Heiserman Perkins, Peter Brown, Cathy Armer, Bob Dall, Elizabeth Christopher, Bill Ellet, Lisa Borders, Anne McPeak, and Claire Rudy Foster. For months of debate about what to call the thing, thanks to Colin Hamell and Derry Woodhouse. For her encouragement and artistic counsel, I'm grateful to Rebecca Berger. I can't overstate the importance of my friend Tehila Lieberman's help in shaping the final draft: She put on her cape and swooped in just when this book needed it. To Lauren, Deb, and Jill: many thanks for listening to me. I'm grateful to the many people who have given me simple encouragement, without which I may have thrown in the towel: Karen Fraser, Marilyn Auclair, Sue Miller (who took time from her busy life to encourage someone she didn't even know), Stephen Russell. There are more—you know who you are. My wicked stepmother, Suzy Fraser, saved me from many embarrassing typos and taught me all I know about the comma. A big shout out to Doug Fraser for his help with the cover image. And, as always, many thanks to Reagan Rothe and the team at Black Rose Writing. I'm happy that my books have been able to call BRW their home.

ABOUT THE AUTHOR

Sara B. Fraser's first novel, *Long Division*, was published by Black Rose Writing in 2019. Her work has been published in *Salamander, the Forge, the Jabberwock Review, Carve, Traveler's Tales,* and other journals.

You can find out more at sarabfraser.com

NOTE FROM THE AUTHOR

Word-of-mouth is crucial for any author to succeed. If you enjoyed *Just River*, please leave a review online—anywhere you are able. Even if it's just a sentence or two. It would make all the difference and would be very much appreciated.

Thanks!
Sara B. Fraser

We hope you enjoyed reading this title from:

Subscribe to our mailing list – *The Rosevine* – and receive **FREE** books, daily deals, and stay current with news about upcoming releases and our hottest authors.
Scan the QR code below to sign up.

Already a subscriber? Please accept a sincere thank you for being a fan of Black Rose Writing authors.

View other Black Rose Writing titles at
www.blackrosewriting.com/books and use promo code
PRINT to receive a **20% discount** when purchasing.